ONE LAST RUN

BRYCE OAKLEY

ALSO BY BRYCE OAKLEY

The Adventurers

Something Far Away and Happy

Against The Grain

Never Mine

Every Version

Latitude & Longing

One Last Run

Shift the Tide

Holiday Romances

Most Wonderful

All Aglow

Ghosted Christmas Past

The Snowy Springs Holiday Romances

Baking Spirits Bright

Rebel Without A Claus

The Kaleidoscope Album

Undone

Bewilder

Midnight

Bloom

Revel

The Kaleidoscope Album Box Set

CONTENTS

CHAPTER 1

DANICA

DANICA WENDELL THOUGHT THAT A SEVEN-HOUR CAR RIDE WAS going to be the worst part of her day, but she was very, very wrong. No, that moment would come later in the afternoon, immediately upon seeing her ex-girlfriend, who she was about to spend an entire week with.

The drive from Denver to Telluride hadn't been terrible, though her motion sickness had gotten the best of her the entire trip. But any time she could steal her best friend away was worth it, regardless of the fact that she almost threw up whenever they went around a hairpin turn. She'd spent most of the windy mountain drive staring straight ahead, silently chewing ginger candies and white-knuckling the acupressure point on her wrist that helped with motion sickness. Of course, Kiera had offered for her to drive, but Danica knew Kiera would be uneasy being the passenger on the mountain roads, so Danica had tossed her keys to Kiera and popped a Dramamine. Danica would rather be dying from motion sickness than make anyone else even the slightest bit uncomfortable.

A text from Maggie popped up on the SUV's media screen, drawing both women's attention. Kiera hit a button to make it read aloud.

"*Text from Maggie: We just got here! The door code isn't working!*" a robotic woman's voice announced.

Kiera cursed, reaching toward the backseat and fumbling to find her phone in her purse.

"I'll get it! You just keep us from falling off the mountain," Danica said, aware that her voice had a pleading note to it. She turned, her stomach lurching with motion sickness as she reached into her own purse, pulling out her own phone. Eddie — her ex-fiancé as of one month ago — beamed up at her from the lock screen, clad in a tuxedo at some expensive gala for kid's teeth. They were officially over, but she wasn't ready to break that news to her friends just yet. One little lie by omission couldn't hurt for a week. She swiped to unlock her screen, barely registering Eddie's blindingly white smile.

"I knew I should have bought those stupid motion sickness glasses I saw on Instagram," Kiera said.

"The big ones with the liquid? I got that same targeted ad," Danica said. "What's the door code?"

"8008135."

Danica blinked, raising an eyebrow. "Are you a pubescent boy?"

"Aunt Jade let me pick whatever I wanted, and it's memorable enough." Kiera grinned, a dimple popping in her cheek.

"Memorable is right," Danica mumbled as she typed the code into the group chat, rolling her eyes.

It had been nearly two years since Danica had seen Kiera. They'd met as college roommates but had become best friends easily. Both Kiera and Danica's parents lived in Denver, and Kiera visited whenever her family was in town for the holidays or vacations. She was the kind of best friend that could be sending videos on TikTok while simultaneously carrying on a serious conversation about childhood trauma over text. The kind of best friend that didn't complain when it had been three months since their last phone call. Exactly the kind of best friend that Danica needed these days.

When Kiera had suggested a retreat to Telluride to stay at her aunt's condo, Danica immediately said yes. Work at the hospital had been grueling lately — they were short-staffed in the NICU where she was a neonatologist, and being the lowest on the seniority ladder meant she spent more time at work than at home in the past few months. Even getting time off for this trip was difficult, and she'd had to cash in a ton of favors to get it covered. As soon as this vacation was over, she wouldn't see daylight from anywhere but the NICU floor windows for weeks.

She hadn't quite wanted to admit to the others that things had ended with Eddie. Wedding planning was stressful for even solid couples, but they had been arguing endlessly. They'd called it quits, but she hated the idea of telling her friends that the relationship had ended and having them give her pitying looks. And worse, to admit to a failed relationship in front of Pete... No, it'd be better to tell them all later and let them think she was fine.

That was why this vacation was important. She needed to reconnect with her friends from college — which was depressingly one of the last times she'd truly felt whole — and get away from the job and ex-fiancé that were causing more than a couple of gray hairs to appear.

She'd been wholeheartedly looking forward to the ski trip, but that was before she saw the guest list. Maggie and even Izzy were welcome additions, and she hadn't seen them since Maggie's wedding five years before, but then she noticed Pete was added to the group chat.

Petra *fucking* Pancott.

Kiera's phone began ringing, and the mental image of Kiera reaching into the back and swerving over the guardrail and the car flying off the mountain flashed in Danica's mind.

"Let me get it." Danica's stomach churned at the thought of turning around again, much less staring at movement on a small screen, but fumbling blindly wasn't getting her anywhere. She grabbed Kiera's purse and dug through the carefully organized chaos within, pulling her friend's phone out of a small child's diaper. Unused, thankfully. The fact that Kiera had two daughters still weirded her out sometimes — she'd seen Kiera shotgun Miller High Life and scream-sing karaoke and lose her flip flops in a gutter, and now she was a mom. Weird. She swiped the call open, expecting to see Maggie's flawless, dewy face smiling back at her.

But there she was. Pete, her dark brown curls perfectly mussed. The kind of perfectly mussed hair you somehow only get after rolling out of bed and leaving someone else behind, satisfied. Danica fought to banish the memory of Pete in bed that suddenly appeared in her mind. Pete laughed, always so unbothered. "It's a no-go on the boobies," Pete said brightly.

Danica nearly dropped the phone. "Excuse me?"

"Oh, hey Wendell. We called Kiera, right? Anyway, the door code. It's not working." Pete smiled in her classic, unintentionally charming way.

Kiera furrowed her brow when Danica glanced her way. "That's what I had her set it as. Our ETA is ten minutes. Can you wait outside?" she said toward the phone, chewing on her lower lip.

They turned off the highway onto a smaller, snow packed road that twisted up toward Mountain Village, a neighborhood of mansions and expensive condos flanked by towering, snowcapped mountains and bare aspen groves.

"Yeah, of course," Pete said, talking over Maggie and Izzy in the background. The three had flown into the small Telluride airport since they weren't local to Denver. Kiera technically wasn't either, but she'd offered to fly into Denver and drive with Danica. The planes that flew into Telluride were tiny death traps, and Danica had very quickly refused that option. Though now, as she held the phone in one hand and stuffed another ginger chew in her mouth, she was regretting the driving part, too.

"We'll be there shortly," Danica said around a mouthful of ginger, the candy nearly burning her tongue with its intensity.

Pete cocked her head to the side, giving her a nod. "Can't wait," Pete said before ending the call — and was it Danica's imagination or did her voice drop an octave, softening into barely more than a low whisper?

A wave of nausea, accompanied by a hot flash, washed over Danica.

"Air conditioning," Danica said, dropping Kiera's phone into the cup holder before cranking the temperature dial on her side. She leaned forward to one of the vents, letting the cool air blast her heated cheeks. The car sickness sweats were the worst. That's why she was flushed. Car sickness. It had nothing to do with the fact that seeing Pete had thrown her out of sorts.

"Jeez, you okay?" Kiera said, adjusting the vents on her side of the car toward Danica.

Danica nodded. "I'm taking even more Dramamine on the way back. Or maybe I'll just never go back. Maybe I live in Telluride now."

"Seriously. I can pull over if you're going to throw up."

"I'll be fine," Danica said, leaning on the cool window as the air conditioning made her hair tickle her cheek. "Just hot."

"Are you pregnant?"

Danica groaned. "No, of course not."

"Aren't you a little young to be going through *the change*?" Kiera teased.

"You shut your mouth," Danica said with mock-affront. They were both 37, which meant perimenopause wasn't totally out of the question, but wow, she was *not* looking forward to that chapter.

Pete fucking Pancott. The last time she'd seen Pete was on the night of their college graduation, when they'd had a screaming match on the quad, drunk and crying and upset. It hadn't been Danica's best moment, and it played over in her mind on nights that she couldn't sleep. Pete hadn't shown up to Kiera or Maggie's weddings, but no one seemed to be holding her absence against her. Apparently, Izzy had flown to Croatia last year to see her, but Danica hadn't asked for details.

She'd known Pete would be on this trip. She'd prepared for it. She'd even assured her therapist that she'd be perfectly fine seeing Pete again. She took a deep breath, tamping down her discomfort. She crossed and uncrossed her legs, suddenly unable to get comfortable.

It had been fifteen years since she and Pete had ended their casual… whatever it was, on the night of graduation. Sometimes it had just been a hookup or a long make out, while avoiding any talk of feelings or the future. Danica had moved on. She'd had a serious relationship, even been engaged. She had a meaningful career, dinner at her parent's house every month or two, and a relatively stable life, broken engagement notwithstanding. She was happy.

Pete had clearly moved on, too. She hadn't reached out even once. She'd always been aimless, uncertain about the future, unable to commit, and had dreams of traveling the world instead of finding a career or settling down. Maybe she'd finally grown up. People were usually idiots at 22, and then reality helped them become real, contributing members of society. Had the same happened to Pete?

The week would be *fine*, Danica assured herself again. She was only feeling uncomfortable because she didn't know what to expect when it came to Pete, and she liked knowing the plan. That was all. They'd ski during the day, drink good wine and eat good food in the evenings, and generally relax.

And she needed that, a relaxing vacation away from the hospital and her life.

Kiera pulled into a parking area and the car slid ever-so-slightly on the snow-packed ground. Danica's stomach lurched right along with it, sending a new wave of nausea through her.

"This is it," Kiera said, coming to a full stop as she pointed to a monstrosity of a building, the gabled metal roof glowing in the late afternoon sun. Massive windows and spacious balconies, many with hot tubs, punctuated the wood and stone facade.

"How many condos are in this place?" Danica asked.

"Oh, this is all Aunt Jade's," Kiera said casually, waving her hand toward the entire building. Danica's eyes widened in shock, and Kiera laughed. "No, I'm joking. I think there's four. The condo at the end is hers."

Danica shook her head, opening the door to take a few breaths of cold air. January was a frigid time to be in the mountains, and the cold stung Danica's cheeks as she sent a quick reply text to her colleague, replying to a question about a patient she'd been closely working with before the trip. Text sent, she shuffled to grab her suitcase out of the back of the SUV.

"Careful, it's icy as hell," Kiera said, holding onto the side of the car as her sneakers slipped. She regained her footing and laughed. "We should have changed into our snow boots just for the ten-foot walk."

Danica stepped carefully, her own white dad-mowing-the-lawn sneakers staying firmly put as she shifted her weight. "Maybe you shouldn't have worn soccer shoes." She pointed to Kiera's low-profile Adidas.

"It's called fashion, Dani. Look it up," Kiera said, dramatically pushing her sunglasses up her nose.

Danica grinned, happy to be out of the car and breathing the fresh mountain air. She expected pine, but all she smelled was... the muskiness of dirty ice and the smoke from wood-burning fireplaces. A slight breeze slipped under the collar of her coat and she shivered, hurrying after Kiera.

"You made it!" Maggie announced. Danica saw that Maggie, Izzy, and Pete were all standing just outside of a tall wooden door that must have sacrificed at least three trees in its origin. Well, Maggie and Izzy were standing outside of the door. Pete was standing on the edge of a planter of tiny ever-greens, her arms high in greeting as if she were about to leap into the sky. Ah, still as weird as ever.

"We made it!" Kiera called back, taking quick, small steps up to the condo door to give the three women hugs.

"Damn, Wendell, you okay? You look white as a ghost," Pete said, and Danica paused in horror.

The first post-breakup run-in with an ex is something every woman has envisioned. Preferably while wearing a Princess Di Revenge Dress. Lacking a suitable reason to wear such an outfit during a road trip, Danica opted for something casual yet stylish, her brown hair styled perfectly, and her lips subtly glossed.

In all of her daydreams of running into Pete again, she'd never imagined the first words she'd hear would be that she resembled the spirit of a dead person.

Danica paused suddenly in her surprise about the ghost comment, and her feet slipped on ice as she stopped. The suit-case fell, abandoning her at a very crucial moment, and she wildly flailed her arms in a vaudeville-style dance, the kind usually accompanied by tap shoes and frantic arm and leg movements.

Suddenly, Pete was beside her, grabbing around her waist.

That somehow made the entire situation worse. Pete was so close. She was warm, and smelled like coconut and sweet apricot, and her face was so close.

"You good?" Pete asked, her warm breath warming Dani-ca's cheeks.

No, Danica Wendell was not good. Because somewhere between the car sickness, the intense flailing, and the arm tight around her waist, the nausea floodgates had swung wide open. Her quick reflexes were her only saving grace as she turned to throw up into the planter. Behind her, Kiera made noises of concern and patted her back, Maggie and Izzy groaned in disgust, and Pete laughed her ass off.

"Does anyone have a shovel? I'd like to be hit over the head with it," Danica said, wiping at her mouth with a tissue Kiera passed to her. She sniffled, mentally noting where in her suitcase she could find her toiletries bag and her toothbrush.

"What about wine-induced amnesia?" Kiera offered, typing into the keypad on the door. It beeped and opened, and Maggie made a weak argument about not knowing she had to press both the asterisk *and* the pound sign after putting in the code.

"That sounds terrible, honestly," Danica said, taking her roller bag from Pete, who had picked it up off the ground for her. She thanked Pete while covering her mouth and scrambled inside to find a bathroom, or any room that had a door with a lock where she could sequester herself for the next thousand years and avoid both her immediate embarrassment and any further run-ins with Pete.

This was going to be a long week, and she'd only just arrived.

CHAPTER 2

PETE

PETE WAS RUNNING ON THREE HOURS OF SLEEP, FOUR ENERGY drinks, and five tiny powdered Donettes she'd bought at the gas station. All in all, a pretty good day. That was, until Danica Wendell showed up.

Pete wasn't big on grudges — she had a poor memory, and usually couldn't remember why the grudge was being held in the first place. This meant she was typically friends with every ex, but she'd replayed every moment of her and Danica's time together so much that she remembered each word of that screaming fight out on the quad at 2 a.m. on graduation night.

It was the last time she'd seen Danica, her hair straight and shiny, still in her white lace graduation dress. The last thing Danica had ever said to Pete was an exasperated, "You're never going to grow up, are you?" That had stung more than any of the horrible other things they'd said to each other that night. That's why Pete had taken it on as a mantra. She *was* never going to grow up, *thank you very much.*

She may not have grown up by Danica's definition, but

she wasn't the one throwing up in a planter box outside a rich lady's condo.

She laughed to herself to even picture it now. Danica, so polished, doing something so disgusting that it would haunt her thoughts for years. She knew Danica well enough to know that throwing up in front of her friends was a nightmare scenario. For Pete, it was something that could happen on a casual Friday night after drinking and eating mystery meat from a street vendor.

As they walked into Aunt Jade's condo — bless Kiera for having a rich aunt — she lagged behind, letting everyone choose their rooms before her. She didn't care where she slept, since she'd hardly be in there. Her intention was to spend the most time she could on the slopes. She shuffled into the kitchen, opening the fridge to find it fully stocked with fancy prebiotic sodas and bottled craft beer. "Don't mind if I do," she mumbled, cracking open the top of a hazy IPA. Leaning against the counter, she took in the kitchen, which was decked out in marble and crisp white cabinetry. Had anyone ever cooked in this kitchen? She highly doubted it.

"Uh, sorry, Pete, but there's only one room left, and it's bunk beds," Izzy called out from the hallway.

"Bunk beds sound fun," Pete called back to assuage any guilt Izzy felt about taking the last room with a nice bed. She walked around the oversized kitchen island to the living room. Floor-to-ceiling glass windows lined one wall, giving a view of Mountain Village, the tourist lodge area of Telluride. Rustic yet modern buildings, wide open slopes, and the main gondola into the ski resort lined the horizon. Bare aspens and snow-draped conifers spread in every direction from the grounds, except over what appeared to be a tennis court covered in a thick layer of snow.

She was still in her travel uniform, comfortable and familiar. Pete shoved her hands into the pockets of her worn tan chore jacket, the heavy cotton fabric soft from countless washes, its multiple pockets perfect for stashing everything from pens to snacks. She'd left the jacket unbuttoned, revealing the faded logo of a faded band t-shirt underneath. Her jeans were cuffed to show her high-top white Converse sneakers, which were scuffed from months of use but still held a certain timeless charm.

"If this is what being a childless, single woman gets you, I'm getting a divorce and giving back my kids," Maggie said, walking into the living area to flop onto the couch. Two over-stuffed chairs sat near the fireplace, facing a worn-in leather sofa. Maggie still looked as effortlessly cool as always, her collarbone length blonde hair still perfectly coiffed even after she'd taken off her beanie.

"Looks like I'm on the right path, then," Pete joked, sinking into one of the chairs and turning to look at the stone-slab fireplace. She reached to flip the switch to turn on the gas, and flames rose immediately over the fake logs. A bit cheesy, but warm.

"Did y'all see the hot tub?" Izzy asked, walking into the room to stare out the window. Izzy, unlike Maggie, was still wearing a mustard yellow beanie over her blonde pixie, an oversized fleece pullover hiding most of her tiny frame.

"That'll be nice for after my snowboarding lessons," Maggie commented.

"You're taking snowboarding lessons?" Pete asked, a brow raising. "Haven't you been skiing since you were like, three?"

"Yeah, but I've never snowboarded, and I feel like this is my one chance to try it without worrying about the kids or my wife being there to need something from me," Maggie said, letting out a deep, long breath.

"How many kids do you have now?" Pete asked.

Maggie smiled in a tired way. "Just the three. Why are you making that face?"

"I'm not making a face." Pete took a long sip of her beer to try to hide whatever expression was giving her away. She glanced toward where Izzy was opening a bottle of red wine in the kitchen.

"You're... grimacing." Maggie's eyes narrowed.

Pete swallowed, trying to hide her smile. "Well, you said *just*, as in, just three. Or, like, not that many, only three. Which, by all accounts, is a lot of kids."

Maggie snorted. "I'm not like a Quiverfull person or whatever. Three kids aren't that... Petra, I swear, if you don't stop grimacing—"

"What's a Quiverfull person?" Izzy interrupted, walking in with three empty wine glasses and an uncorked bottle.

"I think it's a weird religious thing, where you have fifteen kids like they're arrows in your quiver to battle... Satan?" Maggie said, shrugging. "I'm unsure of the specifics."

"Three kids doesn't seem very battle-ready," Pete said with a grin.

"Three kids are plenty for any kind of warfare. Currently, the war is against their own personal demons, like kindergarten and broccoli," Maggie said with the kind of smile that only a mother could have when talking about her kids.

"They'll be shipshape for the Crusades any day, I'm sure." Pete toasted her beer bottle.

"What about you? You were in Croatia?" Maggie asked.

Pete laughed. "Yeah, like a year ago. Since then, I've been in Portugal, Bali, and Mexico."

"Forgive me for not keeping up," Maggie deadpanned, and then glanced toward Izzy. "You went and visited her there, right?"

Izzy nodded. "It was gorgeous. Croatia. Who knew?"

"Anyone who has read Travel+Leisure in the past three years," Kiera said, entering the great room and into the kitchen to grab herself a wine glass.

"No one reads magazines anymore," Izzy said, rolling her eyes.

"I brought four just for this trip," Kiera said, filling her glass with a hefty pour of wine. She tapped Maggie's feet to get her to move them and give her a place to sit. Kiera had changed the most, in Pete's opinion. Her short dark hair was curly, and her wire-framed glasses looked adorable on her round cheeks. She wore perfectly tailored jeans and smelled like she'd just bathed in lilac lotion. Pete found it nice that some things never changed about her old friends.

"Is Wendell feeling okay?" Pete asked.

Kiera nodded. "Yeah, I gave her a Zofran, and she's brushed her teeth four times. I think she's planning to shower off the shame and be out soon."

The mental image of Danica showering was not an unwelcome one, but it felt poorly timed, given she was in a room with other people. Danica in college had been gorgeous, funny, kind, driven, smart... all traits that Pete admired in her. Now, Danica was still stunning, but something was off about her. Maybe it had just been car sickness, but Pete couldn't put her finger on it. She was a doctor now, so maybe she felt stressed about work? Her stomach tightened at the thought of Danica's stupid fiancé, Eddie. A grown man who *chose* to be called Eddie. Disturbing, to say the least. Did Danica really moan *"Oh, Eddie"* when they were in bed? Could an "Eddie" even make a woman moan?

"What's got you all flushed?" Izzy asked her with a wry grin that seemed to suggest Pete had her thoughts written all over her face.

Pete raised her glass. "Telluride is at a much higher elevation, so alcohol hits you quicker."

"Should we talk about dinner or groceries?" Danica asked, swooping into the room wearing a fuzzy, loose lounge set and no bra. No bra. She was holding a bag of thread and an embroidery hoop, like she planned to cross stitch as they all relaxed and caught up. "Did everyone get the color-coded spreadsheet I sent?"

"The one where we were all color-coded and responsible

for one dinner of the trip?" Maggie asked. "Yeah, I... opened it. I think."

Danica pressed her lips into a thin line of irritation, messing with the curtain bangs that kept falling into her eyes. "I thought that might be the case, so I already ordered delivery tonight. We can talk details over Pad Thai." Pete watched her pull something out of her pocket while walking toward the mantle and realized that Danica was cleaning the remote control with a disinfecting wipe. Yep, she's the one who always had small hand sanitizers in her purse for nights out, insisting on hand cleaning before late-night pizza after leaving a bar. Every group had to have that one friend who acted as the mom, ensuring everyone's hygiene and sustenance. The irony wasn't lost on Pete: their group mom, a NICU doctor constantly surrounded by infants, was childless.

"Someone's feeling better," Kiera said with a smile.

"I do apologize for Vomit-pocalypse 2.0 out there. Usually, my ginger chews do the trick, but..." Danica shrugged, offhandedly disinfecting the door handle to the patio beside her, before sitting on the floor in front of the coffee table.

"When was Vomit-pocalypse 1.0?" Maggie asked.

"The Mind Eraser roller coaster at Elitch's. Junior year," Kiera said, shaking her head and laughing as the other three all groaned with the remembrance.

"Unfortunately, my mind was never erased," Danica said solemnly to a round of laughter.

The only updates Pete had heard about Danica had come from whatever passing information Izzy shared about the group. Izzy was the only person she'd stayed in touch with, because Izzy was the only one who respected that Pete sometimes just needed space. Pete had spent the last fifteen years building the Second Star foundation, her pride and joy. She'd started it after selling an app and a few fortuitous investments, but she'd had the right skills at the right time. Now, she spent her time traveling, exploring, meeting extraordinary people, and being the kind of light she'd needed when she was younger.

Danica, with her chestnut brown hair, so rich it almost looked red in certain lights. Danica, with those ocean blue eyes that could always see straight through all of Pete's bullshit. Danica, with that damned oversized top that showed a bit of her collarbone and shoulder, hinting at the pale skin Pete knew extended everywhere, fair and soft. Danica, with no bra.

Had Danica's bra succumbed to the car sickness, as well? Had it disintegrated in her suitcase?

"Izzy, I made sure to get you the vegan Pad Thai. Pete, I have no idea what you prefer these days." Danica's cheeks colored at the innuendo, a light rose brushstroke right under her eyes in a way that Pete found incredibly adorable.

Pete cleared her throat. "I'm not picky."

Danica looked away, fidgeting with her embroidery hoop.

Danica was so different from her. That's what had caused their last fight. What future could two people who wanted such different things actually have? They had been together because of their physical proximity, first on the same dorm floor, then eventually in the same apartment building near campus.

Back then, Pete felt their relationship was a matter of convenience for both. Fun and lighthearted, it required no label. That's what she'd wanted back then, what she thought they'd both wanted. Did that make it hurt any less when they had to come to terms with it? Absolutely not.

And it wasn't any easier now to see Danica Wendell fifteen years later, sitting on the floor with a needle and thread, sipping a stupid prebiotic soda.

Food delivered and wine glasses refilled, they enjoyed their Pad Thai and vegetable spring rolls while allowing Danica to pretend she needed their input for the week of dinners. She planned the entire week, the grocery list, and even put them in pairs to make the cooking easier. Pete and Izzy would have pizza night, Kiera and Maggie were in charge of Taco Tuesday, and Danica was going to cook another night on her own. That left them without dinners for three nights, where they could explore a few local restaurants.

As the women ate and talked, Pete tried to commit the names of Maggie and Kiera's children to memory. Learning that Danica's wedding didn't have a date or venue surprised her, even though their engagement had lasted almost two years. Danica seemed to either avoid or redirect every wedding planning question whenever it came up. Pete masked her surprise and delight by quickly drinking a large gulp of her beer. She was feeling a bit lightheaded by the time they cleaned up their dinner. Maggie, Kiera, and Danica all claimed to be exhausted, and headed towards the bedrooms, making plans for an early morning of picking up their rental gear.

Not ready to end the night just yet, Izzy and Pete grabbed their coats and blankets and relocated to the patio, turning on an outdoor heater to keep them warm. Pete sniffled, the cold air making her nose run. For being a tourist lodging area, it was so quiet outside. Maybe it was the way snow always dampened noise, muffling the sounds of the world. She always loved that the most. The quiet, calmness of snow.

Pete's breath fogged in front of her face and Izzy leaned against her for warmth, holding her wine glass through the blanket. Izzy was like a tiny Polly Pocket of a person, and they'd always been affectionate friends, but Pete realized how much she missed her best friend. She'd spent the better part of a decade quite alone, traveling and throwing herself into running Second Star. "This place is nice," Izzy said in a hushed tone, like she didn't want to disturb the silence too much, either.

Pete made a noise of agreement.

"Is it weird seeing everyone again?" Izzy asked.

"A little," Pete confessed. "Not bad weird. Just weird-weird."

Izzy snorted, sipping her wine with her blanketed hands. "That makes no sense."

Pete sniffled again, closing her eyes and taking in a deep breath of the frosty night air. "We're just such different people now. Kiera and Maggie have kids and spouses, and Danica's a doctor."

Izzy turned to look at Pete, raising a brow. "And what about you and me?"

"We've paved our own paths instead of following orders," Pete said with a firm nod that reminded her exactly how much she'd drank at such a high elevation. Whew. She was definitely feeling that third beer now.

"I'm not exactly sure that being divorced and working at a bar at 37 is really the dream," Izzy said. "It's not like I've avoided settling down on purpose."

"You've just been confusing settling down with settling," Pete said, wrapping an arm around her oldest friend.

Izzy nodded, but her posture shifted as she seemed to pointedly avoid Pete's eye. "How's seeing Danica again?"

"Did you notice she wasn't even wearing a bra?" Pete asked, a cloud of fog forming as she exhaled in exasperation.

Izzy frowned. "No? Was I supposed to?"

"I just thought it was obvious." Pete bristled, taking Izzy's wine glass and stealing a sip. "But you know, it's fine. It's totally fine seeing her again. I'm fine."

"You seem totally fine," Izzy deadpanned. "I mean, I know the breakup was tough, but—"

Pete cut her off with a forced snort of amusement. "Clearly there are no hard feelings because we're both here."

Izzy took her wine glass again, swirling the last sip of liquid around and around. "There are no hard feelings on your part? Really?" She tilted her head, and Pete didn't appreciate the skeptical narrowing of her eyes.

Pete shook her head emphatically.

Izzy eyed her doubtfully but didn't push her for more information. That was why she loved Izzy. She wasn't trying to push Pete too far, or change her, or make her feel bad for falling off the map sometimes. Pete was like a discounted, imperfect piece of IKEA furniture and Izzy accepted her as-is.

"We should get to bed if we're going to beat the worst of the lift lines tomorrow." Izzy said, throwing the blanket off of them both.

Pete shivered and reached to turn off the heater, following her back inside. She couldn't shake off the skeptical look that Izzy had given her. What had Izzy seen that Pete didn't? As with most difficult feelings, Pete had packaged them up and compartmentalized them almost immediately, only to be unwrapped in her sporadic therapy sessions. Her feelings about Danica had stayed in the box for fifteen years, double-taped and super glued shut, and that's exactly where she wanted them to stay this week.

CHAPTER 3

DANICA

DANICA ALWAYS FORGOT HOW MUCH OF A LOVE/HATE relationship she had with skiing. There was a certain kind of bliss in carving down the mountain, enjoying the trees rushing past, shifting your weight and just losing yourself in the flow. Her mind was quiet as she focused on the gliding sound of her skis in the snow, the laughter and shouts of skiers and snowboarders on the lifts and skiing around her, and even the terror-inducing sound of children laughing somewhere behind her. Kids on skis were fearless and always cut way too close for comfort.

On the other hand, her ski boots never fit quite right for the first few hours. She was a bit out of practice and had to keep reminding herself about the ski positions of pizza and french fries, and her face was cold, even under the sherpa neck gaiter and hood she'd brought. Her helmet strap rubbed on her chin, her boots chafed against her shins, and she was painfully out of breath.

It was 10 a.m. and she was already looking forward to the Après part of the day.

People knew Telluride for its expert runs, but she was by no means an expert. Pete and Izzy had disappeared to find the black runs further up the mountain, but Kiera, Maggie, and Danica stuck to the blues. Kiera probably would have been fine with Pete and Izzy, but Danica had a feeling that Kiera was doing easier runs just to stick with her, which was both embarrassing and sweet.

"I'm nervous about how many layers I have on," Maggie confessed on the lift part-way through the morning. Danica clutched the bar, too afraid of heights to look down, and was only half-listening. Was the seat rocking back and forth slightly, or was that just her imagination? Though she was curious about the seat's connection to the lift, she stared straight ahead, worried extra movement would make her sick.

Kiera nodded and laughed. "Is it because you're worried you won't get off all the layers before peeing yourself, thanks to birthing watermelon-sized children? Because that's my problem."

"Exactly. I'm a little afraid I'm gonna pee anytime I fall," Maggie said with a snort.

"I've already peed a little like three times."

"Was one when you sneezed earlier?"

"Yeah! How did you know?" Kiera said, smacking her leg in amusement.

"Because I thought to myself, wow, I'd have peed a little if I had that sneeze," Maggie said.

Although Danica tried not to professionally deal with any human over ten pounds, she was around a lot of mothers and parents who had recently given birth. She'd seen it all. Usually, while telling them, 'Please don't faint, I don't do well with adults.'

"Danica, are you and Eddie planning on having kids?" Maggie asked, leaning past Kiera to look at her. The sight of

Maggie leaning forward on the lift made Danica very, very nervous.

"We never really talked about it," Danica confessed, nervously fidgeting with her goggles that were raised over her helmet. "I don't know if I want to."

"You're engaged and you've never talked about kids?" Maggie asked, her eyes wide.

"We're 37, babe. You're kind of at a point where you'd better figure that out," Kiera said in a way that only Kiera could get away with.

"I knew a mom last year who was 52," Danica said with a shrug as her brain frantically tried to redirect the conversation. "She had twins."

"I'm tired just thinking about that," Maggie said with a sigh. "Don't you love babies, though, since you work with them?"

Danica had been asked that question twelve thousand times. She liked kids, sure. But what made her choose neonatology was that she loved the challenge of preemies, especially the teeny tiny ones called micropreemies. "I have seen too much to try it myself, I'm pretty sure. I think I'm more likely to adopt one of my patients than have my own."

"Oh man, I foster-failed on two dogs, so I totally get that," Maggie said with a sincere smile. "Not that that's the same, but comparatively, they're both cute things that need you."

Danica laughed. "You'd know better than me. I haven't brought one home yet, but I've been more than tempted. I have a colleague who has fostered four of our NICU kids and fantastic families have adopted them."

"I love that, and also it makes me kind of sad to think about tiny babies that need families," Kiera said.

"We also have volunteers who come in and cuddle babies," Danica offered, desperate to move the spotlight off of herself. "They get to just hold a baby for a few hours." Both

Kiera and Maggie respond with meaningful "aww" sounds. Danica was a little jealous of the volunteers that got to snuggle babies. She sometimes helped out with the bedside things in the NICU, taking part in diaper changes or bottle feeding when she wasn't busy, but those times were rare and only when there weren't as many babies on the unit. She had to be prepared in case a patient coded or something else went wrong, and it was difficult to stop a hungry, growing baby when they were halfway through a bottle. Still, there were certain families that she loved more than others, and she made extra excuses to stop in their rooms and chat, even about movies or books. Some families were in the NICU for months and months, and she thought the normalcy helped them just as much as it helped her during those long shifts.

"Did you guys hear Izzy's divorce went through?" Maggie asked as the lift lowered toward the ground. Danica was endlessly grateful to change the subject away from herself and distract herself from the impending challenge of gracefully dismounting from a chairlift. No matter how many times Danica had skied, getting off of the lift gracefully was always something that made her a bit nervous. She could slip and fall in front of a bunch of people, and the lifties would have to come help her, or worse, stop the lift altogether.

"I think I saw it on Facebook? But I've been trying to avoid that hellscape, so I haven't seen much," Kiera said.

"What does she do for work, again?" Danica and Izzy had never been the closest, and she'd only seen her once since college at Maggie's wedding.

Maggie shrugged. "She works in a bar, but I don't know much."

They made their way toward the top of the run they'd picked out, a gradual, chill blue that wouldn't require too much energy, given how tired they all already were.

Danica followed the other two down the mountain, taking her time, breathing deep

Izzy and Pete had been best friends back in college. They'd been inseparable, whereas Kiera and Danica were also closer to one another than the rest of the group. Maggie was close with everyone, like some twenty-year-old Mercutio who had never had a bad word said about her. Maggie got along well with Izzy, but Izzy had never warmed to Danica, regardless of how much Danica tried to get along with her. Kiera had always thought it was because Izzy had feelings for Pete, but Maggie was confident that it was because Izzy was jealous of Danica's grades and achievements.

That theory had never sat quite right for Danica, though. Danica had been a straight-A student on the pre-med track. She'd worked her ass off for scholarships, and she tutored other students on the side. But Izzy was more of a free spirit, a communications major — whatever that meant — and often skipped classes because she was too high to do anything but lie on her bed and listen to music.

Really, Danica chalked it up to the fact that they had almost nothing in common. There was only one tiny sliver of overlap in their friendship Venn diagram, and that overlap was Pete.

Pete was easy to love. She was fun and spontaneous and kind. She was always laughing. It also helped that Pete was stunning, just one of those annoyingly beautiful people. Pete and Maggie had been directly across the hall from Kiera and Danica in their first year of college at Colorado State University. Izzy lived just down the hall, but became practically a third roommate to Maggie and Pete that first year. She slept more often on the futon in their dorm than in her own room. The friendship between the five of them was set in stone on their very first day, when Kiera had suggested they go to the mall to get pet fish for their rooms. They rode the bus to the mall — none of them had brought their cars to school — and bought fish and small tanks. On the bus ride home, the bumpy ride was a death sentence for most of their fish, and their night ended with four fishy funerals in the bathroom. Pete was the only one who had managed to keep her fish alive, and so her fish became their communal fish, a shared daughter who lived three entire years, despite the not-exactly-nurturing environment of a freshman college dorm.

"Hey, what was our fish's name?" Danica called out to Kiera. "I can't remember."

"Gilly Joel?" Maggie called out.

"No, that was our fish in the house during our last year. Pete named the first fish George," Kiera said.

"It was Georgia O'Reef, thank you very much," Pete said, her voice startlingly close.

Having no idea that Pete had caught up to them, Danica jumped in surprise. She didn't consider herself a normally clumsy person, and she hated the way skis and ice had now twice made her lose control of her legs. She lost her balance, flailing her poles as she fell sideways onto her hip, her ankles screaming in pain as they bent in her boots. Damn, she'd been proud of herself for not falling more than seven times already, which was her best record. Being a casual skier, at least in her case, meant that she spent the first two days of any ski trip trying desperately to remember what she was meant to be doing.

Pete looked effortlessly cool as she slid to a stop near Danica, bending down and unhooking her binding before stepping off her snowboard with one boot. "You good?" she asked, reaching out to help Danica up.

Danica waved away the hand that was offered to her. "I was fine until you crept up on me like a... creeping creep."

"A creeping creep," Pete said, her eyes widening in amusement as she lifted her goggles onto her helmet to look at Danica. "Wordsmith Wendell with the deep cuts here."

Kiera, Maggie, and Izzy stood near the side of the run, watching. "Are you hurt, Dani?" Kiera asked.

"Just my pride," Danica responded with a groan, her skis sliding awkwardly as she moved to get up.

Pete reached out again and Danica waved her off, her own annoyance growing. "I don't need you," Danica bit out, then paused at the surprise on Pete's face. She cleared her throat. "I don't need your help."

Pete straightened, looking down at her gloves as if she needed to fix them. Her expression was tight, like she was holding back a reply. She bent and re-clipped her bindings, her dark curls barely peeking out from the bottom of her helmet.

"How'd you even find us?" Danica attempted a graceful redirection away from her annoyed tone while also ungracefully rolling onto her belly and letting her skis fall to either side of her body, their tips facing up. She pushed herself onto her hands, raising her hips in the air as she shimmied her feet closer together until she felt balanced enough to lean back and stand up. Was it dignified? No. Was it the easiest way she knew how to stand up in skis? Yes. She wasn't taking any chances of falling in front of Pete again.

Pete fucking Pancott. Danica hated how she had instantly turned into a mood swinging, clumsy mess around the woman. Pete was an ex she hadn't seen in fifteen years, but those fifteen years made the present moment feel even more odd — she didn't entirely know where she stood with Pete, or if Pete was just going to pretend they didn't have a history together. The most irritating part of being around Pete was how attracted Danica still was, which made her feel stupid. Now, her one chance to look polished and put together, she was tripping and short-tempered and awkwardly trying to stand up with two waxed sleds tied to each foot. It wasn't a recipe for dignified sex appeal, that was for sure. The snow crunched under her skis as she stepped sideways to grab her poles.

"That was like watching a baby giraffe take its first steps,"

Izzy piped up while laughing, and Danica was grateful that her goggles concealed her disdain.

"Maggie shared her location in the group chat," Pete said with a shrug. "We were on See Forever and thought we'd stop seeing forever and instead see if anyone wants to take a break and grab food, though not necessarily in that order."

That sounded heavenly, and Danica glanced toward Kiera and Maggie. "Do you want to take a lunch break?"

Maggie nodded immediately, and Kiera watched her, as if waiting to follow Danica's lead.

"Did you want to stay around the slopes or go into town?" Danica asked.

"Probably slopes," Pete said. "The gondola into town takes forever."

"Dani, you'd mentioned a place you wanted to try in town, right?" Kiera asked, and Danica could hear the unspoken way Kiera was offering Danica an excuse to spend some more time away from Pete if she needed. Danica tallied it as reason number 483 why Kiera was her favorite person: She'd always been able to read Danica like a book.

She was an idiot when it came to that woman, and she couldn't trust herself. As soon as she'd seen Pete the day before, a wave of emotions and attraction and memories flooded her senses. Even now, she realized with dismay that the familiar butterflies of excitement appeared when Pete was nearby.

A half hour later, she and Kiera had ditched their gear at the condo, jumped on the gondola into town, and were walking along one of the main streets of downtown, a charming strip of brick buildings with shops and food that blended small town with luxury resort. Ahead of them, the San Juan mountains were white tipped, their steep peaks reaching up toward the bright blue sky.

"So, want to talk about your little episode on the mountain?" Kiera asked as they walked through the door of a brewpub. Danica had lived in Denver long enough to know you couldn't throw a stone in a Colorado mountain town without hitting a brewpub. Most had good beer but extremely average food. The ambiance of this particular establishment was rustic, with long wooden tables and wood-paneled walls. Ancient skis and snowshoes hung above black and white photos of people skiing or hiking in what looked like the 1940s. Like most brewpubs, it smelled like yeast and fried foods, and the table was only slightly sticky in places.

"Episode? When I fell?" Danica asked, unwinding her scarf and taking off her beanie, running her hands through her hair to revive her hat-flattened locks. The bangs were new, and she wasn't exactly sure how she felt about them yet. She checked her phone to read a text from her favorite colleague, saying that the baby she'd been texting about the day before was still strong and stable. Even hundreds of miles away, she'd never learned to stop worrying about her patients.

"No, when you yelled at Pete for helping you," Kiera clarified, giving her a pointed look that could only come from years of practice as a mother and a middle school teacher.

Danica locked her phone, stifling her grimace at the photo of Eddie she'd put there to keep up appearances. She turned to Kiera, focusing solely on her friend. "I just told her I didn't need help."

Kiera's expression was one of skepticism, and what Danica noted was just the tiniest smirk.

Danica lifted her chin in defiance. "It's so awkward when someone tries to help you stand back up on skis. I would have just taken us both down." Danica adjusted her coat on the back of the chair, then tugged at the sleeves of her base layer shirt.

A server appeared to take their order and disappeared just as quickly. Danica sipped water out of a red plastic cup that had seen better days. She missed plastic straws. Paper straws were a travesty. In the age of space travel and the Large Hadron Collider, why couldn't someone invent a straw that didn't instantly dissolve on your lips, kill sea turtles, or need to be toted around in your purse? Thankfully, the server's return with their beers saved her from further straw grief.

"So, what's really up? You seem off," Kiera said, wiping at the corner of her mouth after taking a large sip of her cloudy beer.

Danica gulped at her own beer, a smooth golden ale. "Isn't it weird that Pete is here after just being absent for fifteen years? No one's even mad that she just hasn't talked to any of us except for Izzy in fifteen years?"

"Yeah," Kiera admitted. "I guess that's a little weird." She raised an eyebrow at Danica.

"I mean, even Izzy comments on my social media posts or sends me a Happy Birthday text. Pete just disappeared and then shows up and acts like we're just as close as we had been."

Kiera made a noise of agreement, thoughtfully looking down into her beer.

"She doesn't even seem to have changed at all," Danica said quickly. Only with Kiera could she be so honest. "She's still impulsive and just doing whatever she likes and acting like those of us with careers have sold out to… the man or something."

Kiera snorted. "Damn the man."

"Hell yeah, except the man signs my checks that pay my mortgage so like, yeah, sure, if that's selling out, then consider me sold."

Kiera looked amused and concerned at the same time. "Wow. You're really riled up."

Danica laughed self-consciously. Kiera wasn't wrong. Her heart was pounding, and she felt a rush of adrenaline from her complaints. "Have you talked to her at all in the last… well, since college and not told me?"

"Uh, no, I was obviously Team Danica in the pseudo-breakup."

"God, I love you," Danica said, grinning. "She does seem like she's happy, though. Annoyingly."

"I'm honestly jealous she gets to travel so much. Wouldn't you, if you had the chance?" Kiera asked.

Danica shrugged. Most days, she preferred her couch and her favorite throw blanket and a cup of tea or wine. "It seems exhausting."

"Nothing can be more exhausting than teaching cells and biodiversity to 85 pubescent middle schoolers all day," Kiera said with a tired grin.

Danica groaned. "Yeah, that does sound... rough." She tipped her glass in acknowledgement. "Major props to you for sticking with that, especially after Covid. No, thank you."

"It has its moments. I'm glad to have work. I can't imagine how Maggie is a stay-at-home mom. I feel like my brain would just melt," Kiera admitted.

Danica raised her eyebrows. "Same, but she seems happy, too."

"Everyone does seem that way, I think," Kiera said, her expression unreadable.

Danica nodded slowly, feeling like she might be the only one who wasn't. Just another reason to not tell Kiera about her breakup with Eddie, she supposed. Honestly, it surprised her that Kiera hadn't already sussed it out. Maybe being around Pete had frazzled Danica so much that Kiera couldn't see beyond her immediate distress. She cleared her throat, shifting the subject just slightly away from herself. "What's new with the girls? Did Lizzie decide what her science fair project is going to be, or is she still overthinking it?"

They talked about Kiera's daughters, two perfect little hellions who Danica adored. They were tiny Kiera clones in every way, from their round faces and dark hair to their snark. Although Danica found that fact perfectly delightful, Kiera found it endlessly annoying.

They finished their meals in better spirits, laughing as they shared stories about work and kids and life while Danica avoided talking about her own relationship. Still, something in the back of Danica's mind knew that the conversation about Pete wasn't over. Kiera had never let her off the hook so easily before, and she doubted that would start now.

CHAPTER 4

PETE

FOR THEIR LAST RUN OF THE DAY, PETE AND IZZY TOOK SEE Forever again, a blue that ran along the topmost ridge of the resort's boundary. The views were incredible and the easier run was perfect for her worn out legs. Better yet, they could board from the top all the way down to the bottom, right into the courtyard in front of the condo.

They explored the runs near Lift 9 along the resort's western edge for most of the afternoon, including a lunch break with Maggie at Bon Vivant, a French restaurant positioned two-thirds up the mountain. You couldn't go wrong in Telluride — it was truly one of the most beautiful places she'd ever been, and having the time to leisurely take in the sights while also flying down the side of a mountain was basically peak happiness. They wove down See Forever toward San Sophia Station, cutting over on Smuggler to Misty Maiden, which would lead them straight into Mountain Village.

Izzy had her earbuds in listening to music — she'd been blasting The Shrikes' new album most of the afternoon, ignoring Pete in favor of soaking up the music. Pete preferred the silence, catching bits of people's conversations and laughter, taking in the rhythmic clanking of the lifts, focusing on the swish of snow under the edge of her board as she carved slow and wide down Misty Maiden.

Her breath fogged in front of her and she flexed her hands in her gloves, winding between the assholes who congregated directly at the end of a run, like people weren't barreling toward them.

"You sure you don't want to hop on 4?" Izzy asked, gesturing to the lift station. In this particular area, several lifts joined together.

"No, but feel free to go it alone," Pete said, bending to undo her bindings.

"Suit yourself." Izzy paused beside her, then unclipped one binding and scooted off in the direction of Lift 4.

Pete cursed her rental bindings. She preferred the ease of step on bindings, but she hadn't had the luxury of getting those at the ski rental shop.

It would have been smart to bring her own gear, but the hassle of bringing all of that baggage on the plane from Seattle would have been too much. She preferred to travel with only her backpack and exactly what she needed, nothing frivolous or annoying. She'd sooner cut off an arm than check a bag, even when living abroad. Especially when living abroad. Watching tourists drag gigantic wheeled luggage over ancient cobblestones made something inside of her die of second-hand embarrassment.

She tucked her board under her arm and walked toward the condo's rear entrance, sniffling in the chilly afternoon air.

"Oh, give me a fucking break," someone said above her and she froze, glancing around. The voice made something inside of Pete's brain snap to attention — she'd know that voice anywhere. What had she done to piss off Danica so badly?

On the balcony above her, Danica leaned her back against

the railing, her chestnut hair peeking out from under a beanie.

Pete paused just below the balcony, out of sight but well within listening distance. It was just simple curiosity, right? No one could fault her for happening upon Danica's conversation. She tried to keep her breathing quiet, which was quite a feat with the lack of oxygen in Colorado. Seriously, how did anyone exercise for a full day at 10,000 feet? It took superhuman strength.

"Why are you calling me?" Danica chided from the balcony above her. "I don't want to talk about this again."

Pete stared up at the balcony in silent intrigue, every fiber of her body buzzing with curiosity.

"We've talked about this." Danica's voice stopped abruptly, and Pete ducked in case she had been caught. A long sigh told Pete that the person had interrupted Danica. "Eddie, seriously, this isn't a good time."

Ah, so Danica was talking to her fiancé. Pete knew that Danica was engaged — Izzy had told her when she'd visited Croatia last summer. Izzy hadn't liked the guy when she'd met him at Maggie's wedding, but she rarely liked anyone, so that wasn't exactly a damning endorsement. Danica knew what she wanted — she always had — and Pete trusted that she had chosen someone good for her.

Judging from Danica's irritation, this Eddie guy sounded needy as hell. Pete cringed, picturing some scrawny dude with tears in his eyes. Who would ever talk to Danica that way? Danica busted her ass to take care of everyone around her. She always had. It was something that had always made Pete feel proud to be her friend.

Well, and more than friends. Whatever they had been. Friends who slept together sometimes. Friends who texted the other at 1 a.m. to come over to each other's place "just to cuddle and sleep."

Everyone always needed Danica, and so Pete was

resolved to never add to that burden. And if that meant staying at arm's length so that Danica never had to worry about taking care of her, then that was the way it had to be.

But that was then. To be honest with herself, a little part of her did feel sad when she found out that Danica was engaged. Sure, they'd never been officially in a relationship, but before their last fight, even after their last fight, she'd always hoped... Well, she'd always held onto the belief that they'd be right for each other someday.

She'd worked hard to make something of herself after college. She'd sold the app she'd made for her senior thesis, a night sky flying simulator called Til Morning, that had been the capstone of her Computer Science degree. Til Morning had been dissected into two other apps by a larger company, and she'd used the money from the sale to invest and travel and experience the world.

Had she ever truly grown up like Danica had spitefully suggested during their last fight? Not in a million years. Change, mature, grow into the kind of person who might deserve a woman like Danica? Well, she'd tried.

Maybe it had been too little, too late. Danica was marrying someone who whined on the phone while she was on a trip with friends. Add that to the red flag category, right under Dentist. A *dentist*. Talk about a career only a psycho would choose. No one — patients or practitioners — truly *enjoyed* dentistry, surely.

"We're *over*," Danica said, and Pete's heart nearly leapt out of her chest. Had she just witnessed Danica breaking up with her fiancé *over the phone*?

Danica was still on the balcony above her, silent and seemingly standing still. Fear of discovery as an under-porch stalker prevented Pete from risking a glance. Nothing said, "I'm definitely worth your time now" quite like crouching under a balcony, breathing heavily while spying.

Danica and Eddie were over... Her pulse jumped and a

little thrill shot through her. Of course, Danica being single did not necessarily give her a chance... but it did not *not* give her a chance.

She adjusted the board in her arms as silently as she could, her hands growing cold inside her gloves from standing still for the past few minutes. The warmth of exercise had worn off. Gone was the adrenaline from hurtling down a mountain, and now she was regretting her decision to linger outside. Thankfully, the balcony creaked above her, and she heard the patio door open and shut. After counting to fifteen Mississippi just to make sure, she snuck in the back door as silently as she could, taking off her boots and jacket in the mudroom.

Pete and Maggie were both startled when Maggie appeared in the mudroom a moment later. "Sorry, I was just grabbing something from my coat," she said a little too casually, reaching past Pete to slip a vape from one of the open pockets. "Want some?" She held out the vape, and Pete could just barely smell the hint of weed.

"Nah, I think that might kill me at this elevation," Pete joked, placing her boots under the bench where they could dry overnight.

"You know, it might be the only thing keeping me alive at this point. There's no oxygen here anyway, so might as well replace it with something else." With a grin on her face, Maggie cracked open the back door, vaped, and let the smoke drift away.

The back door opened again only a moment later and Izzy stomped in, her eyebrows raising in surprise to see them both standing there. Maggie handed her the vape before she even had her board stowed against the wall. Izzy laughed, taking a long pull, then opened the door again to exhale outside.

"This really brings back memories of smoking out the window of our first dorm," Izzy said, handing the vape back to Maggie.

"Room 305 forever," Maggie said with a grin. Maggie and

Pete helped Izzy take off her coat, stepping aside so she could remove her boots with more grace than Pete had demonstrated. Izzy wiggled her toes in her thick Fair Isle ski socks.

"What do you guys know about Eddie?" Pete asked in possibly the least-casual way a question had ever been asked. She couldn't just tell everyone what she'd overheard — one, it would out her as a creeping creep after all, but two, it was Danica's torrid news to tell.

"Eddie, like Dani's fiancé?" Maggie asked, sticking her vape back into the pocket of her coat.

Pete nodded, and Izzy rolled her eyes. "Not this again," Izzy murmured.

Maggie eyed Pete suspiciously. "Not what again?"

"Nothing. I'm just curious. I've never met him," Pete said, stuffing her hands into her pockets. She wanted to get a read on how heartbroken Danica was going to be, but she also wanted to see if this was the kind of breakup that would stick.

Izzy sighed. "You've never met Maggie's wife either," she pointed out, and Pete could tell by her tone that she hadn't meant to make Pete feel guilty for being a bit off-grid with the friend-group, but it had struck a chord.

"He's quiet," Maggie said. "Reserved, but smiley. Like, really tooth-forward, if you know what I mean. Dani has never given me any hints about how he is in bed, despite my asking several times."

Pete wrinkled her nose in disgust.

"Do you think she's happy?" Pete asked, her voice taking on an embarrassingly tender tone.

Maggie and Izzy exchanged a look, then a shrug.

"I guess," Maggie said. "She said they hadn't discussed having kids and that the wedding has no date yet, so my spidey-senses say something is weird there, but with Dani, you never know. She could be sitting in a burning building and tell you she loves the warmth. It's so rare to find out how she really feels about anything."

Hmm. That was a good point. Pete chewed on her lower lip.

Izzy raised an eyebrow, and Pete could tell she knew exactly where Pete's mind was going. Only Izzy knew about Pete's pipe dream that things with Danica could go a different way in the future.

Maggie crossed her arms. "What's going on in that weird little ball of chaos you call your brain?"

"Okay, first, *rude*," Pete said, stifling a grin. "And second, nothing." She wasn't a very good liar, but she attempted to conceal that fact with a bit of over-explanation. "I was curious about our friend. Our *mutual* friend. Our friend who we are all friends with and should care about."

Her intended stern look gave way to a moment of concern that she might seem too intimidating. Well, that was a worry until both Izzy and Maggie laughed.

"Sure," Izzy said with a snort of amusement. "Extremely convincing."

"I had no idea you were still in love with her after all this time," Maggie said, her voice holding a high note of surprise.

Izzy groaned, taking Maggie's vape out of her coat again. Apparently, she'd need much, much more THC in her system to handle this conversation.

"Love is a very strong word," Pete said, holding out her palms to stop that line of thought immediately. "More like a very vague notion, just a hint, really, of interest. More curiosity than anything else."

Neither of her friends seemed very convinced, based on the skeptical and amused looks on their faces.

"You're out of your mind," Izzy said, holding open the door as she exhaled into the cold air.

"No, wait, I actually don't hate this," Maggie said, still

eyeing Pete. "Eddie seems about as exciting as a hard-to-kill houseplant. Where's the excitement in that, you know?"

Pete raised an eyebrow. "Weird metaphor, but—"

"Simile," Izzy corrected, blowing vapor out the door again.

"Whatever," Pete said, rolling her eyes. "And what do you mean? Or are you just trying to meddle because you're boringly happy in your marriage?"

Maggie waved her hands dismissively in the air, hopping on the balls of her socked feet, though Pete couldn't tell if that was out of excitement or feeling cold. "I love to meddle. Meddling Maggie, that's what they call me."

"No one has ever said that," Izzy said, shaking her head with her eyes closed.

"Maybe they'll start now. What if we try to figure out this week if you two could... reconnect?" Maggie offered, still hopping.

"Is that a good idea?" Pete asked, feeling a spark of worry at the excitement gleaming in Meddling Maggie's eyes.

"Uh, sure," Maggie said, watching Izzy take an admirably long draw from the vape. "You good?"

Izzy nodded, coughing and exhaling inside the mudroom, then panicking and hurrying to open the back door.

"I don't pretend to understand how vapes work, but if you could not hotbox Aunt Jade's entire house, that would be helpful." Maggie scolded Izzy with a smile that said she wasn't seriously mad. She looked from Izzy back to Pete. "Okay, let's brainstorm how to figure out this reconnection."

CHAPTER 5

DANICA

How she and Pete ended up alone on a chair lift together, Danica wasn't entirely sure. Kiera had gone off to ski the black runs higher up the mountain. Maggie and Izzy had been right behind her in line, but as the chair swung around and she settled in, it was Pete beside her, not Maggie.

She tucked her poles under her leg and held onto the bar, staring straight ahead.

"These seats are kind of squishy," Pete remarked.

Danica nodded, noticing that her ass wasn't freezing on a hard metallic seat for once.

"So, you've been avoiding me," Pete said playfully.

Danica watched as a skier carved down a wide blue run effortlessly. They looked peaceful all alone. No one else was beside them, cornering them in a vulnerable moment. "I haven't been avoiding you. It's been a busy trip."

The chair swung as it lifted higher and higher, the rhythmic clicking of the overhead cable system the only sound above them.

"I don't want it to be weird between us," Pete said,

leaning back in the chair. She pulled a small flask from her jacket pocket and took a swig.

"Are you seriously drinking right now?" Danica asked, her voice dripping with irritation. "See, this is—"

Pete held out the flask. "You want some?"

"No, I don't want whiskey right now," Danica said, exasperated.

"Suit yourself," Pete said, taking another swig from the flask.

The chair passed another pole, which screeched like some poor dying animal as the chair slowed to a stop. The chair swung, suspended about fifty feet above the ground, flanked on the side of the run by tall bare aspens dotted with conifers. An unexpected mid-air breakdown.

Oh, fantastic, it was her worst nightmare.

"Did the lift break?" Danica glanced up at the pole, then swiveled in her seat to look back. She didn't recognize the snowboarders behind them, like Maggie and Izzy had either left their position in line or were lagging behind. Were they stuck, too?

"I bet someone took a tumble getting off, so they held it up," Pete remarked, unconcerned.

Danica took a deep breath, raising her goggles onto her helmet. She stared up toward where the chair was attached to the cable.

"We're not going to fall," Pete said, nonchalantly resting her elbow on the seat back as if they were comfortably on a sofa, not dangling precariously fifty feet above ground.

Danica's strained voice undoubtedly gave away her uncertainty. "You don't know that. What if we're stuck here for hours?"

"Then it's a nice relaxing spot with a view. We're right next to a pole, so we'll be one of the first to be rescued." Pete looked around, relaxed and enjoying the view like the typical unbothered, unworried person she was.

Danica's chest felt tight and her mouth went dry. "Why isn't it moving yet? If someone just fell, wouldn't it be moving by now?" She didn't know if she was more upset about the idea of being stuck on a chairlift high up in the air or being stuck on a chairlift with Pete.

Pete shrugged — *shrugged!* — and unzipped her backpack, pulling out a water bottle. "You still really hate being out of control, don't you?"

"What's that supposed to mean?" Danica said, short-tempered and anxious and tired, taking off her gloves. "Is that even water?" She was blazing hot suddenly, and put her clammy hands on the metal bar in front of her, cooling them instantly. Her throat felt tight, and she was struggling to take a deep breath. Having a panic attack was inconvenient at the best of times, but being stuck with her ex in a swinging death trap, precariously trapped in what felt like thousands of feet above solid ground, was an even worse scenario than most.

Pete held out the water bottle in an offering. "Want a sip?" she asked, her expression soft.

"I'm fine," Danica said immediately, but then paused and took the water bottle. Her mouth was like sandpaper, her skin felt itchy, and her hands felt numb. The water was cool and soothing, and she gulped it down desperately, trying to convince herself her throat wasn't closing up. Her rational understanding, informed by medicine and history, recognized the panic attack, yet the panic itself felt no less real at that moment.

"Hey," Pete said, her voice gentle as she took off her own glove and reached for Danica's bare hand. Pete's hand was warm as it wrapped around Danica's, and Danica's panic overrode any consideration of what holding Pete's hand meant. "Everything's going to be fine. You're not alone. We're not that far off the ground."

Danica rationally knew all of this, but she could still feel tears welling in her eyes. She looked away from Pete, not wanting her to see how upset she felt. Pete held her hand in silence. Her skin was softer than Danica thought it would be, though she could feel a callous on Pete's thumb where it rubbed the top of her own hand.

Danica let out a shaky breath, unzipping the top few inches of her coat. She watched skiers gliding down the run under them, envious of their freedom. Would they be up here for hours? What time was it? What if they were up here overnight? Would they freeze to death? She knew it was a long-shot, but she wasn't sure how she'd fare with something like survival-cannibalism.

Pete cleared her throat. "Want to tell me about Eddie?"

"I sure don't," Danica answered, biting her lip as she turned away.

"He sounds nice," Pete's voice held the same amount of excitement as if she were identifying a common bird in the pine trees.

"He is nice." Danica was speaking through clenched teeth to keep her chin from quivering. He was nice. He used to be nice.

"Izzy said he's quiet," Pete added.

"Izzy met him once, at Maggie's wedding."

"He's a dentist, right?"

"Yep."

"An admirable profession."

"Why are you like this?" Danica asked.

"Like what?" Pete shrugged.

Danica huffed in indignation. How many more questions about Eddie would she have to dodge if they were stuck here for hours? She studied the ground again, contemplating raising the safety bar so she could just launch herself out of the lift. The hospital provided her with good health insurance. She could work despite having two broken legs, couldn't she? Or, worst case, she could take short-term disability and actually take a few relaxing weeks off without

Pete fucking Pancott questioning her fake-current but really ex-fiancé.

"You know what really pissed me off about how you broke up with me?" Pete asked, squeezing Danica's hand. Her voice was uncharacteristically solemn.

Danica nearly gave herself whiplash with how fast she spun to glare at Pete, forgetting how a sudden movement might make the chairlift rock. "Excuse me?" Pete had a mischievous look as she studied Danica's face. "This is what you want to talk about right now?"

Pete shrugged again. Shrugged! "What better time than when you're a hostage? You've been avoiding me, and I think we should talk about it. Just to clear the air."

Danica wished looks could kill at that moment.

"It pissed me off you were so… final about it," Pete said, sighing. "You just decided there was no future for us, and you wouldn't be swayed."

"*You* broke up with *me*," Danica said slowly, taking a deep, shaky breath that only seemed to stoke the fires of her rage at Pete's statement.

"I said we could see what happened after graduation," Pete said, her eyebrows raised.

"Yeah, because you were so noncommittal that you couldn't even *commit* to breaking up with me," Danica snapped.

"What's that supposed to mean?" Pete raised a brow in disbelief.

"You being noncommittal?" Danica asked, her irritation growing with every word out of Pete's mouth.

Pete nodded, and Danica could still feel the warmth of her hand. She pulled her hand free, waving her hand in the air between them. "In the end you couldn't even commit to calling me your girlfriend." Danica's voice was sharp, her chest aching with familiar hurt. The source and timing of Pete's comments were perplexing. It had been fifteen years since they'd broken up, or rather, not broken up. Since they'd ended things between them.

"You didn't *want* to be my girlfriend!" Pete said, her expression matching Danica's irritation.

"Where did you get that idea from?" Danica asked. "Why do you think I put up with your bullshit for *years*?"

"Because you hate failing at things. That's why you stay with things or people, even when they no longer serve you." Pete looked far too confident in her perception as she said that.

Danica clenched and unclenched her fists. "What is that supposed to mean?" Danica asked. "What does that have to do with us?"

Pete stared her straight in the eye as she said, "We have almost nothing in common. We were bound to find that out eventually, and then it was all going to come crashing down."

Danica blinked. "Are you saying that you wouldn't commit to our relationship for my sake? To save me from failure?"

Pete nodded. "Yeah, I mean, look at you and Eddie—"

"You don't even know him," Danica said abruptly.

"I know enough. He's nice, quiet, probably politically neutral, and he has a good job. He's a safe choice, right?" Pete looked her up and down. "He doesn't challenge you. He doesn't inspire you. You don't sound inspired. You sound like you barely even like the guy. You never bring him up, even when Maggie and Kiera are talking about their partners. Doesn't sound like someone about to marry the love of their life."

Danica opened her mouth to tell Pete she was wrong, but closed it, too exasperated to even get the words out. She wanted to tell Pete she was wrong, even if that would technically be a lie. Even on his best days, Eddie's unexpected call yesterday made her realize she had never even considered getting back together with him. As she was trying to find the right words to tell Pete where she could shove her assumptions about Eddie, the cable above their heads groaned, the pulley system clicking as it started up again. The chair swayed and Danica grabbed the bar again, trying not to lose her balance as the chair slowly lurched into motion once more.

"Hey, it works," Pete said, her mouth splitting into a bright smile.

Danica blinked. Was she on a chairlift with Jekyll and Hyde? She snatched Pete's flask out of her hand and took a swig, the warmth and sweetness surprising her. She sputtered, sniffing the top of the flask. "Is this… honey?"

"My throat gets dry when it's cold. Warm honey water helps," Pete said.

Danica eyed her.

"It's okay. You don't have to say it out loud."

Danica raised one eyebrow, taking another sip from the flask.

"That you were wrong."

Danica rolled her eyes, passing back the flask. "I'll say it out loud when I'm actually wrong." She pulled her gloves back on, focusing intently on tightening the wrist part. She'd assumed Pete was drinking whiskey out of a flask, and there she was, drinking warm honey water like some Golden Girls character. Why did that annoy her so much more?

Pete shifted her goggles back into place. The goggles were absurdly pink and reflective, clashing with everything else about her laid-back style. "How's your panic attack? You feel like you're coming down from it yet?"

Danica studied Pete's side profile for a moment. Her high cheekbones, the slight bump in her nose where she broke it playing flag football in high school. A face once so familiar she could draw it from memory, but she now felt like it was the face of someone she knew but couldn't quite place.

Had Pete picked a fight solely to distract her from her

panic? If so, it had worked. That was the most frustrating part? She hadn't spent the entire stall on the lift panicking, because she'd been so focused on her infuriation. To what extent did Pete's words honestly convey her emotions, and to what extent were they a manipulative tactic to agitate her and divert her attention from their perilous situation in the stalled chairlift? She wanted to thank Pete, but she also still kind of wanted to strangle her. Compromising for somewhere in the middle, she stared straight ahead, pulling her yellow goggles back over her own eyes.

Danica focused intently as the lift lowered into the station, growing more nervous with every moment that Pete continued to lean casually back in the seat. Danica straightened her skis, clutching both poles. Getting plowed down by a ski lift upon disembarking was one of her worst fears, and letting that happen in front of Pete only heightened that worry inside of her.

Pete lifted the bar and let her snowboard land under her at the last moment, expertly balancing and gliding out of the ski lift's way as it continued to move forward. To channel the same level of cool and casual, Danica did not panic and claw her way to freedom with her poles. Instead, she concentrated on keeping her balance and getting out of the way, hoping her reaction looked just as calm and collected. Feeling a bit cocky from her success, she paused, glancing Pete's way. "Which way are you heading?"

Pete stood from clipping in her binding. "I was going to head down Bushwacker," she said, gesturing to the black run behind her. "You coming?"

Danica shook her head. "No way." She pointed to the blue behind her. "Woozley's."

"Coward," Pete teased, her white teeth flashing in a grin.

"Proud to be an alive coward," Danica said back. She leaned forward, pushing off her poles and moving away from the horrifying black runs behind her.

"See you later," Pete called out, then added something unintelligible with a gesture toward Danica.

Danica glanced over her shoulder, confused, just in time to see a herd of children in matching red vests, absolutely invincible on their tiny skis, barreling towards her. They seemed to be racing toward her at an alarmingly fast speed. She froze, clutching her poles close to her body as they raced past. How were kids' clubs even allowed up away from the bunny hill and lower, easier green runs? They split around her, four kids on each side like a school of piranhas, moving as one ferocious organism. A ski instructor whizzed by after them, blowing a whistle and calling for them to slow down. She heard their giggles on the wind as they raced out of sight down the steeper descent of See Forever.

Pete held out a thumbs up questioningly. "You okay? Thought you were a goner."

"It's going to take more than that to take me out," Danica said, her heart still pounding.

"Just a car ride and a slippery parking lot, right?" Pete laughed.

Danica responded with a slightly teasing, "Get lost," as she rolled her eyes and headed in the direction of Woozley's Way. She thought she heard Pete laughing in response behind her, but she stifled the grin on her own face, not ready to outwardly admit she enjoyed their banter.

Fifteen years later, and Pete fucking Pancott still got under her skin like no other.

CHAPTER 6

PETE

PETE SLID OPEN THE PATIO DOOR, THE COLD HITTING HER WITH force as she stepped over the threshold in her swimsuit, a beanie pulled low over her ears. Everyone had gone to bed early after homemade pizza night, but she needed a moment of quiet relaxation before being able to fall asleep. After a long two days of snowboarding, the hot tub was the only cure for her aching body. She hated admitting that she wasn't 22 anymore, that two days of snowboarding could make her feel so exhausted and sore. Her knees burned, her back was stiff, and even her arms felt heavy.

She flipped open the cover of the hot tub, sliding it to the side, and then turned on the jets, adjusting the temperature resembling molten lava. She kept the lights off, preferring the ambiance of the darkness. A moan nearly escaped her lips as she slid into the water, letting the water rise to just over her shoulders. Pete took off her beanie, feeling warm already.

Her eyes closed and she let her head fall back against the cushioned headrest, letting the jets massage her shoulders.

Pete heard the patio door slide open and opened her eyes to see Danica standing in the doorway in a bikini.

"Sorry, I didn't know you were using it," Danica said quickly, reaching to shut the door.

"You're fine, there's enough room," Pete said, trying to keep a casual note to her voice. She didn't want to scare Danica away, but that woman acted like Pete was a bomb with a lit fuse. Pete had felt a bit guilty after picking a fight with Danica earlier, but it had been an easy way to get Danica's mind off of the fact that the lift was stuck for a few minutes. She'd done the first thing she could think of, which was to take Danica's focus and direct it elsewhere, if only for a moment.

It had absolutely nothing to do with Pete wanting the answers to those questions and not knowing how else to ask. Nothing.

"Are you sure?" Danica asked, holding her towel in front of her protectively. Neither one had mentioned the lift conversation during dinner, like Danica would rather pretend the conversation hadn't happened. "You're just sitting out here in the dark?"

"Yeah, quit being weird, Wendell," Pete said, closing her eyes again, but the image of Danica in a bikini was burned into the back of her eyelids. It wasn't the least amount of clothing she'd ever seen Danica wear, but she hadn't expected the sight to affect her so much. Danica had always been soft, but her curves had only gotten sexier and fuller. She casually opened one eye to watch Danica climb over the side of the hot tub, pausing to tie her hair into a bun on top of her head. Pete's own swimsuit was more of a sports bra and boy shorts style, but Danica's bikini had minimal coverage. She could make out Danica's ample cleavage and the pale skin of an ass cheek. She wouldn't object to Danica's exposed body, but maintaining eye contact with Danica's face required effort.

"I can't believe how sore I am," Danica said, sliding her body into the water.

Pete's mouth had gone dry, and she struggled to pull her focus — both her eyes and brain, honestly — to anywhere but Danica's breasts. "Yeah."

Danica let out a long exhale, relaxing back against the wall of the tub. Pete squinted, focusing on how the white snow striped the mountain behind Danica, illuminating the runs. She could see the lights of a snowcat grooming the slopes. Even after 10 p.m., Mountain Village was still lit up like some kind of Rich People beacon to space, but she could still see a handful of constellations and a few planets despite the lights. Mars glowed brightly in the East, right between Gemini and Cancer. Sirius and Rigel were always easy to pick out, and she kept her eyes on them and not Danica's... well, every inch of Danica that would cause her to lose the filter between her mouth and brain and say something she might regret.

They sat in silence, the only sound the jets of the tub and the occasional swish of water as one of them shifted or moved their arms.

The conversation they'd had on the chairlift hung heavy between them, and suddenly, being three feet apart felt more like an ocean stretched between them. Pete glanced toward Danica, surprised to find the woman's piercing eyes watching her, her face in shadow.

Pete's heart ached to realize just how beautiful Danica was after all these years. She looked away before Danica could see those feelings written all over her face.

"Thanks for earlier," Danica said in a casual, if not slightly forced, way.

A nervous laugh escaped Pete's lips as she shrugged. She was worried about revealing her rekindled attraction, afraid of saying something she hadn't thought through fully, afraid of ruining the moment with her vulnerability. "I don't know what you mean." She heard Danica sniffle in the cold air and reached for her discarded beanie. "Want this?"

Danica hesitated for a moment before reaching out to take the knit hat, pulling it down over her ears to ward off the chill. "Thank you."

"Bikini and a beanie. Quite a look."

Danica smiled, swirling her arms in the water. "So, where do you live now?"

"Seattle," Pete said.

"What do you do in Seattle?" Danica asked.

Pete pursed her lips, trying to find the right answer. "Not much. I haven't been there very long, and I don't know if I'll stay."

"Still a rolling stone?"

Pete held up her arms. "No moss yet."

"What have you been doing for the last decade and a half, then?" Danica said, her gaze inquisitive.

Pete had a strange reluctance to tell her about the app sale. It felt kind of tech bro-y in a way that she didn't want to associate with. Way too akin to owning a Cybertruck or growing interested in day trading. Not the vibe she was going for. It felt even weirder to tell Danica that she was running a nonprofit, like she was only doing it for the bragging rights. She preferred to keep most of her life private, even from most of her friends, but especially from Danica. "Um, this and that. You know."

Danica blinked. "I really don't know. Hence why I'm asking."

"Just traveling. You know me, can't stay in one place long," Pete lied, uncomfortable with either looking like she had a savior complex or looking like she'd never faced a responsibility in her life. Better to just let Danica assume the worst, she supposed.

"Why were you in Croatia?" Danica asked.

"Just for fun," Pete lied again. She had spent time in Croatia, visiting two institutions for orphans and vulnerable children run by the kindest Croatian couple she'd ever met. Her goal was to find a way to bridge the funding gaps for the older teens, ensuring they had the resources they needed to live independently.

Danica shook her head. "I don't know how you do it, never staying anywhere for long." Her tone wasn't judgmental per se, but more like she was self-consciously curious.

"Some of us would crumble under the weight of med school, I'm afraid," Pete deflected. An accidental touch of legs in the water sent a jolt through her, reminding her of the mortifying intensity of what felt like a high school crush on Danica. Something had shifted between them. She could feel it in the way their eyes met before they both quickly averted their gazes.

"I nearly did," Danica said, shifting in her seat.

"You? I don't believe it. I bet you graduated top of your class." Pete smiled, watching Danica roll her eyes.

"I was third. Nobody likes a show-off," Danica said with a small stifled smile.

"Of course. And you've been a doctor ever since? Is that how med school works?" Pete asked.

"I wish. After med school, I did a three-year pediatric residency in Philadelphia, then a three-year neonatology fellowship back in Colorado."

"So, of the last fifteen years, you've spent ten of them still in school or training?" Pete asked, horrified at the thought.

Danica nodded. "Something like that, yeah."

Pete cursed under her breath, grimacing. "I can't imagine anything worse."

Danica's laughter erupted, a burst of pure amusement. "Thank you. It's only my life's work."

"Are you happy?" Pete asked, her stomach flipped in

anticipation of Danica's answer. She had begun to realize that yes, she wanted Danica to say yes, that she was happy, but she also didn't want that happiness to be so consuming that it left no room for... other options. She couldn't bring herself to hope that there'd be room for her.

Danica stared at her for a long moment. "With... my career?"

Pete angled her head, the warm water rising around her shoulders as she stretched her legs out across the bench seat. "With your life."

"Who asks someone a question like that?" Danica released an exasperated sigh.

"It's an easy question if you're really happy," Pete said, trying to keep her voice calm.

"Of course I'm happy. I love my job, I love Denver, and I love... my life," Danica said, stumbling over the last phrase.

Pete watched Danica's shoulders tense with each word. She'd spent enough time decoding Danica back in college to know when Danica was lying, because her shoulders always rose closer to her ears as her entire body tensed, like the lie made her physically unable to relax. "Okay."

"Okay?"

"Okay, I believe you," Pete said, biting her lower lip and looking away before Danica could make out her disappointment.

"I don't need you to believe me," Danica said. "I don't care what you think at all." Pete knew that Danica's knee-jerk defensiveness was a sign that she'd been getting closer to letting Danica lower those walls she kept so heavily guarded. The water sloshed as Danica climbed out of the hot tub, grabbing a towel without pausing as she walked back inside, dripping water all over the patio.

Pete stared at the puddles, lights reflecting in the spilled water like the night sky. Her frustrated sigh became fog in the night air in front of her. Pushing Danica too far hadn't been her intention, but she craved to know what Danica was like now. If they had a present, or maybe even a future, instead of just a past.

CHAPTER 7

DANICA

At this moment, Danica was really regretting being such a good friend. Why in the world had she agreed to take snowboarding lessons with Maggie? Last night over pizza, Maggie confessed she was nervous to take the lessons she'd signed up for, and now here was Danica, on a bunny hill, feeling like she might die at any moment.

In all her years of skiing, she'd never been afraid of crashing into a tree, but strapped to this murder board, she just might meet her end.

"Toe edge," the ski instructor, an entertaining and sarcastic Aussie man named Glen, called out. The group was fanned out across the bunny hill, practicing their heel and toe edge balance. Danica thought it could have been an effective torture technique. Her quads burned, her knees hurt, and they hadn't even gone down the entire damn hill yet.

"Naur," Danica whined, flailing her arms and falling to her knees.

"Ah, right, make fun of the person trying to help you," Glen called back.

"Does Australia even have snow?" Maggie complained. "Have you ever even snowboarded? Did you lie on your resume, Glen?"

"We ski, for the record. But the snow is better here. Why do you think I'm not in Straya, hey?" Glen said, giving her a pointed look before walking off to help a younger girl.

Danica hated not being good at things immediately. She pushed herself back up, the board sliding precariously beneath her. Thank goodness it was only Maggie here with her, who hadn't even laughed despite Danica falling every ten seconds since she'd gotten strapped onto this board.

"I'll buy you a drink at the bar tonight," Maggie offered, looking at her with pleading puppy eyes she couldn't resist.

"Ten drinks," Danica bartered, falling backwards again. She concentrated on not putting her arms out to catch herself for fear of breaking a wrist, letting her ass take most of the force like Glen had instructed at the beginning of the lesson. Imagine breaking a bone on a bunny hill without even going down the run yet. Kiera would never let her live it down.

"A million drinks," Maggie said, nodding. Though her arms flailed and legs trembled, she stayed upright — unlike Danica.

Glen appeared above Danica, his ruddy, sunburned cheeks wrinkling at the edges as he smiled down at her. "Come on, you've got this," he said, reaching out a hand to help her up.

"Leave me here to die," Danica whined.

"You've been in this lesson for twenty minutes," Glen chided, laughing. Danica accepted his help, allowing him to steady her as she rose.

"I'm a skier. I know how to ski. I know the skiing moves. I *pizza*. I *french fry*. I do not *heel edge* and *toe edge*. The human body shouldn't be able to balance like this."

"She would know. She's a doctor," Maggie said with faux solemnity.

Danica added a sheepish shrug for emphasis.

"You may be a doctor, but you'll be a boarder before the end of this lesson. Now come on." Glen let go of her and she slid a few inches, wobbling, but remained upright. "That's it. Steady."

The lesson continued in much the same way, with Glen teaching Danica, Maggie, and five others who were alarmingly younger than them how to step out of their bindings and push their board with their free foot to get on a lift.

Maggie seemed to be catching on much faster than Danica, and they spent the next hour of the lesson practicing a falling leaf pattern down the bunny hill. Danica chanted in her head, "Leaves fall, not me. Leaves fall, not me" the whole way down.

They got on the small, slow lift and Danica never felt more at a loss without her ski poles. It was easier to balance with them and she didn't have to hop and maneuver her entire body quite as much to get into position. She awkwardly shuffled onto the magic carpet, a little moving walkway for lift-averse beginners, which was quite possibly the most terrifying thing she'd ever seen.

"They say the learning curve for snowboarding is way steeper than skiing," Maggie said from behind her. Her perfectly coiffed blonde bob remained intact as she removed her helmet and readjusted her ear warmer.

"I believe that," Danica said, her legs like jello as she wobbled a bit on the conveyor belt. "It's way harder to balance."

"Pete said she'll take us up some greens after lunch if we want," Maggie suggested. Greens were beginner trails, so Danica had a chance of staying upright for at least a portion of them. However, inviting Pete along was quite possibly the worst idea Maggie had ever had, second only to these lessons. Danica slid as she tried to climb off the magic carpet, falling onto her knees for the millionth time. Maggie shuffled beside her, lowering to the ground beside Danica.

Danica groaned, pressing her lips into a thin line as she maneuvered to sit down on her ass instead of her knees. "Snowboarding is a young man's sport, Mags. What possessed you to think this was a fun idea?"

Maggie sniffled in the cold air, putting her helmet back on her head. "Life is short."

Danica nodded, knowing that full-well. She'd seen plenty of miracles in her career, but she'd also witnessed a lot of heartbreak and grief. But then again, she had a therapist, so she at least had a place to express the emotions connected to the tumultuousness of having the pediatric patients.

Maggie rested her forearms on her knees as she stared down at the bunny hill before them. "You have kids, and then suddenly your life is only about them. They're parasites who take over every thought in your brain. I wanted to do something just for me. Something I never got to do as a kid, but not something I'm only doing *for* my kids."

Danica turned, picking up on a wistful tone in Maggie's voice. "I think that makes perfect sense, but I have to ask. Is everything okay with the kids?" Maggie had two boys and a girl, all under six. That situation would exhaust anyone.

Maggie waved her hand dismissively. "Oh, yeah. I wouldn't trade them for the world."

"And with Gwen?" Danica added.

Maggie nodded again, but she adjusted her goggles over her eyes so that Danica couldn't make out her full expression.

"Everything's great, honestly," Maggie said, clearing her throat. "I'm just tired. I don't know how Kiera still works while being a parent. Some days it's a struggle just to get everyone changed out of pajamas. I appreciate my parents looking after the kids while I'm away so Gwen could also have a break."

Danica put her gloved hand over Maggie's. "You're doing a really good job."

Maggie gave her a small smile. "I sure hope so. And I hope Grandma and Grandpa haven't let them have too much screen time while I'm gone."

Danica shook her head. "I'm sorry. I didn't realize all of this was weighing on you."

"It's just a constant weight, no more than usual. I'm used to it." Maggie bumped her shoulder. "I'm glad you're doing this with me."

"Me too," Danica said, smiling. "God, you're worried about screen time for your kids while I'm just over here considering if being run down by the chairlift can kill you."

Maggie glanced at the lift above them. "I mean, it's not *not* a death trap."

Glen walked past, holding the hand of a tween boy who was far steadier on his feet than she was.

"Glen, what if we just skip the lift part of the lesson and stay magic carpet riders?" Danica asked hopefully.

"Come on, I've had seven-year-olds braver than you," he responded.

"They have more bone density than me, too," Danica countered, readjusting her bindings. They weren't ready for the lift yet, but it was looming in the back of Danica's mind. There was simply no way she'd be able to do it while standing — how Pete had made it look so effortless, she'd never know.

But then again, Pete made everything look effortless. Back in college, she'd never once seen Pete studying or actually writing a paper or finishing an assignment. She'd seen Pete spend hours with video games, play ultimate frisbee most afternoons on the quad, or read books that weren't assigned for class. Even now, every detail she could glean about Pete's life just seemed as though she was still a woman with her head up in the clouds, never touching down in the real world.

It was impressive in a way, and annoying in another — Pete was smart, but she lacked the kind of ambition that drove Danica. Pete had made some kind of app for her thesis portfolio, but Danica had never seen it, and thought that maybe she'd never even finished it. In fact, it was a bit surprising when Pete showed up in her graduation gown. Had they really let her graduate without finishing her senior thesis?

"Earth to Danica," Maggie said from beside her. "Come in, Dani."

"Sorry, what?" Danica asked, shifting onto her knees to push herself back up to stand. While a bit easier than standing up in skis, she felt far less stable. At the top of the bunny hill, she watched Glen teach the younger group members a balance exercise using their toe edges.

"What were you just thinking about?" Maggie asked, hopping awkwardly with her board.

"Just how much I miss ski poles," Danica said, but in reality, that was what she'd been thinking about for a majority of the morning, so it wasn't entirely untrue.

"You looked really wistful for ski poles, then," Maggie teased.

"I long for the pole," Danica announced just as they rejoined the group lesson.

Glen snorted. "Easy, tiger. The kid's camp can hear you."

They spent the next hour working on maneuvering down the bunny hill without stopping to shift their edge, and Danica cheated, staying on her heel edge for the majority of the run. It was easier to balance leaning her weight backwards than forwards. Before she knew it, the lesson was done and Glen was giving them all high fives and telling them they were now one step closer to being professional snowboarders. Lift crisis averted.

Reaching the cafe at the bottom of the bunny hill, Danica and Maggie walked in and began loading their plates with every carb in sight.

"So, how's wedding planning going?" Maggie asked as they sat down with plates heaped with over-sauced pasta and limp french fries.

Danica pretended to be in the middle of a bite in order to gather her thoughts. "Fine," she said, unsure how to explain the situation. Even during their two-year engagement, they hadn't done much planning. Danica had asked Eddie to hold off on making decisions until things slowed down at work. She wanted to attend some bridal shows and get ideas and really organize her thoughts, she'd claimed. Given that things *never* seemed to slow down at work, they hadn't made much progress before the breakup.

In truth, she'd tried on one wedding dress, and nearly burst into tears in the dressing room from a sudden panic attack. Thankfully, she was there alone, so she didn't have to explain to any of her family or friends why she'd left after only one dress.

They'd been engaged for long enough to raise some questions from family members about their timeline, but Eddie had never rushed her, and she appreciated that, at least.

She thought of him tearing up on the phone the other day when he'd called to ask her if she wanted to come over to get the last of her things.

Eddie was sweet and kind and emotionally available. He had a good job, and he was close with his family. Dogs and kids liked him, which was always a good sign. He'd proposed to her after two years of dating, which had initially come as a surprise, but it didn't feel wrong, necessarily. Eddie was everything she wanted in a partner on paper, and she did still feel sad and confused, but not in a way that made her ever reconsider getting back together with him. He was a good person, but he wasn't her person. She wasn't sure how to explain that to her friends.

"I remember how much of a headache the entire process

was," Maggie said, interrupting her thoughts again. "I begged Gwen to elope like nine times."

"But your wedding was gorgeous," Danica said. "I loved it."

"I love it in hindsight."

"What would you do differently now?" Danica asked, shoving penne into her mouth.

Maggie considered, frowning. "I would have eloped."

Danica laughed. "That bad?"

"No, I'm mostly kidding. It was just expensive and stressful and I didn't even get to spend much of the day with the people I love, you know? I was just running around the room like a chicken with my head cut off, making sure it was perfect and that everyone was happy instead of slowing down to enjoy it all," Maggie said, pausing to dip a fry in ketchup.

Danica nodded, empathizing. "Worth it, though, to marry the love of your life?"

Maggie's smile was genuine as she nodded, her eyes brightening at the mention of her wife. "Worth it."

The look of genuine love on Maggie's face made Danica feel a pang of envy, wondering if she'd ever find someone who made her feel that way.

Maggie raised an eyebrow. "Is everything okay with you and Eddie? You don't really bring him up. Or like, *ever* talk about him at all."

"Yeah, it's fine," Danica said, studying a limp fry.

"Sure, as in, 'yeah, I like vanilla ice cream,' or sure as in... you're sure everything's okay?" Maggie asked.

Danica forced a smile onto her face. "Everything's good. And there's nothing wrong with vanilla ice cream."

"Some people love vanilla things." Maggie feigned seriousness with a slow nod of her head.

Danica rolled her eyes, throwing a fry across the table at Maggie, who laughed and dodged out of the way.

"I mean, he is a dentist. I bet he makes a really high contribution to his 401k, and he's never let his car go one mile past the number for a recommended oil change," Maggie said, making Danica laugh. She wasn't wrong.

"Can you not?" Danica said, though she wasn't upset. She just didn't want to have to defend Eddie against the very truthful allegations and jokes.

Maggie grinned, sipping the last of her soda. "It's not a bad thing. I think that kind of personality suits you."

To quiet the unsettling feeling that statement caused and keep from saying Maggie was wrong immediately, Danica stuffed one last fry in her mouth. Is that what her friends really thought of her? That she wanted *boring*?

CHAPTER 8

PETE

PETE WATCHED MAGGIE AND DANICA, TWO GROWN WOMEN, LIE down on the ground and whine like toddlers. It was an incredible sight. They'd both slipped and stumbled their way up a lift, then unloaded in one of the least graceful displays Pete had ever personally witnessed. At one point, Maggie crawled on her hands and knees, her snowboard dragging behind her.

"I'm going to die," Danica proclaimed as the three of them sprawled at the top corner of Double Cabin, a wide open green perfect for their first time on a real run with their snowboards. They were out of the way enough to not disturb other skiers and boarders, so Pete let them lay and wallow for a moment longer than necessary.

It was an absolutely gorgeous bluebird day, cold but clear, the blue sky stretching wide without a cloud in sight.

"You're both going to do great. We're going to take this nice and slow. You spent the entire morning practicing, so now you get to actually enjoy yourselves."

"I miss the magic carpet," Maggie said, looking over her

shoulder where the lift took braver snowboarders up through a beginner terrain park.

"I miss being able to separate my legs," Danica said, and Pete snorted immediately, trying to cover up the sound of her laugh with a sniffle.

Danica scowled.

"Okay, what's the first rule of snowboarding?" Pete asked.

"Don't fall," Maggie said.

"Don't fall on your wrists," Danica amended.

Pete clasped her hands behind her back, pacing in front of them like a drill sergeant. "Good tries, good advice, but wrong. The first rule is that it's not that serious. You're not a pro. There's no grade at the end of this. No one will be impressed with how good you are. You are doing this for pure joy, no other reason." Pete's own board lay toward the edge of the run. She reached to help Maggie stand, letting Maggie wobble and find her balance, then let go of her to reach for Danica.

"I'm too old for this," Danica whimpered as Pete helped her to her feet. "Why the hell do you do this? It's ten thousand times worse than skiing."

Pete grinned. "Once it clicks, you'll see. It's like... flying."

Danica frowned, tucking her chin back into her face covering.

"Okay, let's take it slow and steady. This is just like the bunny hill. So, let's take it wide as we practice our turns from heel to toe. No need to gain speed right now, we're just getting a feel for a real run," Pete coached, holding onto Danica's hand a little longer than she probably needed. They'd ended on such a bad note the day before, but Danica didn't seem to be holding a grudge. "See the giant opening where this run turns and splits into Teddy's Way? Make your way slowly down and we can pause before the turn."

Maggie and Danica both nodded, and both hopped to get their boards angled correctly to start down. Seeing both of their shaking legs, Pete found them endearing. She didn't know why she felt so much pride in her friends for trying something new and scary, but it made her want to sweep them both up in hugs. Entirely because of her pride, that was all.

Maggie was the first to start her wide falling leaf pattern down the run, taking her time. Danica began to follow the same path, falling almost immediately.

"You okay?" Pete asked, hurrying over to where Danica struggled to get back up.

"I'm fine," Danica said. "My ass is going to be so bruised tomorrow."

Pete laughed. "Yeah, but better a bruise than a broken bone. That was a good fall. Most people fall forward and catch their wrists." She reached to help Danica again, reaching to steady her with a hand on her waist as she wobbled. They both paused, and Pete was grateful her goggles shielded most of her expression.

"I'm good," Danica said, and Pete took a step back, trusting her.

Danica was, in fact, not good, and fell over again almost immediately. Pete heard her muffled curses behind her neck gaiter. "Yeah, you seem good," Pete teased. Danica accepted Pete's offered hand.

"I hope Maggie is having a good time at least," Danica said, steadying herself without letting go of Pete's hand.

Pete glanced over her shoulder to where Maggie was zig-zagging down the run like a pro. "I think she is."

"I'm glad we were able to be here for her. Has she seemed a little... off? We talked about Gwen and the kids earlier and she sounded so weird," Danica asked, adjusting her glove. Her board slipped sideways an inch or two and her hands shot out, grabbing Pete's jacket again. "Fucking hell, did they put extra wax on this or what?"

Pete chuckled, supporting Danica as she recovered her

composure. She waited for Danica to stop wobbling, then added, "I haven't noticed anything. She's been a little more intense, a little wilder than I remember, but I thought that was just like a 'Mom's Big Week Alone' kind of thing."

Danica sniffled, letting go of Pete to steady herself. "Well, I think we should keep a close eye on her."

"You got it, boss," Pete said, taking a step back to look at her form. "Okay, I think you're putting your weight too far back. You don't have to be scared to lean into it. Here, center your weight." Pete reached out, taking Danica's waist in her hands. Despite about seventeen layers between them, touching her like this affected Pete's heart rate and the swirling nerves in her stomach. "See how that makes it so your board doesn't want to slip out from under you?"

Danica nodded. "Glen told us all of this."

"Yeah, well, Glen may have told you, but you aren't doing it, so now I'm telling you."

"I don't remember you ever being so bossy," Danica said with a smirk.

Pete chuckled, watching Danica's feet. "Okay, now shift your weight from side to side." Danica didn't move a muscle, and Pete could feel how tense she was. "Come on. Side to side. Shimmy."

Danica let out a sigh, fogging the air in front of her face. She shifted awkwardly from side to side.

"Jeez, Wendell, loosen up. No wonder you're so bad at this," Pete teased.

"I miss Glen," Danica mumbled, but did as she was told. Pete felt her shift her weight from side to side. As she shifted her weight to her back foot, the front of her board slid forward and she reached out to grab Pete's jacket again, but lost her balance somewhere along the way and ended up wrapping her arms around Pete's neck, their bodies pressing close.

Pete could feel the warmth of Danica's breath on her cheek as she over-corrected, nearly falling backwards.

"You're a mess," Pete chided gently, balancing Danica again. "Loosen up."

"I am loose," Danica countered. "I am fully relaxed. Free as a bird. I'm a chill girl."

"You've never been a chill girl in your entire life, Wendell," Pete joked, and Danica stuck out her tongue. "Watch out. That'll freeze out here."

Danica laughed, and the sound made Pete's insides feel a bit swirly. She hadn't realized how much she'd missed Danica's laugh, an infectious, bubbly kind of sound.

"Okay, now as you begin, I want you to keep your weight mostly centered, with only a slight extra amount on the front foot," Pete instructed, and Danica nodded.

"Thank you for being patient with me," Danica said quietly, like she was embarrassed to say it.

"I have nothing but patience for you," Pete said, realizing that she was admitting far too much with that simple statement. She opened her mouth to add something, unsure if she'd regret it later, but was cut short by the sound of a painful scream.

"Maggie," Danica breathed, looking over Pete's shoulder. She bent, frantically removing her gloves and reaching for her bindings. "Oh my god, I don't know how to do this faster. Can you help me unclip?"

Pete crouched, unstrapping Danica from her board. They ran down the slope to where Maggie lay on the ground halfway down the hill. She was flat on her stomach, still clipped to her board, clutching her wrist. Two others knelt beside her, but stood to make room as Pete and Danica approached.

"Maggie!" Danica yelled from just behind Pete. Pete felt a pain deep in her chest at the worry in Danica's voice. "Don't move her yet."

Pete knelt beside Maggie. "Are you okay? What happened?"

"I fell kind of hard and put out my hands to catch myself and there was this jolt of pain," Maggie said, panting.

"Does anything else hurt?" Danica said, ditching her board beside them as she knelt next to Pete, her eyes scanning Maggie. "Your neck? Your back?"

"My pussy and my crack?" Maggie sang, and it took Pete a moment to register it as a song that had come out when she was a sophomore in high school. She remembered it was so dirty that in hindsight, she couldn't believe 15-year-olds sang it.

Danica pulled her goggles onto her helmet and stared down at Maggie as she sat back on her heels. "Yeah, you're fine."

"Couldn't resist. My wrist really does fucking hurt, though," Maggie conceded, and Pete helped her out of her bindings as Danica took her good arm, helping her sit up.

"Did you hit your head?" Danica asked, her tone serious as she began to check Maggie over. She was in full doctor mode, and Pete had to admit, there was something to be said about watching Danica in her element, completely professional and capable. Danica took Maggie's glove off carefully, gently turning Maggie's wrist over to examine where the skin was already swelling and bruising. Danica murmured a few questions to Maggie, asking her if certain positions hurt more than others, and Maggie nodded or shook her head in response.

"Want me to call ski patrol?" Pete asked.

"No," Maggie said quickly, just as Danica negated her answer with a firm "Yes."

Maggie groaned. "Please, no. I'm fine. I don't need ski patrol. That's so embarrassing."

"I don't think it's broken, but I do think it could be sprained, and we can't risk you falling again trying to get back to the lift. We're a long way from the top of the run, and an even longer way to the bottom," Danica elaborated to a scowling Maggie. She gestured toward Pete's scarf. "Can I have that?" Pete unwound her scarf and handed it to Danica, then watched Danica wrap it over Maggie's shoulder to create a makeshift sling. "This will keep your arm stable and help to reduce any further injury."

Pete pulled out her phone and dialed the number for ski patrol, explaining where they were and what had happened.

"Are they going to take me down on one of those embarrassing sleds behind a snowmobile?" Maggie asked, her voice pitching higher.

Pete shook her head, not wanting to worry Maggie.

Danica did not seem to feel the same way about worrying Maggie. "Probably," Danica said calmly, making another adjustment to the sling as Maggie looked on in horror. "But I'll make sure to take photos so we can never forget it."

"That's really thoughtful," Maggie deadpanned. "You're sure it's not broken?"

Danica looked contemplative. "It could be fractured, but it's definitely not in too bad of shape. You'll be back on the slopes in no time."

Maggie sighed. "Do you think they'll give me a real sling?"

"Probably."

"Nooo," Maggie whined. "Can we at least come up with a really good story for this?"

"You ran into a burning building to save a child," Pete said, nodding emphatically.

"Also, there was a bear," Danica added with a small laugh.

"You're onto something. Definitely a heroic feat," Maggie said, then sniffled, tears welling in her eyes. "I'm so mad this happened. After everything this year, I can't..."

She trailed off, and Danica and Pete exchanged a quick

look of concern. Two ski patrollers appeared in their bright red jackets, one pulling a rescue toboggan behind. Although they were kneeling in the middle of the path, Danica still signaled for them to stop. Pete held Maggie's good hand and watched as Danica explained what happened in a composed voice, sharing her assessment as though she were handing off a trauma patient to an emergency crew. In a way, she was.

Before Pete knew it, they had loaded Maggie onto the rescue toboggan, ignoring her complaints and insistence that she'd be fine just walking miles down to the Meadows first aid station. Pete snapped a few pictures of her, secured to the toboggan with an excessive number of straps and then the ski patrol was off, dragging Maggie behind them like a freshly killed deer.

"That is so embarrassing," Pete said with a small laugh as they watched Maggie descend the slope.

Danica was holding a hand to her mouth to hide her smile. "Poor thing."

"We're never going to let her live this down, are we?" Pete asked.

Danica stifled a laugh, coughing into her hand instead. "Be nice. She's hurt."

"Oh, please. I'm sure Maggie has already made best friends with the patrollers, and the entire medical unit is going to be out at karaoke with us tonight," Pete said, rolling her eyes.

Danica smiled, shaking her head. "I hope you're right."

"You went into like, full doctor mode there," Pete said, turning to Danica.

Two wide blue eyes looked back at her. "It's been a while since I've worked with a patient who could talk back to me, but I tried my best."

"You were brilliant," Pete said, unable to contain a smile and the awe in her voice.

Danica blushed, a small, self-conscious smile playing on

her lips. She sniffled, looking around. "We should text Kiera and Izzy and let them know."

Pete glanced back up the run to where her snowboard still lay discarded near the tree line. "How about we have one last run before we do that?" Her heart pounded in anticipation. Why did suggesting that somehow feel like she was in high school and asking out her crush?

Danica glanced down the run. "I mean, we do have to get down to the medical unit, so we might as well," she said, as if she was weighing the pros and cons of something extremely neutral, like whether to mop the kitchen floor today or tomorrow.

Pete didn't know why that made her feel so disappointed. Sure, it had been fifteen years since Danica had been excited about being on an adventure with her, but a small part of her hoped that Danica still enjoyed her presence, at least.

"Think you can make it the whole way without falling?" Pete said, forcing her voice to stay light.

"Well, I do have new motivation now," Danica said, grabbing her board from where it lay discarded beside them. As Pete angled her head in confusion, Danica clarified, "You know, the whole 'not breaking my wrist' thing."

"Not breaking a bone is the real goal," Pete agreed. "I have to go grab my board up there, so I'll be right back. Think you can get your bindings on by yourself and stand up alone?"

Danica nodded, sitting down to strap into her bindings, and Pete jogged back up the hill. Well, jog was a strong word for any level of activity nearly 11,000 feet above sea level. Trudge was a better description. By the time she reached her board, her heart was racing as she clipped in and started the gentle descent down. Danica was standing on her own and had her arms out wide like an adorable amateur as she began a slow falling leaf pattern down the run.

"You've got this!" Pete called out enthusiastically, and

Danica gave her a wide smile. Pete saw the way she bit her lip in concentration as she leaned into a turn. Pete continued to coach her down the run, and to her surprise and delight, Danica opted to take the harder of the two runs at the fork.

Danica was wobbly and slow, but she made it. By the end of the run, down toward the bunny hill and the medical unit where Maggie was, Danica seemed to be getting the hang of it. She teetered to a stop at the bottom of the run, her arms flying out to catch her balance and steady herself.

"You did it!" Pete yelled, cheering with excitement as she skidded to a stop beside Danica.

"I did it," Danica said, breathless. She put her hands in the air triumphantly, but wobbled on her board and reached to brace herself by hanging onto Pete's jacket again.

Pete laughed, pulling her into a hug before she could think better of it. Danica's arms wrapped around her without hesitation, and the tension in Pete's chest began to loosen. Though several layers separated them, their waterproof exteriors scratching together as they held one another, she still believed that she could feel Danica's warmth. To her surprise, holding Danica again was very comforting. Thrilling and yet familiar at the same time. Danica had always grounded her, and Pete wanted to hold on to the moment just a little longer. She let her eyes close, taking a deep breath in the chilly winter air.

Someone cleared their throat from nearby, and Pete and Danica jerked apart to see Kiera and Izzy standing beside them.

"Maggie texted us that she got hurt," Kiera explained. She glanced from Pete to Danica with a questioning look on her face. "Are you guys okay?"

Danica's cheeks were flushed as she moved her goggles to her helmet. "Yeah, we're fine. Only Maggie fell," she said in a strained voice, not looking at Pete. Awkwardness radiated in the air between them.

Meanwhile, Izzy was staring at Pete without saying anything, and Pete turned, unclipping from her own bindings with a smile on her face. "Y'all get some good runs in?"

"Wait, what happened to Maggie?" Kiera interrupted, watching Danica unsnap her bindings on the ground. "She says they're going to have to amputate."

Pete gasped, turning to Kiera. "Amputate?"

Danica laughed. "She has a sprained wrist. I think her arm will make it through."

"She told me she was waiting for a lobotomy so she could forget that the rescue sled ever happened. Apparently, they were letting the rookie train with the sled on the easy runs, but they went so slow they got stuck," Izzy said with a laugh.

Danica was still sitting on the ground, fussing with her bindings, and Pete knelt, helping her without a word. Danica looked up, a silent look of gratitude on her face.

"Should we figure out how to get Maggie home?" Danica asked, standing and brushing off her pants, the fabric swishing under her gloves.

Kiera had her phone out, her gloves dangling from where they were clipped into her jacket. "She says she convinced someone to give her a ride back on their snowmobile."

"Isn't the condo, like, just on the other side of the Chondola?" Pete said, looking toward the bunny hill gondola ascending to Mountain Village, where their condo was located.

"Classic Maggie," Izzy said, and Danica chuckled.

Danica turned toward where the gondola was loading passengers. "Well, in that case. I think I'm going to go take ten muscle relaxers and be horizontal with my cross stitch until dinner," Danica announced.

"Want to go check out the black runs off Lift 9 with me?" Izzy asked Pete.

Pete glanced back toward Izzy, getting the feeling that Danica wanted to be alone. "Sure."

"You go cross stitch your heart out. We'll be back soon," Kiera said, nodding. "I'll join you guys if that's cool. I've been wanting to try East Drain again since it kicked my ass this morning."

Pete's eyebrows shot up — she was surprised Kiera wanted to spend time away from Danica — but Izzy nodded and said, "Let's go, then."

The four of them walked toward the gondola, climbing into one of the cars. Kiera moved past Pete to sit next to Danica, turning and talking to her in a low voice. Danica explained Maggie's fall again. Izzy scrolled through her Spotify playlists. Pete gazed out the window, a jolt of surprise hitting her as she saw Danica looking back at her in the reflection.

The day was so beautiful, so clear, and while a part of her was worried for Maggie, she was still wound up from her time alone with Danica. Even if they had just spent an hour inching down a run, they'd laughed and joked like they used to. Danica's gaze didn't linger on Pete's again, but that one fraction of a moment was enough — just a flicker of interest that Pete would continue to think about for the rest of the day.

Had Danica felt what she'd felt while they'd hugged, before Kiera and Izzy showed up and turned the moment awkward? So many questions raced through her mind, and she did her best not to feel a stab of regret as the group parted, Danica separated to go back to the condo, and the rest of them hopped on another gondola to connect to their other lift.

Something had shifted between her and Danica. It was exciting. Maybe old feelings would rekindle, or maybe it was something completely new.

CHAPTER 9

DANICA

"HOW DO YOU KNOW THIS BAR EVEN HOSTS KARAOKE NIGHTS?" Izzy asked as the five friends stood on the sidewalk and looked up at the bar's sign. The hokey old timey piece of wood swung back and forth over the door in the chilled breeze of the January night.

Danica shivered, pulled her coat tighter, and winced at some guy butchering Journey's "Don't Stop Believing." What did they ever do to that man to deserve that kind of treatment?

Maggie shrugged. "Google is your friend, Izzy." She gave Izzy a teasing smile as she strutted through the doorway of the bar.

Kiera looped her arm through Danica's and they followed Maggie in, Pete and Izzy right behind them. The bar was dimly lit by an elaborate chandelier that would have been more at home in Disney's Haunted Mansion. Johnny Cash defiantly raising his middle finger on a painting over the stage as the centerpiece of a thrift store art collection on the wood-paneled walls, illuminated by a string of red Christmas lights that twinkled softly. It smelled like cheap beer and the floors were sticky. A lively and diverse mix filled the bar — tough-looking biker women in worn leather sat near tables of young men, their faces bearing the telltale ski-goggle tans.

"I owe you a drink," Maggie said, pointing to Danica with her good arm. The other arm was in a sling, just like Danica had predicted, and wrapped in an ace bandage. Luckily, the wrist hadn't been broken, and Maggie had been sent on her way with a recommendation to rest and ice her wrist.

"I think Pete owes us both drinks, considering she broke your arm," Danica joked. She glanced back toward Pete, but didn't find her. "Where'd she go?"

Kiera pointed toward the stage, where red lights cast a glow on Pete's wild curls. The music had paused between performances, and Pete looked like she was savoring the drama of having all eyes on her. Of course, she'd be the first to run up there, unable to resist a performance.

Pete adjusted the collar of her worn-in flannel shirt. The deep green and navy plaid pattern was faded from years of wear, its edges just starting to fray at the cuffs. Underneath, she wore a simple black crewneck t-shirt, its fabric soft and slightly stretched from frequent use. Her jeans, a pair of high-waisted, straight-leg black denim, were slightly cuffed at the ankle, revealing the worn leather of her sturdy Doc Marten boots. She nodded toward the man running the karaoke machine, then bowed low as she closed her eyes and began to sing, *"Hey now, hey now."*

"Oh my god," Danica groaned, wanting to cover her eyes but unable to look away as the cheesy, over-the-top synths and driving electro beats of Hilary Duff's "What Dreams Are Made Of" pulsed through the room, a wave of early 2000s nostalgia washing over her. The crowd's murmur of confusion shifted to amused recognition as Pete launched into her enthusiastic, almost painfully earnest, Lizzie McGuire-inspired dance.

Danica immediately flashed back to their college karaoke bar. The Inn had been notorious for not caring about fake IDs. It had a shitty carpeted — carpeted! — bar with a half-dead jukebox and bartenders who acted annoyed whenever someone ordered anything but a bottled beer. In the bartender's defense, being the local bar for a college was probably not a profitable or stress-free situation, catering to a crowd of 19-year-olds with fake IDs and a love for dollar beer night.

Those were the days of wearing blazers, layered tank tops, or body con dresses to the bar, topped with a statement necklace and a Bump-It. Pete had gone through a phase of cargo shorts and Abercrombie polos, always with the collar popped. What they lacked in timeless style, they made up for in a startling ability to drink for hours, stay up late having sloppy drunk sex, and then go to an 8 a.m. class the next day. Ah, to have the metabolism and tenacity of a college kid again.

They'd had their first kiss immediately after a duet of this very song. The lingering scent of cheap beer and sweat hung in the air as Pete kissed Danica on stage, the room echoing with applause.

Maggie nudged Danica, and she looked up to see that Pete was pointing at her. "Come on, Wendell, do the Lizzie part," she said into the microphone, causing some in the crowd to glance Danica's way.

Danica shook her head vehemently, her cheeks flaming with embarrassment. Lizzie McGuire in a college dive bar was one thing; Lizzie McGuire in a rich resort town was another.

To Danica's surprise, a random woman from the crowd hopped onto the low stage with the rallying cry, "Sing for me

Paolo!" Pete howled with laughter, leaning into the performance with the woman, who also knew every word.

A server carrying a tray full of tiny plastic containers of colorful jello shots passed near the table and Danica flagged her down, desperate to focus on anything other than Pete and the woman on stage. The last time she'd considered a jello shot had probably been in college, but she needed something immediately. Curiosity and unexpected annoyance made her look back at the stage, where Pete was holding the woman in a prom pose as they sang the last few lines of the song, gazing at each other dramatically.

Something not quite as intense as jealousy simmered under her skin, and she tried her best to shove it far, far down. She and Pete had a history, but were not together in any way. Therefore, she had no right to be jealous of anything Pete did. Still, did Pete have to be so extra, twirling the stranger and lowering her into a dip as the song ended to raucous applause? Pete was just being classic Pete — the life of the party, outgoing, flirtatious. After all, hadn't she pulled a similar stunt with Danica for their first kiss?

Pete made her way through the crowd, grabbing a jello shot off the table and raising it in a cheers motion as Maggie and Izzy gave her high fives. Pete's piercing dark eyes settled on her, one eyebrow cocked in silent question, and Danica felt the weight of that scrutiny. She got the feeling that Pete was daring her to say something, daring her to remember the first time they'd sang that song.

The recognizable first metallic guitar strums of "The Sweet Escape" by Gwen Stefani distracted Danica, and then she saw Kiera on the stage holding a microphone. Immediately upon the realization, Danica turned into a woo girl, shouting as Kiera hit the first few strange "*Woo hoo, yee hoos*" of the song.

"I didn't know Kiera had it in her," Izzy remarked, running her finger around the rim of her jello shot to loosen it.

Danica frowned. "Kiera loves karaoke. Are you kidding? She used to perform this at every karaoke night." Danica turned back to the stage to find Maggie standing beside Kiera and singing the backup vocals. She couldn't help but laugh, and cheered her friend on. Kiera was adorable and in her element, all round cheeks and Mom-bob and goofy dance moves.

"That night at the Inn — you remember?" Pete whispered, too close to her ear.

Awareness prickled along her skin and she turned to look up at Pete. "Nope."

Pete chuckled, rolling her eyes. "Liar." How was her voice a purr as she said the word?

Heat flushed in Danica's cheeks, despite her best attempts to not let Pete's closeness affect her. Of course, she knew what Pete was talking about, but she'd rather gnaw off her left arm than let Pete know that. She shifted, stepping away from Pete as Maggie jumped into a rousing rendition of the *"woo hoo, yee hoo"* hook to close out the song, attempting to wave her slinged arm in the air over her head. Danica tamped down her doctor-panic and instead laughed, shaking her head. The three of them cheered as Kiera and Maggie left the stage, making their way back through the packed tables.

A drink was passed to her, and Danica was surprised to see that Izzy was offering it to her. She mumbled a thanks, watching with piqued interest as Izzy offered Pete the same type of drink. It smelled sweet, and Pete took a sip. "Rum and coke," she explained over the sound of someone else beginning a song.

Kiera reappeared at the table, and Danica squeezed her arm with excitement. "How are we supposed to follow that?" she teased. Kiera grabbed the last jello shot, using her tongue to scoop out the jello, then chewed with a grimace. "You're supposed to just swallow," Danica said, laughing again.

"I can hardly swallow an Advil, you think this cup of jello

is going down in one piece? No, thank you," Kiera said around a mouth full of green jello.

Danica crinkled her nose. "You're a delicate flower."

"I can't believe you missed a swallowing joke there," Maggie said, holding a clear drink. "Low hanging fruit."

"Hey, don't talk about my breasts that way," Kiera said with mock defensiveness.

Danica sputtered, wiping at her mouth, and her gaze caught on Pete, who was standing across the table watching her. Was it curiosity or memory that made Danica's insides tighten with a thrill at the sight of those dark eyes watching her? Kiera wrapped an arm around Danica's shoulders, leaning to take a drink of Danica's drink, and Danica glanced away from Pete, distracted.

Another patron dropped the karaoke song list binder on their table and they flipped through, laughing about what songs they should choose. Maggie immediately claimed a Britney Spears song, and Kiera pleaded with Danica to sing "Islands in the Stream." Izzy chose Alanis Morrisette's "You Oughta Know."

Two rum and cokes later, Danica was being dragged on stage next to Kiera, their clothes awash in a rainbow of colors from an awkward party light. "I changed the song," Kiera told her with a wink, just before the iconic first notes of Shania Twain's "Man! I Feel Like a Woman" began. Danica was delighted and felt the joy rising in her chest like bubbles. She barely yelled, *"Let's go, girls!"* in time.

Maybe it was the song, maybe it was the drinks, maybe it was the freedom of singing karaoke in a town where you knew no one. Or maybe it was the fact that she was on vacation, or that she was back with friends she'd once spent every day with during such a happy time in her life, but Danica could feel the tension dissipating from her body as she sang, not caring about anyone else in the bar, anything else in her life. A great singer, she was not, but she could sing on-key and hit most of the notes. As she was scream-singing about the prerogative to have a little fun, she looked out across the bar, over the tables packed with people who were either singing along or completely ignoring her. Pete, taller than most, watched her with a strange expression on her face, a combination of amusement and something else Danica couldn't quite figure out, something like tenderness.

The song ended and Maggie was on stage singing "Miss New Booty" before Danica and Kiera had even made it back to the table.

A few minutes later, Danica stood in the small, dark hallway waiting for the single-stall bathroom to open up. She fanned her face, flushed from the alcohol or from the intensity of Pete's stare. Her imagination often ran far wilder than she'd wished it would, but she couldn't be imagining the growing familiarity, the rising tension between her and Pete. It was the same spark of attraction that had always sparked between them nearly twenty years before, when they were just eighteen-year-old idiots with bad fake IDs.

Danica ran a hand through her hair, pushing it away from her face. Water, space away from Pete, and time would quiet this feeling. Alcohol had always made her extra stupid about Pete, and she blamed it for a number of wrongs, including their first kiss, the first time she'd ever said I love you, and also the only time she'd ever begged Pete to just be with her, to just *choose* her. Pathetic.

That last time had been only a few months before graduation, and Danica had felt Pete slipping through her fingers already. No matter how tightly she held, Pete was always just out of reach, like she'd been grasping at the shadow of what could be instead of the reality of what was.

The memory ached in Danica's chest even after all this time, and only worsened when Pete turned the corner and entered the hallway where Danica stood. Time seemed to stretch, and she could see every detail of Pete's approach: the way her shoulders moved, the determined set of her jaw, the almost palpable intensity radiating from her. Desire?

"Wendell," Pete said quietly when she reached Danica, Pete's strong fingers wrapping gently around Danica's hand.

Pete's hand, warm and surprisingly rough against her skin, sent a jolt of heat up Danica's arm, despite her thick sweater. Pete glanced around for privacy, then moved to guide Danica further down the hall, out of sight from the main bar area.

"What do you want?" Danica asked, her entire body tensing in coiled anticipation.

"I *want*..." Pete pushed her own hair away from her face, the dark curls taking on a life and a defiance of gravitational law all their own. Danica ached to dig her fingers into those dark curls, remembering exactly how they'd felt in her hands, exactly the way Pete's voice used to hitch when Danica would gently tug on the strands. "Jesus, Wendell, I know exactly what's going through your mind."

Danica forced her face into a neutral expression. "I doubt that." A bad lie, but she had to lie. She couldn't reveal just what she wanted from Pete. Why should she trust Pete? The sparks between them were attraction, familiarity, and intrigue. Nothing serious. But giving into this feeling had serious implications. A girl could daydream all she wanted, but honestly acting on those thoughts? She couldn't, wouldn't, open her heart up like that again.

Pete's tongue darted over her full lower lip, followed by her teeth dragging across the sensitive skin. "Tell me you're not thinking about kissing me," she stated, her voice lower.

"I'm not," Danica protested.

"Tell me you don't want me to," Pete said, stepping forward so Danica's back came up against the wall. Her dark eyes sparkled with mischief and amusement as she leaned closer, all coconut and apricot sweetness directly contradicting the smoldering look on her face.

Danica focused on remembering how to stand, wishing her knees weren't so close to giving out. Her body was embarrassingly melting into a puddle of adoration for this woman all over again, like it didn't remember how quickly Pete had discarded her at the end of college. Memories of the fight on the quad rushed back, and she gave Pete a long, questioning look.

Pete's nose brushed hers, and — goddamn her traitorous body — she was leaning in. Even over the sound of a decent Blondie impersonation, she could hear Pete's breath, rapid and short. Excited.

Knowing she affected Pete, too? That sent a shiver of anticipation up her spine.

Pete bent to brush her lips against the shell of Danica's ear and Danica fought to keep her eyes from closing in delight at the sensation. The hand she'd placed on Pete's chest to push her away closed around the fabric of her shirt instead. Pete's voice was a whisper. "You've been thinking about kissing me for days, haven't you?"

Danica's knee-jerk response was to lie, to tell her no, to cradle her pride close, but she bit her lower lip, stifling a response. And yet, with the way Pete's eyes darkened and slid down to her mouth, that was a response enough.

The door to the bathroom opened, and Kiera stepped out, pausing when she saw the two of them in the dark corner, Pete bent so close. With a jolt, Danica straightened, springing back from Pete; the sudden movement making the air crackle between them.

"Everything okay?" Kiera asked, her voice suspiciously calm.

"Yeah," Danica said, not elaborating as she stepped away from Pete and took Kiera's arm, walking back towards the bar. Her heart pounded and her breaths were shaky, but Kiera was a welcome distraction. Danica didn't dare look over her shoulder, her heart pounding a frantic rhythm against her ribs, the proximity of another kiss with Pete a dangerous temptation.

"I think I'm a little too drunk," Kiera said, glancing over her shoulder toward Pete. "You seem a little drunk, too. Should we call a ride and get back to the house?"

Danica nodded, catching her meaning. Kiera was giving her an out to leave the bar and put some distance between her and Pete. "Yeah, I think that's a good idea."

Of course, Maggie called dibs on one of the two captain's chairs in the back of the minivan rideshare, Izzy sliding into the other. That left Danica squeezed in the back seat between Kiera and Pete. Each time Pete's leg brushed hers, a jolt of awareness shot through Danica, making her breath catch; she stared resolutely ahead, determined to ignore the fluttering in her stomach.

Kiera's phone buzzed with a text from her husband, Alex, who had sent her pictures of the girls in their pajamas, smiling with post-bath combed hair. Kiera turned her phone to show Danica and Pete, and Pete made an *aww* sound of cuteness-approval.

"You did a very good job making them extremely cute," Danica affirmed, laying her head on Kiera's shoulder.

"I did, didn't I?" Kiera responded, and Danica could hear the smile in her friend's voice.

The van stopped in front of the condo and they piled out, Pete taking her hand to steady her as she climbed out the sliding door. She could feel Kiera's gaze on her as Danica took just a beat too long to let go of Pete's hand.

"Who wants a night cap?" Pete said, unwinding her green scarf to hang near the front door.

Maggie and Izzy immediately said yes, but Kiera yawned, pointing to her room. "I think I'm going to call Alex and get the daily report."

"Oh, I guess I should do that, too," Maggie said, frowning.

Danica watched a flicker of concern cross Pete's face as she turned to Maggie. Pete's expression was a mixture of worry and contemplation, clearly considering Danica's earlier comment on Maggie's odd mood.

"Wendell, you in?" Pete asked, turning to smile toward Danica. She glowed when she smiled, those full lips parting in a wide smile, like she couldn't hold back her happiness.

"Nah, I've got a hot date with my cross stitch and solitude," Danica said.

"Loser," Maggie teased, as Danica and Kiera walked down the hall toward their rooms.

"You okay?" Kiera asked Danica once they were out of earshot of the group.

Despite her fluttering excitement, Danica nodded calmly. She just couldn't admit that to Kiera. Not yet.

"What happened with Pete?" Kiera asked, dropping her voice lower. "Did I catch you guys making out?"

Quickly shaking her head, Danica's cheeks flushed once more. "No, not at all."

"Not at all or like, not yet?" Kiera clarified, skepticism in her voice.

"Not at all," Danica said firmly. If she said it aloud, she could begin to believe it.

Kiera nodded, staring her down for what was quickly becoming an uncomfortable amount of time.

Danica held up her hands in surrender. "Seriously, nothing was going on."

"Why were you standing so close if nothing was happening?" Kiera continued, her brow raised.

"Just talking," Danica said, clearly a lie, and she watched Kiera contemplate calling her on it for a moment.

"If you say so." Kiera finally shook her head and sighed, leaning in to hug Danica good night.

Danica walked into her room, feeling relief wash over her as she shut the door behind her. Kiera had made it seem like her surprised presence had been the only thing preventing them from full-on making out in the hallway. If Kiera hadn't interrupted them, what might have happened? Danica touched her lower lip, then took her phone out of her pocket and sat down in the chair near the window. With her room lights off, she could see out over Mountain Village, the snow-cats grooming the trails in the darkness. Her body was unexpectedly sore as she settled in the chair, holding up her phone to pull up Eddie's contact. Her thumb gently tapped the red text of the "Block Caller" button.

The tension that had been dissipating ever since she'd butchered Shania Twain's girl power anthem on stage was beginning to return. If Kiera hadn't shown up... she knew exactly what would have happened. She could picture the hungry, urgent kiss, Pete pressing her back into the wall, her hands roaming freely over Danica's body.

Heat flushed in her cheeks and she touched the cool window to snap herself out of that daydream.

She turned off her phone and tossed it on her nightstand, walking into the en suite to wash her face and brush her teeth. Those moments with Pete still felt surreal. One stolen moment in a bar and she was ready to dive right in. Maybe she *was* a little too drunk.

Her reflection in the dark mirror as she dried her face caught her off guard. She stared at her reflection while she washed her face and did her skincare, surprised that for the first time in a long time, she recognized herself again. How long had she avoided looking at herself before, not ready to face the tired, restless, unfulfilled person staring back at her?

She wiped the water from the counter, now a habit after Eddie always complained about her always making a mess when she washed her face. She changed into pajamas and climbed into bed, staring up at the dark ceiling. It still sometimes felt strange to crawl into bed and not have Eddie beside her, usually ignoring her until he fell asleep while reading some deeply stupid self-help book. She pictured Eddie now, alone in the quiet of their old bedroom, the only sound the gentle turning of pages as he read yet another book promising to unveil the true path to self-discovery. That image did make her feel slightly bad, but not bad enough to make her want to cry. It had taken her years to get over Pete, years of crying and feeling miserable. Why did it seem like there had been nothing to get over with Eddie?

CHAPTER 10

PETE

Riding on the high of a good work call, Pete glanced at the clock on her laptop, which was precariously balanced on her knees. It was just after 3 a.m. — she'd made sure the call time was convenient for Budi, her Balinese contact, but was seriously regretting making it such an odd hour for herself. Now that she was feeling excited and hopeful about the future, it was hard to turn that off and go to sleep. Her time in Bali had been incredible, and she was beyond thrilled to be able to continue working with the organization she'd partnered with.

Pete stretched, her fingertips grazing the rails of the top bunk immediately above her as she looked around her room. Maybe she should take a melatonin gummy and try for a few hours of sleep before Izzy inevitably made her wake up and hit the slopes again.

She made a few quick notes on her computer before setting it aside, standing, and stretching the tightness in her legs. Snowboarding all day was tiring enough, but trying to stand and balance another person on the snow in stiff snowboarding boots was a whole different level of exhausting. Despite the soreness, spending that time with Danica felt incredible.

Her stomach grumbled, and she mentally calculated that it'd been over seven hours since she'd had anything other than alcohol. Her mouth felt a bit sticky at the thought, and she grabbed her water bottle. What really sounded good was ice cream, and she was in luck, because there was some in the freezer from a local creamery in town. That would hit the spot. She grabbed a hoodie and slipped out of her room and up the stairs, trying to be as quiet as possible to avoid waking anyone else up in the house.

A light from the living room made her pause, and then the light... turned toward her? Pete squinted, trying to make out what she was seeing and also avoid being blinded. Her hand shielded her eyes, and she made a confused noise halfway between huh and why.

"Sorry," a voice said in a hushed whisper. Danica's voice. A wave of nervous excitement washed over her at the sight of Danica, yet she composed herself with a deep breath, feigning nonchalance.

The light moved, pointing down, and Pete stepped closer, her eyes adjusting to find Danica sitting on the couch wearing glasses, working on her cross stitch by the light of a headlamp.

"I didn't want to wake anyone by turning on a light," Danica explained as she saw Pete's confusion. "But I had this headlamp, and it's been working okay." She pushed at the bridge of her glasses self-consciously.

"I didn't know you wore glasses," Pete said, stuffing her hands into her hoodie pocket awkwardly.

"They're just readers. Cross stitch is small," Danica said, brushing a few strands of her chestnut hair away from her face.

"Wow, Grandma Wendell," Pete teased. "What are you doing up?"

"My sleep schedule is a little weird," Danica said, shifting in her seat. "Working overnights has kind of made it hard for me to sleep more than a few hours at a time, even on my days off. That, and 2 a.m. seems to be some kind of witching hour for my brain. It decides to be awake almost every night between 2 a.m. and 4 a.m."

"That sounds awful. Is that like a menopause thing?" Pete asked, wanting to recant the question immediately.

"First of all, how dare you?" Danica said, looking up at her. "Why do people keep asking me that? We're 37. I know I may be wearing readers and cross stitching at 3 a.m., but I'm not on my deathbed just yet."

Pete grinned. "No, I just mean, my sister went through menopause early, and that nighttime waking was one thing she always complained about."

"How is Lillian?" Danica asked with a smile.

A trip planned by Pete when she was in college led to Danica and Lillian, her foster sister, becoming close. Peas in a pod, those two. It made Pete grin to remember how they'd spent the entire week ganging up against her and bonding over Settlers of Catan.

"She's good," Pete said, clearing her throat.

"Good."

"Yeah."

An awkward silence stretched between them where Danica set down and picked up her cross-stitch project three or four times. Pete wanted desperately to talk to her about the moment in the hallway, when her sky-high confidence after multiple drinks had collided with her intense, unyielding desire to kiss Danica.

"Why are you awake?" Danica finally asked.

"Couldn't sleep," Pete lied. She turned toward the kitchen. "I was just getting up to make a snack."

Danica waved her hand in the air. "Don't let me stop you."

Talk about hot and cold. Feeling dismissed, Pete turned toward the kitchen and flipped on the under-cabinet light. She could feel Danica's gaze upon her as she grabbed the ice cream container out of the freezer. Chocolate chip cookie dough, her favorite. Danica's too, if she remembered right.

"I forgot we had that," Danica said.

"Want some?" Pete asked, holding up the carton in question.

Danica twisted her mouth, considering. "The sugar might keep me up more."

"Okay, Grandma Wendell," Pete joked, setting down the carton and carefully taking a bowl from the cupboard to avoid clattering the dishes together. She glanced back toward Danica, and in the light, she could see that Danica's eyes were still on her as she scooped out several spoonfuls of ice cream into a bowl. "Mind if I sit on the couch?" Pete asked, while putting the container away and grabbing a spoon.

"Um, sure," Danica said, moving a blanket from her lap and scooting over on the couch.

"What are you making?" Pete asked, nodding toward the cross stitch in her hands. Danica had always been crafty. She had hemmed all of their jeans back in college, and made very impressive Tour de Fat costumes for the niche beer and bike parade held in their college town every Labor Day weekend.

"Oh, it's this cute tradition on my unit. We all cross stitch a square for a baby blanket when one of our nurses is pregnant," Danica said, looking down at her design. Pete could make out a giraffe and some words.

"That's very wholesome," Pete said, taking a bite of her ice cream.

"Yeah, the night nurses are all super into cross stitch, so I just started last year. I'm not very good at it yet, though,"

Danica said. "It's one of those hobbies that really makes you question if you can count properly."

Pete grinned. "And were you prepared for that answer to be no?"

"I was not," Danica said with a sigh.

"You hate not being good at things right away," Pete commented.

Danica narrowed her eyes, but then shrugged. "Yeah, maybe." She eyed Pete's bowl of ice cream, then looked back at her giraffe. "I mean, who likes being bad at things?"

Pete considered as she took a bite of ice cream. "I don't mind it. I bet even Taylor Swift was bad at the guitar at first."

"No, I'm pretty sure she popped out of the womb singing the world's catchiest songs and looking like a goddess," Danica quipped.

"You're smart. You'll master it soon, I'm sure," Pete said. Danica was the smartest, most capable person she knew.

Danica's brows pinched together as she dipped her head and softly said, "Thanks."

Had she just embarrassed Danica with the compliment? She let her ice cream bowl rest on her lap for a moment, taking a deep breath. "Listen, about earlier... I'm—"

Danica's eyes widened like she was immediately worried about what Pete was about to say. All the more reason for Pete to apologize, she supposed.

"It wasn't right of me to talk to you like that," Pete said firmly. "I respect you and I'd never want to be the reason you and Eddie—"

Pete wasn't sure if the snort from Danica was a sign of amusement or anger; the mention of Eddie had clearly struck a nerve, the silence heavy with unspoken feelings.

"I'm sorry, Wendell."

Danica took a deep breath, pressing her lips into a firm line. "I... Well, thank you for the apology. There's nothing to apologize for, though."

"Okay..." Pete said slowly, watching the expression on Danica's face change from uncomfortable to sad. "What's wrong?"

"Nothing."

"You're upset."

"No, I'm not."

Pete took a bite of ice cream, watching Danica. "You look upset."

A muscle in Danica's jaw tensed. "No, I don't."

Pete studied her. "If you say so."

Danica looked back at her for a long moment, then exhaled a long, slow, resigned sigh. "Eddie and I broke up."

Pete nearly dropped her ice cream as she pivoted in her seat, not surprised by the admission itself but definitely surprised by the timing of the admission. "What?"

Danica nodded. "Yeah. I mean, a while ago. Over a month. He broke up with me, originally, but then he called earlier this week and I just... I still feel..." She shrugged, trailing off like she was unsure how to finish.

Pete stared at Danica, her mouth slack with shock. Over a month ago? "Oh, fuck him." She moved to put the ice cream bowl on the table. "Are you okay? Wait, dumb question. Of course you're not." She rubbed a hand over her face. Part of her felt unexpectedly hopeful but part of her ached at the thought of Danica being hurt. Most of her wanted to punch that dentist in his stupid, too-bright, perfectly aligned teeth.

"I'm... I don't know." Danica tossed her cross-stitch hoop onto the coffee table. "Maybe it's just shock, but I feel fine."

Pete nodded, not quite understanding. "I mean, in the short-term, that definitely seems preferable to the alternative, right?"

"Yeah, and he's... um. Sorry, this is probably kind of weird for you to talk about," Danica said, fidgeting with the edge of the throw blanket.

"It's not. I care about you, and I'm happy to talk about anything with you," Pete responded gently.

Danica continued fidgeting with the blanket. "He's not what I actually wanted in a partner."

Pete's voice was low as she asked, "What do you want in a partner?" Her stomach was doing twirls and flips of hopeful excitement, despite her best efforts to respectfully support Danica during such a tumultuous time.

With a small shrug and a frown, Danica let out a breath, the weight of her decision heavy in the air. She looked unbelievably adorable when she did that. "I'm not sure. I just know what I don't want."

Pete raised an eyebrow. "That's hard for me to believe."

"Maybe I'll just adopt one thousand cats and live alone for the rest of my life," Danica said, leaning forward to take Pete's ice cream bowl. "Can I have some of this?" She was asking as the spoon was halfway to her mouth.

"Uh, yeah. Of course. Have it all," Pete said, waving the bowl toward her.

Pete bit her lower lip as her eyes lingered on Danica's mouth for a moment before looking away. So, so many inappropriate thoughts swirled through her brain while watching Danica's lick the spoon clean.

Danica's eyes lifted to meet Pete's as she opened her mouth to say something, but stopped herself.

"What is it?" Pete asked as casually as she could manage.

"You made me realize that, you know," Danica said, not meeting her eye as she took another bite of ice cream.

Pete cocked her head in confusion. "Realize what?" She leaned, tucking her cold feet under herself.

Danica looked at her for another long moment, shaking her head, the spoon held in her mouth. She paused, placing the spoon back in the bowl. "You made me realize what I didn't want."

Pete felt like she'd just been punched in the gut. Her heart sank. "Oof, Wendell. I'm glad I could help you with that, but ouch."

Danica's mouth fell open in horrified realization. "No, not like that. I meant..." She gestured while trying to gather her thoughts, concern on her face.

"What did you mean?"

"Wait, please don't be upset. Can I start over?" Danica said in a rush. In the low light, Pete could tell she was flushed.

Pete was torn between dropping the subject to saving Danica's pride and her intense curiosity to know what Danica actually meant. Judging by the way she had reacted, Pete guessed that Danica hadn't meant to insult her, but she didn't want to speculate about what Danica could have actually meant.

In the end, she crossed her arms over her chest in what she hoped was a good impression of being stern. The mood needed lightening immediately. "Nope, I'm offended until proven otherwise," she said with a long inhale and shake of her head.

Danica watched her as though deciding what to say. "I don't want to get into it."

Pete narrowed her eyes in faux-contemplation. "I don't believe you," she said. It didn't seem like she was going to get an answer out of Danica tonight, but she hoped to learn more later. Despite Danica's seemingly unaffected demeanor following her breakup with Eddie, Pete could remain a good friend, even though the word friend had always had a loose definition between the two of them. What was one more blurred boundary? She turned to grab the remote. "You still like bad reality TV?"

Danica nodded, stifling a smile. "Guilty."

They sat in silence as Real Housewives played on the lowest volume possible on the TV. Pete was aware of every move and shift of Danica's body, even though there was an entire couch cushion between them. As they were watching a particularly silly argument between two rich women, Pete shivered and began looking around for another throw blanket. It seemed like Danica had the only one. What kind of mountain condo only had one throw blanket? She supposed she could get up and turn on the gas fireplace, but she wasn't sure how loud that would be, and Kiera's room was just on the other side of the wall.

"We can share this one," Danica said, pointing to the blanket covering her legs.

"Oh, that's okay," Pete replied, not wanting to make Danica uncomfortable.

"It's fine. I don't mind at all," Danica said, her tone light as she tucked a strand of hair behind her ear.

Pete shifted, lifting the edge of the blanket and placing it over her lap gingerly.

"I'll listen if you want to talk about it, you know," Pete said, not looking away from the screen. She could see Danica glance up at her from the corner of her eye.

"Thanks," Danica said quietly, adjusting the blanket so there was more coverage on Pete's lap. "Just... I'm not ready for everyone to know just yet, okay?"

"Of course," Pete answered. Why didn't Danica want their friends to know she'd broken up with Eddie? Was she afraid they'd judge her? After moving closer together to share the blanket, Pete could feel how tense Danica was.

Pete wished there was something she could do to help relieve the hurt Danica must be feeling. Even the hurt to her ego alone, being broken up with by a dentist, and such a boring one at that. Especially brutal. Even while wanting to support and be present for Danica, she couldn't stop thinking about that near-kiss. Danica had wanted to kiss her, she was sure of it. She could feel the heat of Danica's body, could feel her thigh through her thin pajama pants. It was like her body was on high-alert, noticing every shift in Danica's movement. She couldn't *not* notice her.

Pete took a deep breath and forced herself to relax, letting her head rest against the back of the couch as another episode came on. Bless Real Housewives, there was no shortage of content to enjoy.

She wasn't sure how much time had passed before Danica's soft snores began. To make Danica more comfortable, she shifted Danica's head and propped it up with a small throw pillow against the arm of the couch until the snoring stopped, grinning about how adorable it was that Danica had fallen asleep. She remembered the hours she'd spend in the late nights and early mornings, watching Danica sleep so peacefully, and her nostalgia ached for that easier time. Her own body felt heavy and warm and there was no way she was making her way back down into the freezing basement where the bunk beds were. Pete tucked her hands into her hoodie pocket and let her heavy eyelids close, feeling more content than she had in a long time.

CHAPTER 11

DANICA

Something cold and wet startled Danica awake, and she opened her eyes to find that the cold and wet thing in question was Pete. Worse, it was a massive drool spot on Pete's shoulder, where her head had just been. She was so sore and so stiff; she could barely move. Well, that, and Pete's arm was wrapped around her, their legs entwined. She assured herself that they'd probably ended up in this position for warmth under the thinnest throw blanket in the Rocky Mountain region, but that didn't make it less startling.

She'd said a little too much the night before. Had she still been a bit drunk when Pete had come into the living room? Of all the people for her to confess to, why had she told Pete about her and Eddie?

Pete looked so peaceful like this, her cheek squished adorably against the back of the couch. It was annoying how attractive Pete had remained, how she still had high cheekbones and a perfect jaw, with only small wrinkles at the edges of her eyes, like she smiled enough to create permanent reminders of her joy. Freckles smattered across her nose and cheeks, barely visible except for the fact that Danica was looking at her from three inches away.

"Stop staring at me, Wendell," Pete murmured, her eyes still closed.

Danica startled. "I wasn't."

Pete's eyes fluttered open, heavy lidded, as she looked up at Danica. "It's not time to wake up yet," she said, sleepily wrapping her arm tighter around Danica's shoulders to draw her in. "You're so warm." Pete nuzzled Danica's neck, sending a jolt of ticklish pleasure through her body. Her toes may or may not have curled, but that could have also been from how cold the room remained.

Ignoring the way her heart was fluttering, Danica placed a hand on Pete's chest to create some room for herself. "We fell asleep on the couch. We should go back to our rooms before anyone notices." She tried to pitch her voice low while also attempting to aim her morning breath anywhere but at Pete.

Pete rubbed at her eyes, her eyebrows drawing together in sleepy confusion. "Sorry, yeah, you're right." She pushed at her dark curls that were falling over her face and sticking in a million directions, like a charming yet freshly electrocuted baby bird. She shifted back away from Danica, swallowing and rubbing at her face.

Footsteps drew her attention, and Danica glanced up just in time to see Kiera walk into the great room toward the kitchen. Kiera was probably on a mission to get coffee, and maybe if Danica was lucky, or if the universe was finally on her side for once, Kiera would walk right back to her room without glancing toward the couch where Pete's face was still only inches from her own. From how they were struggling to pull apart their sore limbs and smooth their clothes and hair, she could only guess what it looked like they'd been doing.

"You guys want coffee?" Kiera called quietly from the kitchen.

Danica cleared her throat. "Uh, yeah. Coffee sounds good. Didn't get much sleep."

Pete choked on a sudden laugh, the sound abruptly cut short by a death-glare from Danica that made her hastily clear her throat. "Yeah, we fell asleep watching TV."

Maggie walked into the room, showered, completely clothed and ready for the day, her arm still in its navy-blue sling. Cheerfully, she wished them both good morning without a moment's hesitation or a judgmental look. She sat down on a chair next to the couch, reaching for the remote to change the channel from Bravo to MSNBC.

"Not the news," Pete groaned, and Danica found herself agreeing. "It's like 4 a.m., you monster."

"It's 7 a.m. and I've been up for an hour. I've been waiting for you little cuddle bugs to wake up so I can catch up on last night's Maddow," Maggie said.

A wave of mortification washed over Danica as she ducked her head, not meeting anyone's eye.

"Coffee for the cuddle bugs," Kiera said with over-the-top sweetness as she brought two mugs of coffee and set them on the table next to where Pete's feet rested.

"Oh my god, are they finally awake?" Izzy groaned, walking into the living room, still in her pajamas, to sit down on the couch on Pete's other side. Pete threw a casual arm around Izzy's shoulders and Danica stifled the flare of... was that jealousy? Or possessiveness? Either way, she made herself look away and picked up her steaming mug of coffee.

"You know, you could have just woken us up," Danica said, looking around the room at her friends who were doing their best impressions of people who were trying very hard not to see them.

Maggie waved her free hand. "You two were the picture of cozy. Who was I to ruin that?"

Kiera settled on the floor near Danica's feet, glancing at

Danica's cross stitch project discarded on the floor near her. "Dan, does this really say You Bet Giraffe I'm Cute?"

"It's for a baby!" Danica said quickly.

"I should hope so," Kiera said, shaking her head and grinning. She leaned back against the couch next to Danica's legs. "Aunt Jade needs a sectional. I can't believe she only has one three-seater couch and a chair."

"And she also needs more blankets," Danica added, stretching and realizing just how sore she really was. Snowboarding had made her use muscles she hadn't thought about since med school.

"Well, Maggie's off the slopes today. What should the rest of us do?" Danica asked, glancing around the room. "I think I need a day off, too."

"We could walk around town," Kiera offered.

"We could walk around town and find a spa," Maggie said, and Danica nodded excitedly.

"I want to get as much boarding in as possible," Izzy said.

"I'll go with you," Pete offered, and Izzy smiled at her in response.

Again, Danica stared down into her coffee, forcing herself to take a larger, burning sip, just to replace one uncomfortable feeling with another as the liquid scalded over her tongue. What was going on with her? Maybe it would be nice to have some space to think about what she was feeling and why. Maybe Kiera and Maggie could help her wrap her head around all the events of the past 12 hours.

"Alright, well, that settles it. I'll book us massages at a spa and we can walk around town until it's time for our appointments," Danica said.

"And facials!" Kiera added.

"And pedicures," Maggie joined.

"Wow, that really escalated," Danica remarked, glancing toward Pete and Izzy. "You sure you don't want to join in on this self-care party?"

"Nope. Today's the day I'm going to get through Little Rose without fear," Pete said. "You up for the challenge, Iz?"

Izzy nodded. "You bet. And then Millions and Dynamo after and we'll see how we feel at the bottom?"

"Aren't those expert runs? Like expert-expert?" Kiera asked.

Pete shrugged. "Yeah, I guess."

The idea of Pete on an expert-expert run made something squeeze with worry inside her chest. "Be careful," Danica said.

Pete gave her a thoughtful look, as if trying to figure out the meaning of Danica's tone. "We will be. I promise."

Danica awoke in a strange place for the second time that day, except she was face down on a massage table and a stranger was gently patting her shoulder. Dammit, falling asleep during a massage was the worst. Despite the relaxation, the lack of a tense-to-relaxed transition left her feeling unsatisfied.

"I'm going to step out while you get dressed," the soft-spoken massage therapist said before stepping through the door.

Danica sat up, feeling much less sore than she had that morning. Stretching, she felt a lingering tightness in her abs, a welcome contrast to the loose, amazing feeling in her shoulders and legs. She was a different woman than the Danica that had hobbled into the shop earlier, wincing with each step.

She dressed and checked her phone, noticing that her colleague Annie had sent her a positive update about her favorite patient. Smiling to herself, she turned off her phone and wiped at the drool on her cheek before the massage therapist came back in to escort her to her pedicure. Skipping the facial for an extra thirty minutes of massage had sounded like a great idea, but really, she'd just paid to have a nap.

Keira already sat in one of the pedicure chairs with a

magazine across her lap. "Well, good morning, sunshine," she said, smiling as she looked at to Danica. "Have a nice nap?"

"You could tell?" Danica questioned, flattening her thick, sleep-tousled hair, feeling self-conscious.

"You have your woke-up-cranky look on your face," Kiera said with a knowing grin. "Which means you probably feel unsatisfied about missing out on the whole massage experience, if I know you."

Danica shook her head, climbing into the pedicure chair beside her friend and placing her feet in the warm, bubbling water. "If you ever get tired of being a middle school science teacher, you should be a detective."

"Nah, fuck the police," Kiera said blandly, flipping a page in her magazine.

Danica snorted a laugh. "Maybe a private investigator. A professional stalker, if you will."

Kiera appeared thoughtful, her brow creased. "That does sound appealing. Maybe I missed my calling."

The nail technician offered them both beverages, and they ordered mimosas for themselves and Maggie.

Maggie walked through a doorway from a small room on one end of the salon. Her dewy skin was pink and moisturized, and she walked over to the pedicure chair on Danica's other side. "There's our Sleeping Beauty," she said. "I could hear your snores for my entire facial."

"Could you really?!" Horrified, Danica looked from one friend to another, and Kiera smiled at her, shaking her head gently.

"I'm kidding. You think I could hear anything over the Enya playing in that room?" Maggie said while adjusting settings on the pedicure chair and turning on the massagers.

"Not all spa music is Enya," Danica corrected, flipping through the nail color booklet hooked to the side of the chair.

"Yeah, but all Enya is spa music, so, like, am I really wrong?" Maggie said.

"She does make a good point," Kiera said, flipping another page in her magazine. Two technicians brought the women mimosas, then sat down at Kiera and Danica's feet to start their service.

"So, I think we'd all like to know what exactly is going on with you and Pete," Maggie stated, rolling her pant legs up further as she settled into the foot bath.

"Nothing," Danica said, the single word hanging heavy in the silent air.

Maggie watched her with a knowing look. "Kiera said you guys were making out at karaoke."

"We were not," Danica protested, her voice pitching embarrassingly high.

Kiera playfully scowled at Maggie. "Maggie! You weren't supposed to talk about that."

"I had an abortion in October," Maggie said, holding up her glass. "There, how's that for things we're not talking about?"

Danica took a moment to study Maggie's face, watching her friend for any sign of feeling. "Are we sorry or are we... okay?" At 21, an abortion would have been an easy choice for any of them, but Maggie was 37 and married to a woman. Therefore, any pregnancy was likely intended and wanted.

"I'm okay," Maggie said, though her smile didn't touch her eyes.

"What happened?" Kiera asked quietly.

"Gwen and I wanted to have one more baby, and so we did a few rounds of IUI, and I got pregnant," Maggie said. "There were some complications, though."

"What does... that mean?" Kiera asked slowly. Danica glanced from Kiera to Maggie, trying her hardest not to put on her doctor's hat and begin speculating.

"We had chromosomal testing that showed Trisomy 18, so after a few more scans and tests, we made the decision to terminate the pregnancy," Maggie explained. She looked as if she had explained the situation enough times to take the initial sting out of the words, but the weariness in her face was plain to see.

Danica's heart sank. That kind of testing usually came after the ten-week mark, so Maggie would have been nearly in her second trimester.

"Fuck," Kiera said, shaking her head. "I'm so sorry, babe."

"Yeah, I'm still working through it," Maggie said. "It's hard not to blame yourself for something like that, even though I know in my rational mind I did nothing to cause it. It gets scary when you surprise doctors, you know?"

Danica gave her friend a sympathetic smile. "I get that completely. But you made the right choice. Trisomy 18 is so scary." Birth defects were nothing new to her as a neonatologist, but Trisomy 18 haunted her with its seriousness. She reached to grasp Maggie's hand, her heart aching for her friend. "No one takes that decision lightly. How's Gwen doing?"

Maggie nodded. "It's been hard on her, too, but she's really committed to working through it in grief therapy and it's been good for her."

"We both support you completely," Kiera added. "That's such a difficult kind of pain. I'm so sorry you and Gwen are going through that."

Maggie nodded, her chin quivering like she might burst into tears. Instead, she looked up at the ceiling and blinked quickly. "Thanks," she said in a choked voice. "I was a fucking mess for a while. I was so sad I could barely get out of bed for a week after."

"That's completely understandable. What you went through is horrible, and I'm so sorry," Danica said.

Kiera nodded, adding, "I think I'd be the same way."

"Me too. Do Pete and Izzy already know, or would you rather keep this private?" Danica asked.

Maggie wiped at her eyes, composing herself. "Izzy

already knows. She flew out to Austin to help me with the kids after the procedure."

Caught entirely off-guard, Danica stared at Maggie. "Really?"

"Yeah, she was great. I begged her to move in and be my nanny," Maggie said with a smile. "She even offered to carry for us if we wanted to try again, but I don't think I'm ready for that anytime soon."

Danica nodded, still shocked beyond words, but Kiera seemed to speak for both of them. "Izzy Izzy? Our Izzy? Isabel Tierney?"

Maggie rolled her eyes. "Yes, our Izzy."

Danica squeezed Maggie's hand again. "I wish I had known. I would have flown down there in a heartbeat."

"I know, but you're big and important and I knew work was stressful and you were working overtime. And I wasn't going to take Kiera away from the girls to babysit me," Maggie explained.

"I would have made it work," Danica said. "And I'm still around if you ever want to talk it through. I know that our social workers have the names of a few support groups, if you or Gwen ever need."

Maggie squeezed her hand again. "I do think when I'm ready, it'd be nice to talk to other folks who have gone through the same thing." She sniffled, then wiped hastily at her eyes. "Okay, tell me something salacious so that I don't cry through this entire pedicure."

Danica paused, basking in the calf massage part of the pedicure that had just begun. She was warring with whether to jump in with the news about Eddie, but didn't know if it was really the right time. What Maggie had shared was so heavy, and she was resistant to turning the spotlight on her instead.

Kiera sighed heavily, speaking first. "Well, while we're sharing, I'm next. I think Alex is cheating on me," she said, taking a sip of her mimosa. Her tone was the same as someone remarking on unremarkable weather, casual and bored.

Danica paused, her own drink halfway to her lips. "What?" Her mouth hung open in shock. Kiera and Alex had been married for nearly ten years and had two kids together. Kiera was beautiful and smart and funny and who in the world would cheat on such an angel of a person?

"Yeah, I guess I shouldn't say 'I think.' I know. I went through his texts on the iPad." Kiera stared down at her feet, watching the pedicure technician start with the nail polish.

The image of Kiera poring over texts on an iPad sent a pang of heartbreak through Danica. She reached to her other side, taking Kiera's hand.

Maggie shook her head slowly. "Oh, Kiera. I'm so sorry. That's awful. Do you know… who?"

"A coworker." Kiera swallowed visibly, a muscle in her jaw working.

"Damn," Danica said solemnly. It was always a coworker. Danica's mind briefly wondered if Eddie had ever had feelings for a coworker, but she didn't even feel jealous thinking about it. As a dentist, he was surrounded by female assistants and hygienists, but teeth made for a pretty unsexy work environment. She couldn't remember what Alex actually did for work as a Civil Engineer.

Maggie chimed in. "Do you need help hiding his body, or would you prefer an alibi?"

At least that brought a small smile to Kiera's lips. "Neither. Yet. But maybe in the future. I'm not sure if I should just not mention it and pretend it never happened, or confront him so we can work through it. Divorce seems so… exhausting. And the girls are so young. I can't traumatize them like that."

Danica's immediate reaction was to realize if she ever found out Eddie was cheating on her, she would have left him immediately. Hell, if she found out Pete was seeing someone else, it'd be over. Wasn't that just common sense? She supposed people worked through affairs all the time, but she never thought that her best friend was that type of person. Danica spoke up, adding, "As a child of divorced parents, I can assure you it sucks, but it would have been worse to see my parents fight and be miserable all the time." Her own parents had divorced when she was six, and her father drifted in and out of her life after that. She never blamed either of them for the divorce, though. Sometimes relationships just didn't work out.

Kiera shook her head. "I don't want a divorce."

Danica's eyes widened in surprise as she glanced back at Maggie, whose own expression mirrored her astonishment at the unexpected statement.

That wasn't like Kiera. She was stubborn, sure, but she wasn't a doormat. The Kiera she knew was strong and independent. Danica nodded, carefully trying to phrase her response. "Okay. I'm here for whatever you need, and I'll support you through anything. How are you doing? Are you okay?"

"I don't know. I think I'm okay? I'm still… figuring it all out, I guess, which is why I hadn't told you sooner." Kiera chewed on her bottom lip.

Danica nodded. "I can understand that. And if you want me to tap Alex with my car, I'm ready at a moment's notice."

"I'll be in the passenger seat," Maggie added.

Kiera's mouth formed a sad smile. "Please don't run over my husband."

"I only said tap." Danica held her palms up in defense.

Maggie added, "You said you didn't want a divorce, but you never said you were opposed to being a widow."

Kiera rolled her eyes.

If she was ever going to admit to being single, now was the time. With her friends' vulnerability fresh in her mind, her pulse roared in her ears. But as she opened her mouth, Maggie squealed with delight at the glittery pink color on her big toe, and Danica just... stayed silent. She felt like a fraud and a coward as she forced herself to laugh along with her friends.

Their pedicure service wrapped up, Danica choosing a subtle nude, Maggie going with cherry red, and Kiera choosing neon green. As they walked out of the spa and salon, Danica stopped them both on the street, grabbing each by an arm of their ski jackets. "I really love you both."

"Is this a group hug moment?" Kiera said with a quirk of her lips.

"This is definitely a group hug moment," Maggie said, launching herself to wrap her one free arm around Kiera as she collided with Danica.

Danica laughed, despite her lingering discomfort about keeping her own secret.

"Should we grab lunch?" Maggie asked, pointing toward a faux-rustic sandwich shop next door.

"Actually, I think I'm going to go back to the house and call the girls and then take a nap," Kiera said, her tone more withdrawn than Danica was used to hearing

"Suit yourself," Maggie said flippantly, linking her non-sling arm through Danica's.

"You'll be okay getting back? Do you want to take the car and we can call a ride?" Danica asked, touching Kiera's elbow gently.

"I'll call an Uber," Kiera said. "It's no big deal."

"Share your ride location with me so I can be sure you don't get murdered," Danica instructed. Telluride to Mountain Village was a short Gondola ride, but the ride the night before had taken awhile.

Maggie grinned. "I'm glad you never stopped being our mom, Dani."

Danica smiled, patting Maggie's head and then pinching her cheek.

"Alright, ride info is shared," Kiera said, looking at her phone.

"Want to come back and join us after your nap? We can Après without the whole skiing part," Maggie said.

"Maybe," Kiera said noncommittally. She looked up from her phone toward where a car was pulling over. "That's me. See you guys later."

"Text us," Danica said. "To let us know you got back home safely."

Kiera gave her a nod and climbed into the back of the car.

Maggie and Danica hurried inside the sandwich shop to get out of the cold, stomping their boots on the mat near the door. They ordered at the counter and found a seat near the window.

Danica unwound her scarf and wiped her nose with a tissue. Cold air always made her nose run in a very unattractive way. "Is it just me, or did Kiera just sprint away as fast as possible?" she asked, glancing at the taxidermy elk head staring at her from behind Maggie.

"She's going through it, it sounds like," Maggie said, turning to follow Danica's gaze. "Oh, hello. That thing is, like, way too close to my head. Didn't know this spot was already taken."

"Imagine its judgment if you'd ordered the elk burger," Danica said. "I just can't figure out why Kiera would stay with Alex. Would you stay if Gwen cheated?"

Maggie shook her head. "No, but I can see why someone might stay because of the kids. Kiera has a job, which would make leaving easier, but leaving a partner when you're the homemaker? I'd have a hard time leaving Gwen if I needed to, since I feel so reliant on her financially, even though I trust her completely. If I didn't trust her and still depended on her like that… It sounds so daunting."

"That's a good point, but you'd still find a way to leave, wouldn't you?" Danica asked, knowing Maggie was taking time off from her career to raise three kids, which sounded like a fuller-than-full-time job.

"Yeah, but Gwen and I have a pre-nup. You and Eddie are probably planning on having one, right?" Maggie asked, glancing up as a server placed their beers on the table, assuring them their food would be out soon.

Danica wasn't sure how to answer that... Instead, she lifted her vanilla porter to her lips to give herself a moment to think.

Maggie eyed her critically. "Haven't you been engaged for almost two years?"

Danica sipped her beer again. "Uh, I mean. Yeah. But that's not that long. We still have plenty of time to plan... everything."

"You haven't planned anything in two years?" Maggie pressed, sipping her own milk stout.

Danica shook her head. Her guilt and awkwardness from lying was weighing even more heavily on her. She opened her mouth to say something, but Maggie cut her off.

"I don't think you should marry Eddie," Maggie said directly, watching her closely for a reaction.

A gasp escaped Danica's lips as she stared, utterly taken aback. "Wh-what? Why?"

"You don't love him." Maggie pressed her lips into a firm line, looking at Danica as though she were piecing together a puzzle. "I can tell. I have seen you in love, and you don't love him. Eddie just isn't right for you."

Danica blinked, tears welling up in her eyes.

With an unnerving persistence, Maggie continued to watch her, her gaze unwavering. "How long have you..." she trailed off, her hand gesturing vaguely, a silent question hanging in the air.

"Wh-what do you mean? I'm not—I mean, why would you even say that?"

"Did you cry when you broke up?" Maggie asked, her tone gentle, like she was holding Danica's hand as she dragged her out of the dark cave of her lie.

"Goddamn, Margaret. Yes, I cried." Danica shook her head, grimacing as a wave of discomfort washed over her.

"Wanna start at the beginning?" Maggie continued with the gentle tone.

Danica glanced up toward the ceiling, trying to avoid Maggie's eye. She took a deep breath, then let it all spill out. She detailed the engagement, the breakup, the aftermath, and the phone call earlier that week.

When she was done, Maggie squinted in concentration. "Let me recap. You're not actually that upset about the break up? Dani, it's okay if—"

"Where are you getting that?" Danica asked, not wanting to hear the end of that sentence. "Are you psychoanalyzing me?"

"No, I know you. You feel things very deeply. You always have. And to be honest, I've never gotten the sense that you've been madly in love with Eddie." Maggie looked at her with a pitying stare.

"Just because we were a bit more subdued with our affection doesn't mean we weren't in love," Danica insisted.

"When did the sex stop?" Maggie asked, apparently not feeling even an ounce of shame as their plates were being set down, and they could be easily overheard. She picked up a potato chip and tossed it casually into her mouth.

Danica tried to roll her eyes. "That's not an indication—"

"Six months?" Maggie interrupted.

"Eight," Danica croaked, then finished her beer in one large gulp. "Eight months."

Maggie's mouth formed into something resembling a *"yeesh"* grimace.

"Sex isn't everything, you know?" Danica was really fighting for her life in this damn sandwich shop.

Maggie nodded, not saying a word as she picked up her turkey Reuben.

"I thought we were talking about Kiera's issues, not mine," Danica grumbled, lifting her veggie burger with both hands.

"Kiera isn't here to defend herself. You are," Maggie stated, as if it was obvious. "So, what happened? Are you okay?"

Danica nodded, staring down at the burger in her hands. "Okay, fine. I felt relieved. When he finally broke up with me, I felt like a weight was lifted off my shoulders. And when it was over, the first thing I thought was..." She paused, not sure if she wanted to continue. "I don't know."

"Your first thought was Pete," Maggie said around a mouthful of sandwich.

Danica glanced away with a huff of exasperation. "No." She set down her burger, suddenly losing her appetite. She wiped her hands on her napkin and fidgeted with her silverware. "It wasn't."

Maggie's soft expression was non-judgmental as she watched Danica.

"Don't look at me like that," Danica said, looking up at the elk instead. Its glassy eyes and nose were shiny in a discomforting and uncanny way.

Maggie wiped at her mouth with her napkin, then took a deep breath. "Look. I was there in the beginning. I remember how you and Pete were together."

"We were young."

"And I see the way Pete looks at you now," Maggie continued. "And the way you look at her."

Danica flushed. "I have no idea what you mean."

Maggie smiled back at her. "Just think about it."

With a sharp shake of her head and a flat tone, Danica

declared she would do no such thing. "Let's hold off on telling Kiera about this for now, okay? With all of this affair and Alex stuff, I don't want that to be on her mind."

Maggie gave her a small, sad smile. "Your friends should help you through the hard times."

"Well, if that isn't the pot calling the kettle black," Danica said, but her words didn't carry any sting.

Maggie waved a hand dismissively, but her eyes twinkled with a teasing gleam. "Yeah, yeah. 'Do as I say, not as I do.' Oh, look who else can deflect with an adage?"

CHAPTER 12

PETE

PETE WAS GRATEFUL FOR A QUIET NIGHT STAYING IN AFTER THEIR karaoke night full of drinking and poor sleep. The group sat around the dining table sipping drinks as Danica fussed over a white chicken chili across the kitchen island. Outside, giant snowflakes floated down from the sky, blanketing the world in a fresh layer of snow. Tomorrow would be a truly epic powder day if this kept up.

"My knees were shaking. I was so scared," Izzy said with wide eyes, recounting the tale of how they'd tried a few expert runs that day. "We were doing fine until Pete's spectacular yard sale."

"A what? Yard sale?" Maggie repeated.

"When you fall so hard, your gear flies all around you, making the area look like a yard sale," Pete explained. Her ass hurt and she'd probably need to stick to easier runs the following day, but what was the point of being at one of the most gorgeous ski resorts in the country if you didn't try something new? They still had two days of vacation left, three if she was counting the day they all had to head back home, and she had to get out her restless energy somehow.

Because constantly daydreaming about pinning Danica up against a wall and actually getting to kiss her. Letting her mind wander to what else might happen. Waking up beside Danica, albeit in an awkward position and apparently to an audience, had reminded her what it felt like to be close to Danica, to be pressed against her.

Danica probably needed time after her relationship before getting involved in something new, and Pete could give her that, but she wanted to be on Danica's mind. Pete wanted to follow Danica's lead and be ready whenever she was.

She stole a glance toward the kitchen where Danica was tasting directly from the stirring spoon. They locked eyes and Danica gave her a wry smile as heat spread through Pete's entire body. With a playful wink and a secretive finger to her lips, Danica dipped the spoon back into the pot.

Pete grinned, sipping her wine and admiring the way Danica was in her own little world, dancing to the Shrikes album playing in the background while cooking.

The sight made her ponder what sharing a home with Danica could be like — cooking together, sharing jokes, dancing on the kitchen tile... taking a break from cooking to lay Danica back on the kitchen counter and—

"Isn't that right, Pete?" Izzy asked.

Pete glanced back to the group to find three sets of eyes staring at her. "Yeah. That's right." She had no idea what she was agreeing with.

Kiera rolled her eyes and Maggie openly laughed while sipping a soda. So, she *wasn't* supposed to agree with whatever Izzy was saying.

"Happy thoughts?" Izzy inquired, looking innocent.

"Wh-what? No," Pete said, and she could feel her cheeks flushing. Damn wine. This was somehow entirely the wine's fault.

"The Happy Thought run, weirdo," Izzy said, rolling her eyes. "We were talking about that run through the trees."

Pete shook her head to clear her thoughts, focusing solely on the rush she had felt while boarding through the Happy Thought woods — less of a run and more of a portal into a winter wonderland — weaving between gigantic evergreens laden with fresh snow. It had felt magical. Otherworldly. For a run called Happy Thought, the only thought in her mind the entire time had been Danica.

Distraction plagued Pete all day, and by early afternoon, Izzy's patience was exhausted, causing them to end their day after Pete made a rookie mistake and fell. They had come back to the condo and overheard Kiera yelling at someone on the phone. Kiera had sounded livid, and they'd hidden from her bad mood by taking naps downstairs in Pete's bunk beds.

Danica and Maggie had come home in the late afternoon with shopping bags and wind-flushed cheeks. Danica had kept things short with her, going to take a nap in her room before coming out to dinner wearing a new sky-blue sweater. Maggie made her catwalk through the living room to show it off. It matched her eyes perfectly.

Izzy waved a hand in front of Pete's face. "Did you hit your head when I wasn't looking today or what?" she snapped.

"Sorry, I'm just tired," Pete said, sighing. She tapped her fingers on the table, her gaze resting on the exhausted faces of Kiera, Maggie, and Izzy. "We should play a game."

Kiera glanced around the room. "Maybe a puzzle. I don't think Aunt Jade has any board games."

"We could do an extreme puzzling session where we try to finish the puzzle in under an hour," Pete suggested. "They have these competitions—"

"Pass," Izzy said, leaning back in her chair.

"We could play charades," Pete offered.

Kiera shook her head.

"Let's play truth or dare," Maggie exclaimed, looking mischievous.

"No way," Danica said from the kitchen. "Remember that time you dared me to run through the boy's floor in just my bra and underwear?"

"Oh my god, I'd forgotten about that." Kiera turned to Danica, laughing. "Didn't you trip and fall?"

"Some idiot had left a big puddle on the floor outside of the bathroom, and I pulled an accidental Risky Business slide into the RA's door. I had a bruise on my cheek for days," Danica said, shaking her head.

"Which cheek?" Maggie teased.

"You know what, maybe we should play truth or dare. Maybe it's time for payback. This is a fantastic idea," Danica said, pointing the soup spoon at Maggie.

Maggie tapped her fingers together in an evil, plotting way. "Bring it on."

"I still can't feel my tongue," Kiera complained, chugging water.

Danica's soup had proven to be extremely spicy, but absolutely delicious. Kiera, Izzy, and Maggie had all added cream cheese to their portions to try to dampen some of the heat, but Pete scarfed a full bowl and went back for seconds.

Izzy was still wiping her drippy nose, eating straight out of an ice cream carton in an effort to quell the heat.

"Sorry, I guess I forgot you're all babies," Danica said with a grin. "Except Pete."

"I thought it was perfect," Pete said with a smile, looking toward Danica at the head of the table.

"Okay, Danica, truth or dare," Maggie said, leaning to take a bite from the ice cream carton Izzy had been hoarding.

"Let's lay out some ground rules," Danica said, holding up her fingers to count them off. "Nothing that will get Aunt Jade evicted."

"Very wise. I approve," Kiera chimed in.

"Everyone has a right to refuse their dare. We're nearly 40. We have free will," Danica added.

Pete nodded. "And if you don't want to do your dare, you have to either sing your favorite song at the top of your lungs or eat a spoonful of a mystery substance that the rest of us choose," she said.

The sound of Danica's giggle, sweet and infectious, completely captivated Pete.

"Only edible things for eating," Danica emphasized. "Okay, truth."

"You chicken," Maggie said. "Alright. Have you ever had a sex dream about me?"

A snort of surprised laughter escaped Danica's lips, a mixture of amusement and disbelief. "I have not."

"Your loss," Maggie said with a grin.

Danica nodded, feigning gravitas. "I'll try to remedy that as soon as possible, I promise. Okay, Kiera, truth or dare."

"Dare," Kiera said, looking ready for a challenge.

"Speak with a Scottish accent for the next three rounds," Danica said immediately, like she'd been waiting for this exact excuse.

Kiera laughed. "Aye, I will." It was a terrible accent in just three words, and Pete grimaced into her glass of wine.

Over the next few rounds, Izzy had to wear a clean pair of Danica's neon green ski socks on her hands for the rest of the game, Pete had to dance in silence for a full minute while standing on her chair, and Maggie had to swish Danica's spicy soup in her mouth for thirty seconds.

The unspoken rules of the night seemed to be silly, low-stakes fun, with everyone fully clothed, a sense of playful abandon hanging in the air. That was, until Maggie leveled Danica with an intense stare. "I dare you, Danica Mae Wendell, to go make a snow angel on the deck in only your underwear."

A full-on Wild West showdown began as Danica and

Maggie stared at one another. Pete could have sworn the theme from some old Clint Eastwood movie began playing in the background as tension and phantom tumbleweeds filled the room.

Kiera sighed, glancing between Maggie and Danica. "Well, do you want to eat a spoonful of wasabi or do a naked snow angel?"

"I said her underwear could stay on! And her bra. I'm feeling quite generous," Maggie feigned innocence.

Slowly, Danica began to move with a resigned look on her face, her chair scraping dramatically against the wood floor as she stood, reaching for the hem of her sweater. Pete stood up so quickly her chair fell backwards, startling everyone into looking at her. "I'll be your proxy."

"What?" Danica asked, pausing, the skin of her stomach showing a few inches below the hem of her sweater.

"I'll do it instead," Pete said. "Sounds fun."

Danica seemed confused. "It's my dare. I can do it."

Izzy stood up. "I'll do it, too."

Kiera looked around the table. "So, we're all doing this? I thought we weren't getting Aunt Jade evicted."

"Group dare, I guess." Maggie laughed.

The women laughed as they turned off the lights — a concession they agreed to in order to stay in the neighbor's good graces — and stripped down to their underwear. A gust of wind blew snow inside as soon as Maggie opened the door, and all four shrieked as they ran onto the patio.

Another stare down began as they all paused, arms clutched around themselves, alternating from standing on one foot and then the other, waiting to see who would go first.

Pete backed up from the group and let herself fall backwards into the snow, waving her arms and legs to make a snow angel. She heard squeals and yelps as the rest of the women followed her lead. Warm fingers brushed against hers and she turned her head to see Danica's open, grateful expression.

"Okay, that's enough of that," Kiera said after a few minutes, standing up to run back inside. Maggie and Izzy were almost immediately behind her, and then Danica was standing over her, holding out a hand. It was not lost on Pete that Danica was only wearing a thin bralette and a pair of white underwear, less opaque than they had been before. She took Danica's hand, jumping up to hurry them both inside.

Maggie tossed Danica a towel. "Truce?"

Danica laughed. "Oh, not even close."

As Danica handed Pete the towel, she saw Kiera watching them closely, seemingly curious about the shift in their interaction. Everyone took a moment to find dry clothes and change into pajamas, then agreed to get whatever extra blankets they could find in the condo to get cozy in the living room and watch a movie.

Danica was the last to return, and Maggie moved from where she was sitting beside Pete, shifting instead to sit in the chair, saying she could see better from that angle. Pete didn't think Maggie could be any more obvious at trying to make sure she and Danica sat together.

Izzy, Pete, Danica, and Kiera all sat on the couch, crammed together with their blankets. After an epic round of rock, paper, scissors, Danica picked a Wes Anderson movie they'd all wanted to see together in college, but it had come out after their graduation.

Izzy fell asleep almost immediately, and Maggie conked out right after her. Kiera stayed awake until about forty-five minutes into the movie. Pete sat as still as she could, not wanting Danica to move away with any kind of touch or contact. She was keenly aware of just how close Danica was, how her hair smelled like rosemary shampoo, how she awkwardly rested her hands on her thighs like she might also be afraid of accidental contact with Pete.

Danica laughed at a particularly silly scene in the movie and Pete couldn't help glancing toward her, taking in the way the reflected light bounced off her cheeks, making the long, elegant curve of her neck stand out. She was even more beautiful than Pete remembered.

Noticing Pete's gaze, Danica's blue eyes widened. "What?" she asked self-consciously.

"Everyone's asleep but us," Pete pointed out in a whisper.

Danica nodded. "Yeah, we should turn it off and head to bed, too."

"It's still early enough," Pete said, her voice still quiet. "I was thinking it might be kind of magical to sit in the hot tub while it snows."

Danica watched her for a long moment, then turned away, clearing her throat. "Sounds fun. Enjoy."

Pete's voice was barely audible as she leaned forward so Danica could hear her. "You don't want to join me?"

Danica crossed and uncrossed her arms, looking adorably nervous. "What do you want me to say right now?"

Pete's gaze was steady as a wry smile lifted the corners of her mouth. "I think you already know what I want."

"Let's get everyone off to bed," Danica said.

Pete wasn't exactly sure what that response meant. She shook Izzy's shoulder, ignoring her protests of being comfortable. Kiera claimed she hadn't been sleeping, but her groggy voice said otherwise. Maggie jolted awake, startling everyone, and then speed walked out of the room without a word. Danica got Kiera a glass of water and handed Izzy a few Ibuprofens for her incoming hangover, and as their friends shuffled off to bed, Pete turned toward Danica. They were finally all alone, standing in the dining room.

There was an awkward sort of anticipation lingering between them, like two people on a first date who didn't know how to interact with each other.

"I'm too tired to change," Danica said, glancing over her shoulder. "I might just go to bed."

"Hmm. Truth or dare?" Pete asked with a mischievous quirk of an eyebrow.

Danica frowned at her, then sighed. "Don't you dare."

"So, it's a dare, then?" A grin tugged at the corner of Pete's mouth.

Danica shook her head slowly, not breaking eye contact with Pete.

"I dare you to go skinny dipping in the hot tub," Pete whispered conspiratorially.

"I thought we weren't getting Aunt Jade evicted."

"With the lights off, no one will see us," Pete said. "Unless you're too chicken."

Danica paused for a long moment and appeared to be weighing the pros and cons of the situation. "Can I wear a beanie?"

"I suppose."

As Danica watched Pete, taking her time, Pete's stomach flipped with anticipation of her 'yes'.

"I will if you will," Pete said.

Danica pulled at the hem of her shirt. "Alright. Fuck it."

Pete laughed at Danica's playful tone. "Done." Pete pulled her shirt over her head, only tensing her abs a little bit as she did. She slowed her movements, feeling Danica's eyes on her. This was an interesting game they were playing, but one that Pete didn't want to concede. "I could have said naked snow angel," Pete said.

"Frostbitten vulva isn't on my bucket list." Danica began to lift her shirt, then paused, pointing at Pete with mock-confrontation. "No funny business."

"Sure, Wendell," Pete said with a smirk. She shimmied her pajama pants over her hips, hooking her thumbs in her underwear to pull them down, too.

Danica turned around to pull off her shirt, but if she

thought that would stop Pete's eyes from roaming every inch of her shoulders and back, she was woefully mistaken. She tugged off her pants in a quick and inelegant maneuver, and Pete tried very hard to remain appropriate and not stare at Danica's ass, but she could hardly be blamed. She'd seen Danica naked so many times before, but it had been fifteen years. Now, her body was lush, all soft curves.

"Don't forget a towel." Danica cleared her throat, grabbing one from a pile. She wrapped it around herself quickly, then grabbed a beanie from the table next to the door, pulling it over her head. "Ready?"

Pete nodded, not even trying to cover herself with her towel. It would only slow her down from getting into the warm water as fast as she could.

Danica's gaze trailed downward, but snapped back up to meet Pete's eye. "Ready?" Pete nodded, and Danica opened the door to let her go out first. She shut the door as quietly as she could, and they raced barefoot and bare-assed across the patio and rushed to take the hot tub cover off.

"Fuck, it's way colder than I thought it would be," Danica said, her teeth clenched as she held her towel with one hand and worked to remove the cover with the other one.

"Way colder," Pete agreed with a chuckle, shoving the cover aside unceremoniously. "Okay, get in, get in, get in." They dropped their towels and climbed into the hot tub, sinking down so only their heads were out of the water. As the water stilled, Pete could hear the gentle shushing of the snow falling around them.

Danica was looking up at the sky, a soft smile on her face as snowflakes landed on her cheeks. Seeing her smile, completely enthralled by something so simple and lovely, caused a painful yet tender feeling to bloom in Pete's chest. Snowflakes landed on the wool of her beanie, the fluff of the pompom on top. Danica looked at her and smiled her soft, heart-melting smile. "It looks like you have a halo."

Pete reached up to touch the snow landing in her dark curls, then shook her head and watched the tiny droplets fly.

Danica laughed, a sound like bells in the winter night, her voice fogging the surrounding air. "I'm glad you made me do this."

"Me too," Pete said, leaning back against the side of the hot tub, finally warm enough to consider not being entirely underwater. She propped an arm up on the edge and watched as Danica's gaze trailed down to where the water covered the top of her chest, then back up again.

"I'm sorry I've been so..." Danica gestured in the air between them.

Pete raised an eyebrow. "Warm and welcoming? Bright and bubbly?"

"Awkward and standoffish?" Danica said.

Pete dipped her chin in acknowledgement. "Ah, that."

"I didn't know what it would be like to see you again," Danica said, her voice lower. She looked down into the water, tendrils of hair free from underneath the beanie and brushing against her cheeks.

"And? What is it like?" Pete asked, her heart thumping with expectant hope.

"I think sometimes I forget you were one of my best friends," Danica said, still looking down at the water where she was swaying her arms back and forth.

Pete made a sound of understanding and nodded. Maybe it was their proximity and their nakedness, but Danica still had a nervous energy about her. Pete remained still, watching the way Danica's brow wrinkled as she seemed to weigh her words.

"I mean, things did end badly between us, but this week made me realize how much I've missed..." Danica paused again, looking up at the falling snow again. She squinted, as though looking for the right word.

Pete had never wanted to hear the word 'you' so badly in

her life. She wanted to hear that Danica missed her, that she'd never stopped thinking about her.

"Our friendship," Danica said carefully and slowly.

Ouch. Pete tried not to let the sting of the words show on her face. But she had missed their friendship, too. And if all Danica wanted was friendship, it might hurt, but she'd rather have Danica in her life as a friend than not at all.

"I've missed you, too," Pete said, the words tumbling out in a rush, betraying the carefully constructed composure she'd tried to maintain.

"Where have you been for the last fifteen years? I feel like you just disappeared," Danica asked, her voice thick in the cold night air.

Pete held out her hand to catch a few snowflakes as she contemplated what to say. There was just something really lame about saying that she'd been experiencing the world, or exploring, or that she was working tirelessly on building her nonprofit into something that would actually help vulnerable and parentless children.

"You don't have to tell me, unless you're a super-secret spy or something. Then you definitely have to tell me," Danica said, watching her closely.

"Not a spy. I've just been traveling and working," Pete said as honestly as she was comfortable with.

"What are you doing for work?" Danica asked.

Pete let her hand drift back under the water. "Odd jobs," she said, and that was the truth. She'd worked on organic farms in South America while waiting for an organization connection to pan out fully, and she'd been a ski instructor for rich kids in the French alps out of sheer boredom for two winters when things were slow with making connections in Europe. She'd always taken her time vetting new partner agencies and organizations, making sure they were really helping kids and not just taking the money for themselves.

Danica frowned. "Why are you being so cagey?"

"It's just not that interesting, I'm afraid. Tell me about your job," Pete said, trying to change the subject.

"Also not that interesting," Danica said with a shrug.

"Liar."

Danica watched her for a moment, then turned her face back to the sky. "It's hard. It has its rewarding moments but it feels really heavy sometimes. And the hours are hard for a relation—" She stopped herself, contemplating. "Well, I guess that's not something I worry about anymore."

Pete nodded, not wanting to break whatever spell was making Danica open up to her. "How are you feeling about that?"

Danica lifted one shoulder in a half-shrug. "Weirdly... fine?"

"Do you think you'll get back together when you get home?" Pete asked, her chest clenching with concern.

"No, I don't... I don't want to. I know it's relatively new in the grand scheme of life, but it doesn't feel raw, you know? It doesn't feel like heartbreak has felt before, not like I just broke up with the love of my life or something," Danica said with a heavy sigh.

"Heartbreak?" Pete questioned before she could help herself.

Danica leveled her with a stare. "Are you fucking kidding me?"

Pete's eyes widened in surprise. "What? Where'd that come from?"

"Oh my god, never mind," Danica said, rolling her eyes and crossing her arms over her chest.

Understanding washed over Pete as she watched Danica; the realization striking her with intense clarity. "Wendell," she said, her voice softening and lowering to barely a whisper. "You mean *us*."

Danica glared at her, and Pete could have sworn she could see the bricks of her walls starting to rebuild.

"Hey," Pete said, leaning forward in the water to touch Danica's arm, looking into her eyes. "I didn't know you felt that way."

"Yeah, well... I did," Danica said, glancing away from Pete's intense stare.

Pete wished she was good with words. She wished she had some grand speech to explain to Danica that she wouldn't take back the world-crushing heartache she experienced, because it fueled her to work harder to achieve her dreams. She'd never prioritized a relationship because she never stayed anywhere long enough to grow roots. Instead, she'd blamed never having a deep soul connection with anyone on the fact that she was always leaving soon, always one foot out the door. Not because some part of her had always hoped she and Danica would find their way back to each other.

They had to break their hearts to grow up, to grow into better versions of themselves.

But she wasn't the kind of person who could say all of that aloud just yet. Instead, she said what she could manage in the moment. "Danica," she whispered, closing her eyes for a pause before opening them, looking directly at her. "I'm sorry for what happened between us then, but I'm here now. We're both here now."

CHAPTER 13

DANICA

DANICA'S BODY FELT FLUSHED AND TINGLY WITH ANTICIPATION AS Pete slid closer to her. Their bodies drew together like magnets, leaning into one another. Pete's nose slid down the side of hers, only an inch between their mouths as she listened to Pete's shaky breath.

There was still a chance they could let the moment pass without ever leaping over that final hurdle. There was still time to pretend this never happened, to stop this from happening.

Danica didn't know exactly what she wanted. Her mind was quiet, but her heart was beating wildly out of her chest as Pete's hand slid up the side of her neck to cradle her cheek.

They were drawn to one another — they had always been pulled toward one another like magnets — and somehow it felt inevitable that they'd end up like this again. Pete's thumb slid over her jaw, gently angling her face up. Every breath was a whisper against one another's lips, a promise, a prayer, a warning. She shouldn't let this happen, she thought through a haze. Pete's nose touched hers, a familiar warmth spreading through her, making her forget any lingering resolve she'd been holding onto.

Her heart thrummed a hard and fast rhythm as they both moved slowly, carefully, snow gently falling upon their bare shoulders as the air fogged from the hot tub and their bodies and their shared breaths.

Pete seemed to wait for her to close the distance between them, for her to take the lead, like this kiss was a *when*, not an *if*. Danica craved more. Chemistry had never been their problem. The memory of their tiny dorm rooms, the hushed whispers and frantic heartbeats, came back to her — hours spent kissing, exploring, drunk on lust and the incredible feeling that this gorgeous woman actually liked her.

She felt that same giddiness now, like it was the first time all over again. Danica's tongue grazed over Pete's lower lip, barely tasting the cool, melted snowflakes, and Pete caught Danica's mouth with hers.

It was a kiss so soft, so slow, it felt like a whisper against her skin. Then another, with a little more confidence, a little less tentativeness. Danica threaded her hands into Pete's hair. This was happening. This was really happening.

Pete let out a sigh, and when her lips found Danica's again, the kiss was deeper, slower. Pete shifted closer, their kiss lingering only briefly before she gently brushed her thumb across Danica's lower lip, the light catching the brightness in her eyes as they studied one another. Kissing Pete felt like re-reading a favorite book — comfortable, familiar, and exciting all at once. Danica shivered in the cold air, snowflakes dotting her bare shoulders, filled with excitement, and maybe a little bit of terror. She was scared how Pete had always held her heart so gently one second and precariously the next, how much her body ached for Pete's touch, how right this felt.

Pete's tongue slid over Danica's, and their kiss deepened like she was reclaiming what had been missing for so long.

Danica nipped at Pete's lower lip, her arms sliding around Pete's neck as their bare chests made contact out of the water. Pete let her hands fall to Danica's hips, then pulled her closer until Danica was straddling her, a knee on either side of her thighs. The warmth of the water, the way Pete's skin felt both soft and slick, the chill of the air — Danica's body was going haywire with sensation, with the contact that she so desperately needed.

Each gasp they took between kisses was as tantalizing as the way Pete's lips danced over Danica's, leaving her feeling exposed and vulnerable.

Pete pressed her face into Danica's neck, licking and nipping at her skin, and Danica tangled Pete's hair in her hands to keep from moaning so loud that she'd wake up the entirety of Mountain Village.

Pete pulled back, her chest rising and falling with rapid breaths as she pressed her forehead to Danica's. "Is this still okay?" she asked Danica in a hushed voice.

Danica could hardly find the words to voice that this was the best kiss of her entire life. That she had no idea that just kissing could be so good. That she could spend hours in this hot tub kissing this woman, holding her body close. Words were the last thing on her mind as Pete's breasts brushed against her skin, as Pete's hands slid over her back and hips, as Pete grabbed at her ass. Danica could only nod, catching Pete's mouth again with hers.

"I could kiss you forever," Pete murmured against Danica's lips, and Danica moaned in agreement. Why had they spent so many years *not* kissing?

In all her years with Eddie, they had never just kissed like this. Why had she so quickly forgotten what such a satisfying kiss had felt like? Why had she let herself settle?

An overwhelming feeling crashed into Danica, part shame, part self-loathing, part voice in her head screaming, *What are you doing?!* And what *was* she doing? Her ex-fiancé had broken up with her only a month before, and now she was in a hot tub making out with another ex. She was making all the same mistakes, being so reckless with her heart all over again.

She needed space from Pete — it was like the nearness to this woman blocked all rational thoughts from her brain. Pete had broken her heart once, and once was enough. With Pete, things felt too complicated to move forward, to let herself get heartbroken again. She pulled backwards, her breath shallow and quick.

"What's wrong?" Pete asked, reaching to tuck a stray lock of hair back into Danica's beanie. "Are you cold?"

No. "Yeah," Danica answered. "I think we should go to bed."

Pete watched her face carefully, Danica's expression infuriatingly neutral and unreadable. "To... bed?"

"To sleep. Separately," Danica said, standing suddenly. Pete stared at Danica's body, her eyes roaming everywhere, very obviously taking in Danica's breasts, then lowering... "To sleep," Danica reiterated.

Pete nodded, reaching for their towels to hand one to Danica, then climbed out and Pete paused to replace the hot tub cover. Danica hurried back inside, ice already forming on the fine hair at the napes of her neck. Danica shivered, pausing to grab her pajamas from a dining chair where she'd discarded them before. She was going to have to get in the shower to warm back up before bed. The thought of asking Pete to join crossed her mind, but she tamped that urge down just as quickly as it popped into her head.

"Goodnight," Danica said, the word coming out a little harsher than she'd intended, seeing Pete's confused and hurt expression.

"Goodnight, Wendell," Pete said softly, her gaze lingering on Danica, eyes wide with unspoken emotion.

Danica let herself zone out under the warm water until

she grew self-conscious of personally causing a water shortage in Mountain Village. She climbed into bed, staring at the ceiling in the dark. Hours passed as she tossed and turned, oscillating between self-loathing and confusion. Somewhere around 4 a.m., she got out of bed and quietly opened the door to Kiera's room. Kiera's presence had always calmed her, and there had been more than a few times in college where they had climbed into each other's bed for the comfort of being near a friend.

From somewhere in the dark, Kiera said, "Dani? What's wrong? Come here." She held open the covers for Danica, and Danica quickly climbed into the bed beside Kiera. Kiera's voice was still groggy and half-asleep as she asked, "Do you want to talk about it?"

"No," Danica admitted, and Kiera let her hand rest on Danica's arm.

"Want me to sing you the girls' lullaby?" Kiera asked.

Danica smiled in the darkness, sniffling as tears stung her eyes. "Sure."

Kiera hummed Brahms' lullaby, and Danica felt instantly calmer and less alone. She could feel her mind quiet any lingering panic about what she'd just done. Perhaps it was the lullaby or the closeness or the company, but nothing seemed to be catastrophic enough to keep her from sleep. The gentle vibrations of Kiera's humming faded as she drifted off, a peaceful stillness settling over her.

CHAPTER 14

PETE

"I JUST REALLY PREFER TO KEEP MY LEGS TOGETHER," PETE SAID.

Izzy laughed. "Liar."

Pete shot Izzy a glare, sliding her skis back and forth in the lift line. Izzy was sticking with her trusty snowboard, but Pete wanted to check out a few of the expert runs on skis. After an hour or two on blues, of course. It had nothing to do with the fact that Danica was on skis, and mostly stuck to blues. It had nothing to do with the fact that Danica and Kiera had joined them for the day. Maggie had stayed at home, curled up on the couch with some book that was, in her words, "Deliciously smutty."

The only bad part of having Danica and Kiera with her today was that every time she checked out Danica, Kiera would notice and give her a pointed look, like she was some sort of morality enforcer.

That morning over breakfast, Pete saw a hickey on Danica's neck, dark red and glaringly obvious. When Danica caught her eye, she gave a little smirk — clearly not *that* bothered by the previous night.

Which was interesting, given how Danica looked panicked and upset the night before after they'd kissed. Pete had tossed and turned for hours in that stupid tiny bunk bed, worried that she'd done something wrong. But then she'd remember the way Danica's hips were grinding into hers, the little moans that escaped Danica's swollen lips as Pete had given her that damn hickey, the way Danica's body pressed so tightly against hers — and it definitely didn't seem like Danica was doing anything she didn't want to be doing. Maybe she just changed her mind, which she was perfectly allowed to do. Pete just worried that she'd done something to make Danica change her mind.

It had always felt so right with Danica before, like a part of her knew, or at least hoped, that they'd come back to one another. Even after a brief period when Danica had gotten a girlfriend for a few weeks, or the few one-night stands Pete had taken home from the bar — Pete had never questioned where she stood with Danica. They were friends with major benefits and without any complications. Or so she'd believed while they were together.

In the months after college, after that fight, after Danica had made it clear they were over until Pete got her shit together, Pete crashed on Izzy's couch in San Francisco a few times before finishing and selling Til Morning. She'd get drunk on bitter, cheap whiskey and ask Izzy if it was stupid that she was still so heartbroken over a person she'd never even technically dated. She'd never forget the way Izzy once said to her, "What if she was the right person at the wrong time? Maybe the right time just hasn't happened yet."

It had taken years to not love Danica, and she wasn't sure if she had even achieved that. It had taken nearly a decade before she stopped thinking, "I wish Danica was here" while watching the sunset over a beach in Bali, or overlooking miles of lush jungle in Costa Rica, or at an incredible art gallery in Budapest.

Losing Danica once was awful. If Danica gave her the chance, if she could show Danica that she'd changed from the immature, directionless person she'd been... She wouldn't make that same mistake twice. If Danica was willing to explore a future together, Pete was not going to waste it this time.

When Maggie had reached out to invite her on the trip, it had taken only Danica's name on the guest list to convince her. Of course, it was a plus that Izzy and Maggie would be there, and even Kiera, who had her fun moments. The thought of seeing Danica again... well, she had a feeling she'd either get closure or confirm what a mistake it had been to let Danica go. Then, when she'd heard Danica and Eddie arguing, when Danica had confirmed they were over... It wasn't closure she was after, suddenly.

And that was how Pete ended up on skis.

Danica had laid out the plan after Pete had insisted that she didn't need to start with greens, the easiest runs. They'd do these blues until Pete felt more confident to take the slightly longer and harder trails. They'd grab crepes and lunch at the Bon Vivant restaurant, and then could split up for the afternoon. Pete, Izzy, and Kiera would hit the harder black trails and Danica could go back to the condo to hang out with Maggie. Danica said that she was still sore from snowboarding, but Pete knew that she just didn't want Maggie to be alone all day. Classic Danica, always worried about everyone else.

They stood at the top of Peek-a-Boo, and Pete had nearly forgotten what it felt like to be on such a wide-open run. Still, Telluride was the kind of magical ski resort where the views were incredible on every slope. Surrounded by stunning snow-capped peaks that pierced the clear blue sky, she could enjoy the easy run and take in the breathtaking views.

They started slow and easy, with Izzy carving wide, long paths, Kiera right behind her. Danica stayed near Pete, but muscle memory was beginning to kick in. She'd always taken easily to anything athletic, and she'd had roller blades and skateboarded as a teenager before learning how to snowboard after coming to Colorado for college. She'd tried skiing first — Kiera and Izzy had taught her freshman year — but snowboarding had been so much more exciting.

Her knees were going to hate her tomorrow, she could already tell, but Danica was right about her boots needing to be tighter. She was used to her boarding boots, where she needed a little more give as she leaned forward and back, but she needed much less of that on skis, letting the pressure to turn on her edges come from the angle of her knees and ankles instead. Not that she was on her edges yet. She was very much pizza-ing this entire run, her ski tips nearly touching as she made her way slowly down the eight-lane highway of a run.

"You're doing good," Danica encouraged.

"Skiing isn't hard," Pete said off-handedly.

Danica nonchalantly raised her shoulders. "It's plenty hard for the average person."

"Wendell, did you just call me not-average?" Pete joked, like she was gushing over a compliment.

"No, you're insufferably good at everything," Danica said with a groan. Pete would take the compliment, regardless of how it was delivered.

"Did you see your folks for Christmas?" Pete asked a little further down the run as the slope leveled out and they could slowly keep pace with one another. "Or did Eddie drag you to see his parents somewhere like Cape Cod? Martha's Vineyard?"

"I saw my parents," Danica said casually, like it was the most normal thing in the world to have a family to spend the holidays with. And to her, it was.

"Are they still in Denver?"

"Yeah."

"Still in that tiny little house near the zoo?"

Danica huffed a small laugh and slowed, cocking her head toward Pete. "They are."

"I loved that house," Pete said, her voice tender and nostalgic. Danica had let Pete join her for Christmas every year in college, and they'd always treated her like one of the family. Her mom had even embroidered her the cutest, coziest felt stocking with beads and sequins by the third year, and remembered Pete's favorite chocolates to put inside. Pete remembered a specific chilly Christmas morning where she had coffee on the patio with Danica's dad, listening to lions roar from the zoo.

"Did you do anything fun for Christmas?" Danica asked when they caught up again.

Pete had spent Christmas in Seattle, video chatting with her sister Lillian, and eating Vietnamese takeout. "The usual."

"Lying on some tropical beach with an umbrella in your drink?" Danica quipped.

"Is that what you really think I do? Relax all the time?" Pete asked.

"Well, you refuse to answer any questions about your job, so I'm just guessing that relaxation has a lot to do with it," Danica countered.

"I work at a non-profit." A half-truth, but she wasn't about to say she *founded* a non-profit.

"What kind of work does your non-profit do?" Danica pressed.

"Work that's not for profit," Pete said with a grin behind her scarf.

Danica sighed, skiing ahead again, past a group of people who were milling about toward the end of the run.

Pete didn't know why opening up to Danica was so difficult. Why some part of her wanted to keep all the boring achievements under wraps. She was proud of her work, proud of her foundation, but she wasn't in it for the praise.

She was in it for the kids. She was in it for the young girl still inside her, being shuttled from foster home to foster home, knowing she'd never have a real family and petrified to let anyone in. Well, until she met Lillian at one of her last foster homes, a placement she'd had in her late teens. They'd both been there until they were eighteen, officially aging out of foster care.

She'd gone to a small liberal arts college in Colorado on scholarships and financial aid, wanting something more for her life — and also not knowing what else to do. Finding this group of friends in college had been one of the first times where she'd really felt like she had a family. Finding Danica back in college was the first time she'd ever met a person who felt like home.

She didn't want to lose that again.

The four of them slid into a lift seat together, and Pete tucked her poles under her leg like she'd seen Maggie, Kiera, and Danica do dozens of times. Danica pulled down the bar before they were even out of the lift station. Kiera had situated herself directly between Pete and Danica, and Danica bent forward to look toward Pete and Izzy.

"Is it like, extra cold today or what?" Danica said, sniffling and tucking her nose back into her neck gaiter.

Izzy paused as she fixed her hair, pulling two longer strands of her bangs out on either side of her face. "I have some whiskey shooters in my bag if you need a warmup."

Danica grinned. "Ooh, sure."

Pete's jacket made a plasticky swish as she turned in the lift chair so quickly it made the seat rock. "Oh? What was it you told me a few days ago? You don't need whiskey to ski?"

Danica rolled her eyes, but was clutching the safety bar as the seat rocked. "That was a flask. This is very different."

Even Kiera took one of the shooters from Izzy, and they all toasted on the lift before swallowing the burning liquid. It was cheap liquor — nothing expensive came in a plastic one-ounce bottle, of course — but it did the trick. Pete could feel warmth flooding through her chest and into her stomach.

"How many shooters do you have in there, Izzy?" Kiera asked.

"Enough," Izzy said enigmatically, zipping her bag and turning her head as if she wouldn't take any more questions.

"Is this hair thing, like, a cool thing the youths are doing or what?" Danica said, gesturing to Izzy.

"They're my slut strands," Izzy said.

"Your what?" Kiera asked, amused.

"So, everyone can know I'm a girl, and so ski patrol won't call me sir, and other boarders won't call me bro." Izzy's expression looked like she was explaining that the sky was blue.

"Oh, do I need them?" Danica asked, touching her face with her heavy mittens.

"You're wearing a bright purple jacket. I think you're okay," Pete pointed out, but couldn't help her smile as she studied Danica's worried expression.

"Kiera, you need slut strands," Danica said playfully, nudging Kiera in the side. Unlike Danica's bright purple jacket, Kiera's coat was navy. It was fitted, though, showing off her curves.

Kiera shook her head, though Pete could tell a hint of a smile was pulling at her mouth. "I've portaled whole ass humans out of my body into this world. I don't care if ski patrol misgenders me."

"That's a perspective," Pete laughed.

Izzy shrugged. "There's just something about being called sir that really bothers me."

"I get it," Danica said, nodding. "I don't like it either. Like, why is sir the default?"

"I'd honestly rather be called sir than ma'am any day," Pete said, and her friends groaned in agreement.

The lift dipped down, and Pete felt a rush of nerves about

successfully getting off the lift without falling in front of Danica. She hadn't been nervous about a lift in years, so it was a disorienting feeling, the way her stomach flipped as the lift lowered down. Danica always waited until the last possible second to lift the bar, and Pete held her poles tightly, praying to the ski gods not to let her make a fool of herself. Kiera tapped Pete's ski with her own, and Pete realized she hadn't been holding them parallel. She mumbled a thanks to Kiera as their skis touched the ground, and she planted her poles, pushing with all of her might to get out of the way of the moving lift seat.

Except, all of her might was a little too much, and she nearly slammed into a group of teenagers who had gotten off the lift before them. Her cheeks flushed in embarrassment, but she narrowly avoided bowling down the kids.

She looked at her friends to see if she had any witnesses, but only Danica was turned toward her. Pete could have sworn she saw a sparkle of amusement in her eyes as she pulled her goggles over her eyes.

"Do you still feel good?" Danica asked, eyeing her critically. "I don't think your boots are tight enough."

Pete looked down at her boots, her skis sliding as her balance shifted. "What's wrong with my boots?"

"Izzy, you can bend a little easier than the rest of us. Can you notch her boots just one click tighter on the top?" Danica pointed with her mittened hand.

Izzy glanced from Danica to Pete, undoubtedly waiting for Pete to argue with Danica. Pete nodded for her to go ahead, and Izzy kneeled in front of Pete to tighten the straps. Pete pretended to knight her, tapping her on each shoulder with a ski pole. "Arise, Sir Izzy, Protector of Shins, Knight of the Bent Knee."

"It's *Dame* Izzy," Izzy said, pointing to the strands of hair poking out from her helmet.

"Right, so sorry, ma'am," Pete teased. "I mean, Dame Izzy of the Slut Strands."

Izzy and Kiera glided down the run ahead of them, and Pete stuck close behind Danica, shamelessly admiring the easy way her body balanced and shifted.

When they got further down the run, they found that Izzy and Kiera had paused at the top of a black run called Allais Alley, which veered down so steeply that standing where they were, Pete could only see the bottom.

"Hey, so, I know we said we'd stick to blues... but... what if we just tried this one?" Kiera asked as they paused atop one of the black runs that veered off from the long blue run after the lift.

Pete felt a slight bundle of nerves in her stomach, but as she glanced toward Danica and saw the panic on her face, she realized that she'd have to be the strong one. She forced a nonchalant tone in her voice. "Yeah, looks fun."

"You're suggesting we ski down *there*?" Danica squeaked, pointing her ski pole toward the steep trail pitching down at an intense angle. "I don't... I don't think that's right. Or legal. But definitely not right. Didn't we say blues for Pete at first?"

"It's okay, Dani. You can take See Forever to get back to the condo, or Woozley's Way and meet at the lift station," Kiera said reassuringly, pointing toward the two other runs that ran parallel.

Perhaps Kiera was attempting to kill her for all the times she'd caught Pete staring at Danica's ass today. Perhaps Kiera was trying to pressure Danica into leaving the group, and therefore Pete. Pete *knew* Danica could do this run. Danica was far better than she gave herself credit for. She turned, using her poles to push herself closer to Danica. She lowered her voice as she leaned closer. "You've got this."

"I most certainly do not," Danica said, shaking her head.

"I'll — *we'll* — be right there with you," Pete said. "You're a good skier, Wendell. You just need to trust yourself."

Danica looked from the trees back to Pete. "I don't know."

"You can just go a different way," Kiera said impatiently.

"You two go ahead. We'll be right behind you." Pete forced a smile toward Kiera and Izzy.

"You sure?" Kiera asked, turning to Danica.

Danica nodded, tucking her chin back into her neck gaiter.

Izzy and Kiera straightened their gear and then dipped over the horizon line, Izzy's whoops of excitement echoing and making Pete feel giddy with anticipation.

"Want me to go down Woozley's Way with you?" Pete offered in a quiet voice.

"I'm really more of a groomed, gentle slope kind of girl," Danica said, still staring down the run. "Moguls seem... really scary."

"You're good enough to do this," Pete pointed out. "Moguls aren't that bad on skis. I don't know how Izzy is doing it on a snowboard."

"This is how people die at ski resorts. This is how you go too fast and hit a tree," Danica said, and Pete reached to take Danica's mittened hand in hers.

"The steep groomed runs are how people end up going too fast. I promise this run is more like a puzzle, where you get to choose several different paths. And the snow from this morning is probably still gorgeous and fluffy here. And all of that said, I'll go with you down any other run you want," Pete said.

The cold wind whipped around Danica as she shook her head, her breath misting in the air.

"Are you really that afraid of hitting a tree when skiing?" Pete asked gently.

"No. I mean, yeah, *always*, but not for this. It's just..." Danica took a deep breath, letting it out slowly as it formed a foggy cloud in front of her face.

"Why do you only do blues when you're such a good skier? Why stick to what's safe?" Pete asked.

"I hate being bad at things." Danica's confession came out in a mumble.

"What do you mean?" Pete lifted her goggles to put them on her helmet, looking at Danica with confusion.

"I just don't." Danica said.

Pete frowned, the faintest hint of a suspicion pulling her brows together. "You were bad at snowboarding at first."

"Yeah, but Maggie was there with me and no one was *expecting* me to be good at it. I can practically feel Izzy watching me, and Kiera doesn't really think I can do this, either. You heard her. '*Oh, go on See Forever and go home.*'" Her Kiera impression was a little too condescending but otherwise spot on.

"You're that afraid of failure?"

Danica shifted, shrugging her shoulders. "I mean, yeah, where people can *see* me fail."

"In front of *me*?" Pete asked, completely thrown off.

"*Especially* in front of you," Danica said, stabbing at the ground with her pole.

Pete laughed. "That's one of the stupidest things you've ever said to me."

Danica threw her arms up in frustration. "I never said it was rational. I just hate this panicky feeling inside of me right now."

Pete took Danica's hand again, looking her in the eyes. Danica's eyes were bluebird sky bright, rimmed with tears. "Hey, it's just me. Izzy and Kiera are long gone. I don't think there's anything braver than being willing to learn new things, or being willing to be bad at something enough times to figure out how to be good at it. That's... *life*, Wendell. Sometimes you have to fall on your ass skiing."

"Well, what happens when I inch through this and you're also long gone and then I'm just alone?" Danica asked. "What if I fall in a tree well and I suffocate because no one can find me?" She frowned down toward the trees.

"Not going to happen. And I'll be right behind you. This is my first time trying a mogul run on skis, too," Pete assured.

"And if I'm really bad at this, you won't tell a soul?" Danica asked.

Pete nodded. "I am *very* good at secrets."

Danica snorted. "Yeah, tell that to the hickey you left on my neck."

Pete grinned. "I didn't say I'd keep *that* a secret."

She could have sworn Danica was smiling behind her neck gaiter, maybe even blushing, but that could have been from the chill they had after standing around for so long.

"I really will go down one of the other runs with you if you don't want to do this," Pete said.

Danica took a deep breath, staring down at the tracks ahead of her in the trees. "Will you go first so that I can follow your path?"

The tone of her voice melted something within Pete, and she smiled gently. "Of course." Danica was so rarely this vulnerable in front of her. "But it's not going to be pretty. We're in this together, slow and steady and ready to ruin the day for the poor bastards stuck behind us." She settled her goggles back in place and then twisted to adjust her skis. "You ready?"

"Yeah, just make sure you don't run off." Danica looked at her, then nodded. That small show of strength made Pete feel warm with pride and excitement.

"I'll be right there."

Then they were off. Pete dipped into the flatter beginning part of the run, then pitched forward and revealed a path of moguls and the ski marks that ran through them, like every turn was a choose your own adventure. It was a little dicey, and she purposefully took it slow, glancing behind her every few moments to make sure Danica was okay. Giddiness fluttered in her chest, and she set off again, a little more confident knowing that Danica was right behind her. She could hear the swoosh and crunch of Danica's skis in the snow, and it took a lot of concentration to keep her eyes ahead, focusing on the moguls instead. Izzy and Kiera were so far ahead that it truly felt like they were in their own little world, far away from the rest of the mountain, just two people exploring and adventuring.

That was what she wanted most of all — an adventure partner. Sure, Danica pretended to be averse to new things, but she was so smart and so competent that she learned quickly. Pete had always had to muscle her way through academics, but it had all come easily to Danica. She'd always been a little jealous of that. Now, Pete saw that her own ambition was a positive trait, not just another downfall of not being the smartest person in the room.

She glanced back behind her, seeing Danica concentrating but still managing to work her way through the puzzle. She was fully in control, stable and strong. When she saw Danica glance up to follow her, she nodded her head for Danica to follow, then veered off into the trees that lined the run, a tiny trail already paved by a skier before them.

The trees were dense with no obvious path, but Pete picked her way around, much easier on skis than a board.

"Now, this is definitely illegal. We're going to get kicked out," Danica's voice shook a bit from close behind her.

"We can't go past the ropes," Pete said, pausing to rest under the bough of an evergreen. "Did you see any ropes?"

"No." Danica glanced back over her shoulder, then pushed with her poles to stop beside Pete.

"I have an avalanche beacon if that's what you're afraid of," Pete stated.

"No, I'm much less afraid of an avalanche and much more afraid of getting caught," Danica said, her head twisting back and forth as if trying to see if ski patrol was about to kick them out.

"This isn't out of bounds. You're such a stickler for the

rules, Wendell." Pete grinned. She loved to push Danica out of her comfort zone, especially when it resulted in a quiet moment alone, watching Danica look around the dense trees in wonder.

"Did you need a break from the moguls?" Danica asked.

"No, I just needed a different kind of adventure for a moment," Pete said like it was obvious. She lifted her goggles onto her helmet, leaning against one of the trees, watching Danica.

Danica lifted her own goggles, raising an eyebrow in question. "You're going to go to ski jail just for a little adventure?"

"Only if you'd visit me in ski jail and hold your hand up against the glass while we're on the phone," Pete said with a grin.

"I'll bake you a cake with a file. That's the most I can promise for now." Danica said, reaching up to bat snow off a tree branch. It felt like they were deep in the forest, far away from Izzy and Kiera and their past...

"I'm sorry if last night was too much," Pete said quietly.

Danica shook her head. "I panicked."

Pete's stomach dropped. "I'm sor—"

"No, I'm sorry. I don't know why I panicked. It's just... It was fun, and I don't know why I... do anything that I do, I guess," Danica said. She looked so sad.

Pete leaned forward to tap the front of her helmet to Danica's. "Hey, it's just me. You know me."

"That's the problem. I know you, and I want you," Danica admitted breathlessly. Her eyes darted down to Pete's mouth, the air felt charged between them again, and Pete's mind felt clear — no worries, no thoughts at all, really — as she reached for Danica.

Their bodies knocked back into a tree, and the only warning of what was to come was a slight whispering hush as a clump of snow fell off a branch high above them, landing directly on their heads. Danica gasped with surprise, brushing snow from her face and helmet, and Pete laughed, wiping at her eyes.

Danica straightened, shaking her head. "Was that the universe's idea of a cold shower?" Pete laughed, leaning down to grab her poles as they awkwardly untangled their skis. Danica pushed backwards, angling away toward the ski tracks pointing out of the trees. "Loser buys crepes?" She asked in a playful tone.

Before Pete could say a word, Danica pulled down her goggles and pushed forward to take off down the trail and out of the trees. Pete wasn't exactly sure what had unleashed this unexpected excitement in Danica, but she liked it. She pushed off, willing to follow Danica anywhere.

CHAPTER 15

DANICA

With a tactical plan in place, Danica and Maggie crouched on the balcony, waiting for the others to get within throwing distance. Maggie packed snowballs — no small feat with one hand still mostly out of commission — building a small pyramid of ammunition, and Danica kept watch, peering between the rungs of the raised deck railing and tracking Kiera's location on her phone.

Danica had come back after lunch, where she'd eaten so many crepes that she could have burst. Of course, they'd been on her dime, since she'd lost the race to Pete, who fearlessly flew down the mountain to beat her to the bottom. Danica had been right behind her, heart racing, lungs burning, head still reeling from that near-kiss under the snowy trees.

She and Maggie had spent the afternoon reading and cross stitching in Maggie's bed while drinking hot cocoa, before Danica took a long bath and a long nap. Overall, a damn good day. They were going out for dinner, saving Danica a trip to the store, so they had come up with a plan to ambush their friends with a snowball fight.

"I think I see Pete's turquoise jacket," Danica whispered, even though the trio they were waiting for was still hundreds of yards away.

"Of course you do," Maggie said with a teasing grin.

Danica angled her head, one brow raising in silent question.

"So, what exactly is going on there?" Maggie asked casually, packing a snowball in her good hand.

"Nothing," Danica said lightly.

Maggie made a "hmm" sound, still not looking at her.

Danica eyed Maggie with skepticism. "What do you know?"

"I know that she's been staring at you and practically drooling this entire trip," Maggie said, finally looking up

"She has? Really? Has she said anything?" Danica asked, packing a new snowball with increased fervor.

Maggie shrugged. "Nothing specific, but I know you both, and I'm pro-whatever this is. I mean, I just think it could be fun, right? A little vacation fling before you have to go back to real life, you know?"

Danica grimaced. "Really? Kiera hates the idea."

"Kiera is just salty because she's staying with a dirtbag who cheated on her," Maggie said.

Danica's mouth popped open in a silent gasp. She agreed with Maggie, completely, but even so, hearing someone put it so bluntly was still a surprise. "I mean…"

"I know you agree with me."

How could Danica word this delicately? "It's, uh, it's not a choice I'd make."

"Yeah, because we're not straight women, so we don't have to lower our standards until they're basically down in hell," Maggie said, rolling her eyes. "But enough about that. You and Pete. I don't think it could hurt." The glint in her eyes was a little too knowing for Danica's taste.

"Of course it could hurt," Danica said, shaking her head.

"We have two nights. You can't get that attached in two nights." Maggie's tone implied the statement was obvious. "You always play it safe, Dani. It might be nice to do something a little wild for once. You know Pete, she's a safe choice to have fun with. You two already have lots of chemistry. After all, when else are you going to get a chance to have sex with someone hot without adding to your body count?"

Danica groaned. "Body counts are bullshit."

"What about body counts?" Pete called from below the deck.

Maggie and Danica both startled, looking out through the deck railing to see Kiera, Izzy, and Pete standing below them on street level.

"Whatcha doing?" Kiera asked, angling her head and narrowing her eyes with suspicion.

"Security breach! It's every woman for herself," Maggie called out dramatically, grabbing a snowball and flinging it toward a surprised Kiera.

Danica grabbed two snowballs, throwing them at Pete. Izzy had already ducked and was preparing a return of fire.

"So not fair," Kiera yelled back, throwing a loose snowball that broke apart mid-air to shower snow over the patio.

Once the snowballs started flying, allegiances were quickly nullified, and everyone was a target. Danica squealed in a decidedly embarrassing way, running across the deck to hide behind the hot tub as Izzy and Pete stormed the stairs, arms loaded with snowballs.

Kiera got a few good shots in at Pete and Izzy, but it only seemed to distract Izzy. Pete was on a mission, her eyes sparkling with delight as they stayed focused on Danica, who was cornered between the condo wall and the hot tub.

"I surrender, I surrender," Danica pleaded, holding up her hands.

Pete's eyes softened as she approached. She reached as if to shake Danica's hand, then pulled her off-balance and stuffed snow down the back of Danica's coat. Danica yelped in surprise and Pete threw her head back, laughing, only to be hit squarely on the ear with a snowball thrown by Izzy. With Pete distracted, Danica scooped a new snowball, reaching to grab Pete's jacket and repay the favor.

Pete's feet slipped, and they both fell to the ground with shrieks of laughter. As Kiera, Izzy, and Maggie shouted and laughed nearby, Danica paused, still lying mostly on top of Pete, her chest heaving, lungs burning with the cold air. Pete smiled up at her, reaching to tuck a stray strand of hair behind her ear. Their warm breaths fogged the air and the world around them seemed to quiet and blur, leaving only the way Pete's dark eyes searched hers for an answer to the question they'd been silently asking all week.

Danica's gaze darted to Pete's mouth, her stomach tightening with nervous anticipation, and just as she was sure that Pete was going to lean in to kiss her, a shock of cold made her jump. Pete cackled with delight, and Danica realized belatedly that Pete had dropped a handful of snow on the back of Danica's neck. It slid down her shirt and she jumped up, pulling at the hem of her base layer to get the snow out of her shirt.

"I win!" Pete exclaimed, standing up to brush snow off her pants.

"Let's just say revenge is a dish best served cold, my friend," Danica threatened.

Pete grinned. "We'll see about that."

* * *

"I really thought this place would be gayer with a name like Tomboy Tavern," Pete said as they slid into a booth for dinner. The large leather booth wrapped around a table, and Maggie awkwardly repositioned everyone until Pete and Danica were next to one another, herself in between Danica and Kiera.

Danica eyed Maggie as she sat down, unwrapping her

scarf and raking her hands through her hat hair. Maggie was a masterful matchmaker, wasn't she? The woman looked absolutely shameless as she gave Danica a wink, then picked up the drink menu. "Alright, people, I skipped my ibuprofen so I could have a nice cocktail."

"That's not..." Danica started, but paused, shaking her head. "You know, I'm not putting on my doctor hat tonight."

"I'm picturing a really cute scrub cap as your doctor hat," Pete said.

Danica bit the inside of her cheek to keep from beaming up at Pete with all of their friends around. "It *is* pretty cute."

Chandeliers made of brown beer bottles hung above tables in the dimly lit dining area, made even darker with weathered old wood floors and chocolate brown leather seating. Kiera idly played with the edge of a curtain that was pulled back by the edge of the booth.

"It doesn't give me completely straight vibes," Izzy said, looking around.

"Bi-curious, maybe?" Maggie asked. "Like Kiera in college."

Kiera gasped. "It was *one kiss*. Hardly a phase."

Pete leaned back in the booth, murmuring, "Uh oh," under her breath so only Danica could hear.

Danica looked between Kiera and Maggie, confused. "One kiss? What kiss?" She glanced back at Pete, who only offered her an unhelpful shrug.

Kiera crossed her arms over her chest. "I kissed Izzy once."

The server came right then, interrupting as the group fell into an awkward silence. He took their drink orders, and Danica chose a few appetizers for the table, knowing both how hungry *and* how indecisive they were.

Once the server left, Danica looked at Izzy, her eyes widening in surprise. Izzy, to her credit, only gave her a small shrug. "We were drunk at a party," Izzy explained.

"What party?" Danica asked.

"I think it was the one where we made that drink in a bucket," Maggie said, glancing between Kiera and Izzy for confirmation.

They'd thrown a few parties in college, but the wildest were the parties with their signature drink, "Hop, Skip, and Go Naked," which they traditionally made in some kind of large punch bowl or bucket. It included a six-pack of cheap beer, a bottle of vodka, blue Hawaiian punch, and frozen lemonade concentrate. Danica felt a little queasy even thinking about the horrific hangovers that drink gave her, but it also lived up to its name.

"Wait, wait. So, you two kissed, and everyone knew?" Danica asked, looking at everyone at the table. She glanced back at Pete, who had her arm outstretched on the back of the booth behind Danica. Pete lifted a shoulder in response. "Izzy told me later. I think you and I, uh... skipped most of that party."

Danica's cheeks flushed, but she forced herself to turn back to Kiera. "And you never told *me*? Your resident bisexual best friend?"

"It wasn't that big of a deal," Kiera said, and Danica knew she was forcing the casual way she was speaking. "It was just one time."

"But you never told me," Danica repeated.

A strange quiet fell over the table as Danica glanced back at Izzy, who had a blank expression on her face as she stared down at the menu as if preparing for an exam.

Danica felt Pete's hand on her back and, turning, saw a knowing look that hinted at later revelations.

The drinks came at one perfect moment to switch topics away from Kiera and Izzy's kiss. They talked about the menu and ordered, then relaxed back to sip their cocktails.

"Here's to Danica's first black run today," Pete said, lifting her glass.

"And here's to Pete being back on skis," Danica added, lifting her own glass.

Pete's gentle expression as she looked at Danica made Danica all-too aware of how close their bodies were in the booth. How Pete's arm moved to casually brush her shoulder and back, how Pete's knee was so close to hers.

"Ugh, get a room," Maggie interrupted with a laugh as they all clinked glasses in a cheers.

Their food arrived shortly, along with another round of drinks, and Pete and Danica ended up splitting their salmon and chicken plates, sharing the meals with one another. It felt comfortable again, apart from the obvious tension surrounding the revelation that Kiera had once kissed Izzy and never told Danica. Not that Danica had the right to know everything, but it was odd that Kiera hadn't at least mentioned it.

"Should we go back to the karaoke bar?" Pete asked as the server took their plates.

"I'm tired," Izzy and Kiera said in unison, and everyone laughed a little uncomfortably.

"I think I overdid it with the snowball fight and need to go ice this thing," Maggie said, pointing to her wrist tucked into its sling.

"You guys are so lame," Pete said, turning to Danica. "You in?"

"Maybe not for karaoke, but I'd have another drink," Danica said, then turned back to Kiera. "Only if you guys think you can get home okay? I could walk you if you want." The condo was nearby, only about a ten-minute walk through Mountain Village's shopping district.

"We'll be fine," Maggie said, rolling her eyes. "But I will take some hand sanitizer if you have it."

Danica dug out the small spray sanitizer she always kept in her purse, spraying everyone's outstretched hands.

"You sure staying is a good choice?" Kiera asked as she and Danica slid out one side of the booth.

"Yeah, it'll be fine," Danica assured her, giving her a hug as they parted ways. She watched Maggie link arms with Izzy, bumping her shoulder into Kiera as they all walked out of the bar.

"Want to grab a seat on that couch near the fire or at the bar here? It's kind of busy in here. We could go somewhere else?" Pete asked.

"The couch is fine," Danica pointed. A worn leather couch, its surface softened by years of use, faced a large brick fireplace where warmth radiated into the room. They ordered two Old Fashioneds at the bar and sat down on the couch, keeping a few inches between them. As soon as Danica had taken one sip, she set down her glass and turned to Pete. "Okay, spill what you know about Izzy and Kiera."

Pete groaned. "You really want to talk about Izzy and Kiera?"

Danica raised her eyebrows. "Yeah, obviously. What did Izzy tell you?"

A slow sigh escaped Pete's lips, her mouth twisting to one side in thought as if she was contemplating what to tell Danica. She took another sip of her cocktail, her thumb tapping on the diamond-etched lowball glass. "Okay, it wasn't just one kiss. It was like a full make out. All initiated by Kiera."

Danica's eyes widened in surprise and she leaned closer. "Seriously?"

Pete nodded solemnly. "Yeah, Izzy was pretty sure there was going to be a next time when she originally told me. Maggie had said they were all over each other. Izzy seemed pretty excited about it, and then Kiera just always acted like it never happened. But here's the kicker... Kiera was completely sober."

"What? How do you know she was sober?" Danica asked, her head shaking in disbelief, her eyes wide with shock.

"Both Izzy and Maggie were positive. Kiera had just gotten there and kind of... pounced on Izzy, apparently," Pete said.

"Maybe she pre-gamed?" Danica questioned.

Pete shook her head. "Pre-gamed a party with her own friends? Nah."

"I can't believe you never told me!" Danica said, smacking Pete's knee.

Pete laughed, reaching to take Danica's hand. "We had more important things to talk about back then." Pete said quietly, leaning in to slide her hand along Danica's cheek, her fingers tangling in Danica's hair as Pete brought her mouth to Danica's, just gently brushing their lips together.

"Yeah, you do have a good point," Danica whispered, her fingertips touching her mouth where Pete's lips had just been. Pete tasted like smooth whiskey and bitter orange and warmth and promise.

Pete reached across the back of the couch, her fingertips idly playing in Danica's hair. "I've missed this."

"Kissing me in crowded bars?" Danica asked.

"Well, yeah. But mostly just... you. I've missed you," Pete said.

Danica smiled into her drink, unable to stop the flush rising on her cheeks. She nodded in agreement. Being near Pete again was as intoxicating as the whiskey in her glass. Danica felt an inexplicable magnetism towards Pete, an unwavering attraction that burned as bright as the flames in the fireplace before them.

Kiera's voice in her head told her she needed to be careful. And Maggie's voice was there, telling her to go for it. That she had nothing to lose. In two days, Pete would go back to Seattle, and she'd go back to Denver, and there'd be no hard feelings. She knew better this time than to expect anything more from Pete than a good time. Just because they weren't planning a future together didn't mean they couldn't enjoy each other's company and many, many talents in the meantime?

Maybe both Kiera and Maggie were right. Maybe it was a bad idea, but maybe it would be fun. She'd spent her entire life making the right choices — making the boring, safe choices. Why did she always have to be responsible? Of all the bad choices she could make, this was still a relatively safe one. No one would get hurt if they weren't making promises they couldn't keep.

She curled up closer to Pete, resting against her shoulder as they sipped their drinks in companionable silence.

"I have an idea," Pete said.

"Oh?" Danica tilted her head to look up.

"Do you trust me?" Pete asked, a mischievous smile growing on her lips.

"Not one bit," Danica said, grinning.

Pete eyed her, then smirked. "Finish your drink. I want to show you something."

CHAPTER 16

PETE

"I SHOULD HAVE EXPECTED YOUR PLAN WOULD GET US arrested," Danica said, looking up and down the street. Pete's boots crunched in the snow as she maneuvered her way down the small path to the frozen pond on the edge of the shopping square. The pond was cleared of snow, except for the light flakes that had begun to drift down from the sky. "There's a sign that says it's closed," Danica added. "It closes at sunset."

"You can't close a pond," Pete said, as she took a tentative step onto the ice of the pond. She'd seen ice skaters out here, so she knew technically it was okay to walk on, but maybe spending all this time with Danica was making her play it a little safer.

Pete slid her boots back and forth on the icy surface of the pond, smooth and slippery, especially with the fresh dusting of snow. Her hand stretched out toward Danica, palm up. "Come on," she said. "Water's fine."

"Listen, if I fall through this surface and go into shock, I'm going to need you to take the appropriate steps to save my life," Danica said, holding up her mittened hand as if she was about to start listing the steps on her fingers.

Pete laughed. "Stop thinking so much."

"Do you think we'll get kicked out?" Danica asked, glancing back and forth as she took one small step toward Pete. Even that made Pete's heart race with a sense of thrill. It was always so fun watching Danica break a rule, like she was peeling back the layers of Danica's carefully constructed Good Girl personality to find the interesting parts beneath.

"Kicked out?" Pete asked, trying not to laugh.

"Yeah." Danica seemed so earnest.

"Of a pond?"

"No, out of Telluride." Danica looked completely serious, which only made Pete want to kiss her rule-following face even more.

"You can't kick people out of a town." Pete chuckled, then spun in a circle with her arms flung out to either side.

Danica exhaled a huge sigh, then walked toward Pete. Danica's woolen mitten fit right into Pete's palm. "I seem to have forgotten my ice skates back at the bar," Danica joked. She was wearing dressier boots that were definitely more ice-skate adjacent than snow-ready.

"We'll just have to make do," Pete said, twirling Danica in a circle, then letting go of her hand to race across the pond and out of the obvious lights of the nearby shops.

She could hear Danica laugh, followed by the scratch of her boots scuffing across the ice. Pete leapt and slid as far as she could, turning to see Danica do the same.

"Do you remember that time we went ice skating?" Pete asked as they twirled and slid in circles.

"I remember bruising my tailbone and needing to sit on a donut pillow for weeks," Danica said with a shake of her head, catching Pete's hand.

Pete chuckled. "I forgot about that." She pulled Danica

into her, brushing some of the snowflakes from Danica's beanie and hair. Danica shivered against her, and something about her rosemary shampoo and the cold night air made this a distinctly intoxicating moment that made Pete want to hold her close forever, here, just like this.

"That's because you always remember only the good parts," Danica stated.

"I remember lots and lots of the good parts, it's true." Pete brushed a strand of Danica's hair away from her face. "I don't remember your broken ass, but I do remember how much you laughed that day. You said your face hurt from smiling so much."

Danica smiled now, looking up at her. "Do you remember any of the bad parts?"

Pete ran her thumb over Danica's cheek, over that freckle on her left side that always drew Pete's gaze. "Nope."

"So, you're like an elephant wearing rose-colored glasses," Danica said, furrowing her brow.

"Did you just call my nose big?" Pete joked, holding her fingers to her own nose.

Danica gasped. "No, because of your memory — oh, you're messing with me."

They both grinned like fools, holding one another on the frozen pond, snowflakes falling all around them like they were in a snow globe. Alone in their own little world, despite the occasional burst of voices from those walking past, or cars in the parking lot, or restaurant doors opening and closing to give a brief flash of bustling noise.

"I remember it all," Pete whispered, her gaze searching Danica's.

Danica watched her for a long, silent moment before biting her lower lip.

"I really, really want to kiss you right now." Pete's heart thumped with nervous energy in her chest.

Danica pulled back just enough to tilt her head up to look

at Pete, and Pete tensed, ready for a lecture about timing. Instead, Danica pushed onto her tip-toes, angling her face up. "Then kiss me."

Pete's heart nearly galloped out of her chest, and she wasted no time in following Danica's command. She closed her eyes, leaning into Danica, only to find that Danica had her hands on Pete's chest to stop her.

"Wait, no, hold on, let me wipe my nose," Danica laughed, pulling a tissue out of her pocket. "That was like a super romantic moment and I don't want my snot to ruin it."

Pete laughed as Danica handed her a tissue as well. "Always prepared, Wendell." She wiped her own nose.

"Okay," Danica said, clearing her throat and tucking her tissue away into her pocket again. "Now." She pushed back onto her tip-toes and Pete held her tight again, kissing her slow and heavy, lingering and unhurried and enjoying the moment. Their coats made soft shushing sounds against one another as they shifted, fitting into one another.

There was no hesitation in this kiss, no hesitation in the way they reached for one another, like they weren't worried about the time they had together. Lost in the deep, passionate kiss, she felt Danica's warm hands replace the chill on her face. She wasn't sure when Danica shed her mittens, but the tender touch soothed her skin. It was a caress that spoke of cherishing and protection.

They were awkward on the ice, and Pete held Danica close to her, keeping them both steady and stable. It was the kind of kiss a woman could get used to — the kind of kiss she'd think about for hours, or days, even. She remembered all the best kisses with Danica, but this one ranked high.

"I'm so glad you're not getting snot on me right now," Pete whispered against Danica's mouth as they both paused for air.

"Ooh, dirty talk." Danica smiled back against Pete's lips.

"I actually did want to show you something," Pete said as she sank to her knees. She tugged Danica down with her, then rolled onto her back. The chill of the ice bit into her body, even through her ski jacket, but Danica laid down next to her, even while asking repeatedly what they were doing.

From the far side of the pond, the lights from the shops weren't so noticeable. Despite the resort and Mountain Village lights, she could still make out her favorite constellations, their faint light twinkling against the brighter backdrop.

Their warm breath swirled in front of their faces as they stared up at the night sky.

Danica pointed toward the southeastern sky. "There's Sirius. Which makes that Canis Major. Your favorite."

Pete turned her head, watching Danica. "You remember my favorite constellation?"

"Don't get a big head about it. It's the dog and Sirius is one of the brightest stars," Danica said, but Pete could tell even in the darkness that she was smiling.

"And your favorite, right there," Pete said, pointing to the south edge of Canis Major. "Lepus."

Danica laughed.

"What's so funny?" Pete asked.

"I never cared about Lepus. I mean, the hare is great, but I only said that it was my favorite to impress you," Danica admitted.

Pete let out a small gasp, and turned her head to the side to see Danica's face in profile, her wide smile visible even in the dark. "Seriously?"

"Yeah. It was closest to your favorite, and it was easy to find because it's kind of halfway between Sirius and Rigel," Danica said.

"You are ridiculous. I can't believe you did that," Pete said, reaching to squeeze Danica's hand. "You never had to lie to impress me, Wendell."

"Yeah, tell that to dorky eighteen-year-old Danica," Danica said.

"You were never dorky," Pete said, scooting to be closer to Danica, who was laughing in disbelief. "Okay, maybe like, a little dorky, but mostly just cute."

"You were cool and knew all the names of stars and where the constellations were and which stars were actually Saturn. You had a favorite constellation that wasn't Orion's Belt or Cassiopeia, and I really wanted you to think I was cool, too," Danica said, holding a mittened hand over her eyes. "It sounds so dumb when I admit it now."

"I always thought you were cool in your own way," Pete said.

"Ouch."

"No, I mean it. Don't make that face. That's not like a participation trophy compliment. You were so sure of who you were and who you would be. I had no idea what I was doing, and I found that confidence and drive very attractive. And, to be honest, I always thought you liked Lepus because you're basically a hare. Always going, always ambitious, always very aware of everything going on around you," Pete said.

Danica turned to look at her. "That's... strangely very sweet."

"Anyway, I wanted to make you lay on this freezing cold pond and look at the stars because... well, do you remember that app that I built? The night sky one, where you could simulate flying among the stars?" Pete asked.

Danica's brow furrowed. "I remember it, but I don't remember you ever finishing it."

"I finished it after we graduated," Pete said. "And then I sold it to a UK-based developer who was working on something similar."

Danica's eyebrows rose. "Really? That's so cool. Are you still making apps, then?"

"Yes and no. Mainly no," Pete said, her stomach twirling with nerves. It felt like she should be honest with Danica, but she also wasn't exactly sure what to tell her.

"Ah, cryptic as ever," Danica said, turning back to the sky.

"I negotiated a really, really good price for the night sky app, and I put most of it in savings, but I bought some Bitcoin. Gross, I know. At the time, Bitcoin was kind of dumb but a smart friend suggested it, so I bought it when it was fairly cheap, and then sold it at a good time."

Danica's gaze sharpened. "How much Bitcoin did you buy?"

"Only about 1500. It was only about thirteen dollars for one at the time."

Danica choked. "That's a lot of money."

"It was worth 20,000 dollars when I sold it," Pete said quietly.

"You made 20,000 dollars off of Bitcoin? Holy shit."

"No, I mean, each Bitcoin was worth 20,000 dollars."

"So, you're saying you sold 1500 Bitcoin for 20,000 dollars each?" Danica asked, pushing up onto her elbows. "That's... a lot of money."

Pete shrugged self-consciously. It was, indeed, a fuck ton of money, but she'd been living frugally to put almost all of it into the foundation. "I've wanted to tell you, but it makes me sound like some crypto tech bro, and—"

A light shone on them, temporarily blinding her with a number of lumens second only to the sun itself. She held up her hand, shielding her eyes, as Danica cursed.

"We're too pretty for ski jail," Danica groaned, sitting up.

"Hey, the pond is closed at sunset!" a male voice called out.

"Sorry! We think she dropped her keys earlier," Pete called out. They helped one another up and linked arms and shuffled off the ice toward the man with the blinding light. Both of their heads ducked in the embarrassment of being caught.

"You can look in the morning," the man said flatly. Extremely helpful.

"Sure, thanks," Pete muttered, as they stepped foot back on the regular walking path.

"That was nice." Danica wrapped an arm around Pete's waist, holding her closer as they walked together. Pete held Danica close, thankful for the warmth of her. "I can't believe you led me to believe your favorite constellation was Lepus when it wasn't."

"And I can't believe you didn't tell me you were a multi-millionaire, so we're even," Danica said with a joking smirk.

"Not even, not even a little bit," Pete said with a laugh. "And I'm not, actually... It's kind of a long story."

"You spent it all on blow and strippers already?" Danica asked, bending to adjust her boot.

"Yep. I'm sorry you had to find out this way." Pete made a big show of sighing.

Danica stood again, wrapping her arm back around Pete. A small maniacal giggle was the only warning Pete got before something cold and wet began to slide down her neck and into her coat. Pete shrieked, arching her back to try to get the snow out of her shirt as quickly as possible.

Danica cackled. "Payback!" She ran a few steps ahead of Pete, laughing.

"Oh, you are *so* getting it now," Pete warned, chasing after her.

Pete was still laughing as she and Danica pushed open the door of the mud room on the lower level of the condo, even as Danica tried to shush her. They were wet from the snow they'd been throwing at each other on their walk back, cold from lying on the frozen pond, and yet Pete was sure antici-patory steam was coming off her skin. Danica paused in the mud room, stripping off her coat, then leaned on the wall to pull off her boots without sitting.

Danica's white sweater looked soft and inviting, and Pete longed to touch her, to not be separated by coats and mittens and layers of clothing. Memories flooded her of the night before, of Danica's warm, wet skin against hers in the hot tub. She pulled her own coat off, willing herself to not be such a horny teenager, but when she looked back up, Danica's blue eyes were smoldering with what she knew were the same thoughts.

Danica's lips parted as though she was about to say something, but no words escaped as Pete moved to kiss her, crashing together in a kiss so inevitable and impatient that some magnetic force had to be at play.

Pete struggled to kick off her boots, laughing against Danica's mouth as she tried. Danica's hands were in her hair, her entire body pressed against Pete's with a kind of desperation that Pete mirrored. Pete lifted Danica into her arms, feeling Danica's legs wrap around her hips as she held her, kissing her up against the wall.

"Do you think we can sneak up to my room?" Danica whispered.

"Depends on how quiet you can stay," Pete said and Danica moaned into her mouth.

"You're right. Bunk beds it is," Danica responded, reaching for Pete's mouth again, nipping her lower lip.

Still pressing Danica up against the wall, Pete sucked Danica's lower lip into her mouth, teeth scraping her flesh. Danica crushed herself closer, her fingers tangling in Pete's curls as she rocked her hips into Pete's.

Pete let herself take everything Danica was willing to give. Every touch felt more urgent. She'd been waiting for so long that one more second might make her combust.

"We'd better get to your room," Danica gasped in between kisses, and Pete gathered all of her resolve and self-control as she carried Danica toward her room, stumbling and trying to be quiet as they made their way down the hall. Pete shut the door behind them, immediately pressing Danica back against it.

Danica's chin tipped up and Pete's tongue found her skin, salty and sweet and irresistible. Her hands drifted lower. Danica's legs unwrapped from Pete's hips as they moved to stand. Pete's knee pushed between Danica's legs, her hands sliding past Danica's waist toward her hips as Danica rocked against her knee.

An extremely sexy and quiet moan slipped from Danica's lips as Pete held Danica's hips tightly against her, leaning forward to nibble on her neck, her ear lobe, her jaw. She ached with need, her pulse throbbing in her ears, her mouth, her entire body.

Danica seemed to feel the same way, moving against Pete's knee, making those quiet moaning noises that made Pete smile against her mouth as their lips met again. She'd missed this. She hadn't let herself miss it until this very moment, but she'd missed everything about Danica. The way Danica's soft hair felt wrapped around her fist, the frantic way Danica always chased release, the way her moans seemed to vibrate through Pete.

She wanted more of Danica. She was desperate to replace her knee with her hand, her tongue. She wanted all of her. If Pete wasn't careful, she'd be taking Danica messy and eager and up against a wall.

Of course, that all sounded extremely appealing now, but she'd waited all this time. Now that she had Danica in her arms, writhing in expectation, she wanted to take it slow and savor every moment.

Pete's hands moved to dip below the bottom hem of Danica's sweater, pulling it over her head with an excited anticipation as though she was unwrapping a present.

"You are so gorgeous I can hardly think at all," Pete said, taking in the thin, flimsy fabric of her bra.

Danica's forehead pressed against Pete's, her ocean blue

eyes sparkling in the dim light. Pete ran her hands over Danica's skin, so soft and perfect. She took a step back, taking Danica's hand as she walked backwards toward the bed, unwilling to take her eyes off of the woman in front of her.

"Bunk beds are the least sexy bed choice," Danica teased as Pete pulled Danica down to straddle her lap, careful not to hit her head on the bed above.

"I don't know. They provide plenty of handholds," Pete said with a wicked grin.

Danica raised a mischievous eyebrow, reaching forward to grip the frame of the top bunk. "They do, don't they?"

Pete leaned forward to let her hands slide across the smooth expanse of Danica's back, her mouth gently pressing against the thin fabric of Danica's bra. She reached to unhook it, and Danica lowered her arms from the bed frame to let the straps fall. Pete discarded the bra and guided Danica's arms back to the upper frame, grinning at Danica as Pete's thumb brushed against her nipple, her touch sending a thrill through her. Danica's eyes fluttered closed and her back arched ever-so-slightly, a silent plea for Pete to continue.

Danica's knees trembled as Pete dropped her head, her tongue and lips trailing down from her collarbone, wet kisses on delicate skin. Pete's lips enveloped Danica's nipple, causing Danica's skin to tighten and pebble. One of Pete's hands slipped lower, following the curve of Danica's waist and hip, over her thighs to tease against the seam of her jeans. Danica rocked into her, making a quiet, frustrated huff.

Pete turned them both, letting Danica fall onto the bed under her. Hands braced on either side of Danica's shoulders, she skimmed her nose against Danica's, their breath warm and smelling faintly of whiskey. Pete's tender, kiss-swollen lips tingled.

"I've been craving the taste of you for so long," Pete breathed, her voice more a growl than a whisper. Taking delight in the way Danica's eyes darkened with desire at her tone, Pete couldn't help but grin again. God, she loved it when she could turn Danica on with just her words, like she had that night in the hall at the karaoke bar. Pete nipped at Danica's lower lip. "Tell me you want it, too."

The sheets twisted around Pete's fingers as Danica pushed herself up, arching her back as if in a desperate need. "Yes. Please. Yes."

CHAPTER 17

DANICA

As Danica said yes, Pete's tense shoulders relaxed, and a sigh of relief escaped her lips. Like there was even an ounce of chance that she'd say no to Pete right now. As Pete's lips brushed against Danica's skin, a shiver of goosebumps erupted across her body. Pete's lips and hands, moving with a gentle urgency, explored the curves of her body, leaving a trail of warmth in their wake.

Pete undid the button of Danica's pants, sliding them down over a pair of fluorescent green knee-high ski socks. "Ooh, these are definitely staying on," Pete teased, and Danica felt her cheeks grow warm as she laughed, tension coiling low in her belly.

Despite the room's warmth, Danica shivered again, seeing the desire and intensity in Pete's eyes. The undoubtable want and need. "Pete." A request? A demand? She wasn't sure. She only knew she felt with the same desperate want. Pete's kisses burned a trail across her skin, then paused as they brushed the elastic of her underwear, teeth teasing the fabric before her fingers, quick and sure, slipped beneath the waist-band, teasingly slow.

Pete paused, as if to ask if Danica was sure, and Danica arched her back, her hips pushing against Pete's hand in a silent plea.

Understanding, Pete tugged Danica's underwear down her thighs with tender care. Nestled between Danica's thighs, she lowered herself onto the bed, stretching out on her stomach. Pete's warm lips traced a path up Danica's inner thigh, leaving a trail of kisses, her tongue darting out to taste her skin, making her shiver with anticipation. The sensation of Pete's gentle nip on Danica's thigh was both pleasurable and slightly painful, prompting a whimper to escape Danica's lips. With one hand, Pete hooked Danica's right knee and those hideously bright socks over a shoulder, spreading her legs wide open. Danica held her breath, the air thick in her lungs, as Pete's breath whispered a silent promise against her skin, stirring the ache within her.

At the first swipe of Pete's tongue against her, Danica nearly arched off the bed. She could feel Pete's broad smile even between her thighs, Pete's strong hands wrapping around her hip to hold her in place, pulling her even closer. The sensation overwhelmed her, and she fisted the sheets in her hands, savoring the broad strokes of Pete's tongue sliding through her wetness. Pete licked a long, slow path from Danica's entrance up to her clit, then dipped two fingers inside of her, eliciting another whimper of pleasure. Pete's fingers curled inside her, her mouth and fingers finding a familiar rhythm that would make Danica see stars.

She glanced down at Pete, finding those intense brown eyes locked on her. Pete grinned up at her devilishly, and the sight of Pete's mouth on her, the movement of her arm as she felt those fingers so expertly pushing her to the edge… Danica could barely remember to breathe.

Danica's back arched against the mattress as Pete expertly

pushed her over the edge, her thighs quivering as she climaxed. Overwhelmed and too sensitive, Danica's weak tug on Pete's hair was punctuated by a barely audible whimper. Pete didn't move an inch — instead, keeping her fingers firmly in place, her tongue continuing to elicit nearly overwhelming and delicious sensations.

Just as Danica was starting to recover from her first orgasm, Pete rocketed her into another one, her teeth grazing Danica's sensitive clit. Stars exploded behind her eyelids, constellations of pleasure and sensation and emotion. She cried Pete's name in between gasps, and could feel Pete's eyes on her as that delicious sensation continued long and slow until all the tension released from her body. She untwined her fingers from Pete's hair as she fell back against the bed, sweaty and spent. Pete sat back, eyes sparkling as she kneeled between Danica's thighs with a grin, her face still slick and wet.

Danica's heart ached at how beautiful Pete looked. She had that familiar cocky, self-satisfied look in her eye, that distinctly-Pete expression on her face. The fact that all the swagger came from how well she'd pleased Danica… How she'd missed this, not just the sex, but everything about Pete. All the multitudes of Pete. As her brain started working again, her body still pulsing with each beat of her heart, Danica reached for her and Pete prowled up the bed, all arrogance and lean muscle and undeniable sex appeal.

"Just as good as you remember?" Pete whispered, her nose nudging Danica's.

Danica, still completely jelly-limbed and worn out, snorted and rolled her eyes. "You're shameless."

Pete raised an eyebrow, pushing up on one elbow. "I'll take that as a yes."

Danica couldn't help the smile raising the edges of her mouth. "It was fine."

Pete's eyes widened with indignation. "Fine? Do I need to

get back down there and remind you how it was better than fine?"

Danica laughed, reaching to run her thumb over Pete's still slick mouth. Pete leaned down, her lips brushing Danica's, and as her tongue slipped inside Danica's mouth, Danica could taste herself there, all the layers of musky, tangy sweetness.

"You taste as good as I remember," Pete breathed against her mouth, and Danica pulled her closer, her hands weaving into Pete's hair once more. Their kiss deepened, exploring and reminiscing at the same time, and Pete moved her hips against Danica's thigh.

Danica pulled away and reached for the hem of Pete's shirt. "Is this okay?" she asked.

Pete nodded enthusiastically.

With Pete's help, Danica pulled off her shirt and sports bra, running her hands over the familiar lines of Pete's lean body. She was a work of art, even after all these years, strength and softness mingling to create the woman of Danica's dreams. Danica unbuttoned Pete's pants, the zipper the only sound in the room apart from their heavy breaths. Pete shimmied out of her pants, her eyes lifting to Danica's as she held the waistband of her boxer briefs. "These too?"

"All of it," Danica confirmed, reaching to help Pete pull the fabric over her long, lean legs. "It is truly unfair how attractive you are."

Pete laughed, the sound deep and musical. "I'll take that as a compliment from the most gorgeous woman in the room."

"Oh, hush," Danica said with a grin. Her heart stuttered, and she leaned forward to brush her lips against Pete's again, pushing her to lie back as Danica leaned on her elbow. She trailed her hand down Pete's body, sliding over the dark curls between her thighs. Pete gasped as Danica's finger ever-so-gently traced over her clit, and Danica wanted to moan with how wet and ready Pete was for her.

"Oh my god," Pete said, turning to bury her face in Danica's shoulder, and Danica leaned down to take Pete's mouth, deep and slow, as she made her fingers mirror the movements of her tongue. She wouldn't rush this — refused to let this be as ephemeral as it already felt. Her fingertips remembered every nuance of Pete's body, every detail familiar as she pressed two fingers inside, her thumb brushing Pete's swollen clit. Pete's hips raised ever-so-slightly, a soft moan of pleasure heating their kiss.

"Fuck me," Pete whispered against Danica's lips. "Harder. Please. I can't wait."

Danica curled her fingers, her thumb pushing with more force against Pete. "Is this how you like it?"

Pete threw her head back, squeezing her eyes shut as she rode Danica's hand. The position gave Danica the perfect view of where her fingers disappeared between Pete's thighs as Pete bucked against her, needy and desperate. Danica hid her smile as she focused, keeping the pressure steady and intense, wanting Pete to come just as hard as she had. She could feel Pete begin to tense in those delicious few moments before climax, and she leaned down, her tongue drawing against Pete's hardened nipple, her teeth grazing the pebbled skin. Pete cried out, her entire body shaking as she came around Danica's fingers, her thighs clamping together. Danica's rhythm slowed as Pete relaxed.

Pete twisted her hips in silent confirmation she needed a break. "I'm going to die if you keep going," Pete said with a huff of laughter.

Pete slumped against the mattress, her breathing still labored, her legs tangled with Danica's. Her flushed complexion was glossy with sweat, starting at her hairline and continuing down to her navel, which rose and fell rhythmically with her breathing.

Danica had never seen a sight so lovely in her entire life. She curled into Pete, her body molding into its familiar place at Pete's side.

"I can't believe we've wasted fifteen years not doing that," Pete said with a laugh, tracing circles on Danica's bare shoulder. Danica was practically draped across Pete, her head on Pete's chest, listening to her breathing. Steady. Comforting and familiar.

"Or at least the last six days," Danica agreed.

Pete furrowed her brow with feigned seriousness. "I think we'd better spend the next 36 hours making up for lost time."

Danica lifted her head to grin up at Pete. "Sleep is for the weak."

"Sleep is for the losers who don't have a gorgeous, naked Danica in their bed," Pete said, kissing Danica's temple.

"You don't have to flatter me," Danica teased. "You're super rich, right? You can just buy me a car to say thank you." She paused, playing up a moment of consideration. "Or maybe I should be buying *you* a car to say thank you for that thing you did with your tongue."

Pete rolled her eyes, snorting. "I really promise you it's not like that."

Danica pushed up onto her elbow. "Then what's it like? You just travel the world, surviving off of your investments? That's what you've always wanted, isn't it?"

Pete's mouth tightened, and Danica noticed the way Pete felt suddenly very far away. "It's not like that. I'm not just some..." Pete gestured vaguely. "Purposeless human."

Danica raised an eyebrow. "Then tell me what it's like."

Pete's cheeks were flushed, and not just from the exertion. "I am extremely privileged to have the life I do now. I bought Lillian a house, I paid off all my student debt... These are things I could never even imagine doing back when I was still just a depressed teenager in foster care. I didn't have some desire to code forever, to hoard wealth like all the assholes I was meeting in the tech world. When I was traveling, I started connecting with all of these incredible people who were doing amazing things for kids in children's homes and foster care. And the one problem they all had was funding for any kind of extracurriculars, or any extras of any kind. Grants are exhausting to apply for, and it's hard to find the time to work toward things that might not pan out when you already have so much to do and organize, you know?"

Danica nodded, her brow furrowed in concentration as she tried to piece together what Pete was telling her. "You started funding orphanages?"

"Not exactly. I started funding programs *for* children's homes. I never wanted anyone to feel lost and alone like I had growing up. There was never extra money to go anywhere or join sports or buy musical instruments, so that's what the money goes toward. Basically, just enriching the lives of kids, funding hobbies or anything that can help them feel like they matter. For me, it was more important to show vulnerable kids that their interests matter, not just job training. You know, just exploring and having fun." Pete took a deep breath. "Anyway, yeah, that's... that's what I've been doing for the last ten years."

Danica was stunned, sitting up to look more directly at Pete. Here, she'd been assuming Pete had some weird hippie working on organic farms in Thailand and hitchhiking through life. "Why didn't you want to tell me this?"

Pete smiled disarmingly. "Does it matter?"

Danica angled her head. "Yeah, *it does*. You're incredible, Pete, and I don't give a fuck about your tax bracket. You've come up with this amazing idea that honestly saves kids' lives. You should be crowing from the rooftops about it."

Pete scrubbed a hand over her face. "God, no."

Danica pushed up onto her knees, cupping her hands around her mouth to loudly announce, "Petra fucking Pancott is amazing."

Pete's eyes widened, and she grabbed Danica, flipping her onto her back in a fit of laughter. "Stop that! The people of the world can't know I'm selfless *and* pay my fair share of taxes. I'd never be able to leave my house again for fear of being mobbed with adoring fans."

"Ah, there's the cocky bastard I know and love," Danica said with a grin, kissing Pete's nose.

"Love, hmm?" Pete repeated, quirking her mouth to the side.

"Oh, shut up, not like that," Danica said, though something inside of her leaped at the thought. Nope. She didn't know why that had popped up, but she pushed that emotion way, way, way down. A flicker of something crossed Pete's expression, just a slight increase of intensity in her gaze as she stared down at Danica, her hair wild from Danica's hands. Well, and Danica's thighs.

"Sure, Wendell. You think you can butter me up to buy you a car," Pete teased, touching Danica's nose with hers.

Danica pushed up, giving Pete another kiss before laughing. "It was worth a shot."

"Here, I'll give you this: I noticed you need new snow tires when Kiera drove your car up that first day, but that's on you. You're a doctor." Pete tickled Danica, and she writhed until the feeling of their bodies against each other took over all other thoughts, their mouths and hands and bodies slowly exploring one another over and over again.

Danica was putting an obscene amount of dry shampoo in her hair when she heard a knock on the door frame of her en suite. Kiera stood there with a smile and a mug of steaming coffee, looking as put together as ever. She wore a turtleneck sweater, perfectly tailored jeans, and trendy boots that Danica eyed and mentally marked as borrow-worthy. Danica felt very suddenly frumpy in her thrifted Levi's and oversized fisherman's sweater.

"Good morning, sunshine," Kiera said, passing her the coffee.

Danica took the mug of coffee gratefully. "Morning," she said, pausing to sip the coffee.

"How'd you sleep?" Kiera asked.

"Great, thanks," Danica lied. "How about you?"

"Better without you starfishing," Kiera teased.

Danica grinned, catching Kiera's eye in the mirror. "Thanks again for letting me sleep in your bed."

"Want to talk about it?" Kiera asked, leaning against the bathroom counter.

"I was just feeling weird, and you always make me feel better," Danica said, trying to massage her bangs into submission.

"Mmhmm," Kiera said, pointedly looking at Danica's perfectly made bed.

Danica met Kiera's eyes in the large bathroom mirror.

"What's on your neck?" Kiera asked, angling her head to see.

Danica could feel her entire body flush with embarrassment as her hand shot to her neck, remembering how she'd found the hickey after the hot tub... and then probably added to the collection last night. "I burned my curling iron."

"You burned your curling iron," Kiera repeated, deadpan.

"No, I mean, I burned my curling iron with myself." Danica wasn't a very good liar at the best of moments, and when she was flustered, it was even worse. She checked her neck in the mirror, seeing a bright red spot exactly where she remembered Pete's mouth. Really, it was impressive that she didn't have more of them.

"You hussy!" Kiera chided.

Maggie popped her head into the room. "Hey Dani? Are you — wait, who's a hussy?"

"Danica the hussy is in here," Kiera said, pointing emphatically into the en suite. "She has a *hickey*."

Danica set down the coffee cup and held her hands over her face as Maggie walked into the bathroom and sat on the edge of the bathtub.

Maggie giggled, kicking her feet. "From *who*?"

"Well, it wasn't from me," Kiera said.

"Wasn't me," Maggie said quickly. "Did a hot stranger visit you after the bar last night?"

Danica suddenly wished she'd drowned in that frozen pond. "It's nothing." Her hand moved down to cover her neck.

"Tell us everything," Kiera said, shutting the door of Danica's bedroom quietly and then hurrying back to the bathroom. "Wait, they aren't from Pete, are they?"

"You two are the worst," Danica said with an uncomfortable laugh, rifling through her makeup bag for concealer. Her cheeks were on fire. Maggie was giddy with anticipation, but Kiera looked somehow both curious and judgmental. Danica applied the concealer with a few taps of her fingers, buying herself time. "Okay, fine, Pete and I... rekindled things," she said. Both women had an immediate and exaggerated reaction. Maggie clasped her hands to her mouth, her eyes sparkling with delight. Yet Kiera looked ready to launch into a lecture about why this was a bad idea, with a PowerPoint presentation to match.

"Who kissed who?" Maggie asked, eager for the details.

"It was kind of mutual," Danica said, biting her bottom lip to stifle a grin. "It started two nights ago in the hot tub, and then last night..." Her shoulders nearly touched her ears as she shrugged dramatically.

"Did you have sex?" Kiera whispered conspiratorially.

Danica looked between her friends, her face splitting into a wide smile. Guilty as charged.

Maggie was bouncing — *bouncing!* — in place with excitement. "And how was it?"

"You are way too excited about this, Mags," Kiera said,

looking from Maggie back to Danica. "Are we just not going to talk about how Dani is engaged?"

Maggie made a dismissive noise.

"I can't believe we're seriously talking about cheating on Eddie as if it was a fun, lighthearted time," Kiera said, an expression of confused contemplation on her face, like she was trying to decide if she was translating the situation correctly.

"Just tell her," Maggie said to Danica, letting out a long breath.

Danica pursed her lips. Maggie was right, and she couldn't just expect Kiera to let it go without the full story.

"Tell me what?" Kiera asked, her confusion turning to suspicion.

"Eddie and I aren't together anymore," Danica said in a rush, saying the entire sentence as if it were one long word.

Kiera blinked. "You what? When did that happen?"

Danica closed her eyes. "I'm sorry I didn't tell you sooner." She took a deep breath and recounted the big details to Kiera, who watched her with an intense stare.

Kiera stared at her with a concerned look on her face. "Are you okay?"

"I'm not really that upset," Danica admitted. "I feel kind of... relieved."

"So, is Pete like, a rebound thing? Are you ready for that?" Kiera asked, her voice quiet. "Are you okay?"

Maggie waved her hand in the air. "She's just having a bit of fun. Tell us more about it. I'm boring and married. Let me live vicariously through this."

"It was..." Danica cleared her throat. "Yeah, it was good."

"I always imagined Pete to be a good kisser," Maggie said wistfully. "And like, really good in bed. She has that energy."

Danica snorted in amusement, and almost told Maggie she was exactly right, but quelled the urge.

Kiera shook her head, but Danica could detect a bit of amusement. "Can you not?"

"You wouldn't get it because you're woefully straight," Maggie said with a heavy sigh. "It's a thing."

Danica did not think it was entirely appropriate to agree with Maggie's questions about Pete's skills in bed, but she caught Maggie's eye and gave her a small wink when Kiera began to pace the room.

"So, what happens now?" Maggie said with a giddy grin. "You gonna make out again today?" She waggled her eyebrows. "Going to go to fourth base?"

"Home base," Kiera corrected.

"Whatever," Maggie said, shrugging. "I thought it was nicer than asking if she was ready to get railed on a bunk bed again."

Danica choked, but Kiera finally laughed. "I did not need that mental image."

"I don't... I'm not entirely sure. Maybe?" Danica said after a moment to think. "Probably."

Kiera and Maggie voiced immediate and opposing opinions.

Danica pulled at a loose thread in her sweater. "I don't think it'll turn into anything serious, you know?"

"You've already had a thing with Pete, so it doesn't have to be that serious," Maggie stated. "Besides, Pete is like the Mayor of Unserious Town."

"I think you're being pretty casual about the fact that a month ago Danica was going to get married to someone else," Kiera argued.

"Is it that weird to have a few carefree days before having to go back to real life?" Danica asked, feeling defensive.

Kiera sat on the edge of the bed again. "We're in Telluride, not Vegas."

"I support women's rights *and* wrongs," Maggie said with a firm nod.

Kiera crossed her arms. "I worry about you, Dani. I was there when Pete broke your heart. I saw what it did to you."

Danica deflated. Kiera had a point.

Maggie frowned, leveling Kiera with a look that said she thought Kiera was being absurd. "Yeah, but she was twenty-two. So, now Danica knows that Pete doesn't want anything more than a casual thing, and Danica doesn't need anything serious, either. Why can't she just enjoy herself judgment-free for a few days?"

Maggie and Kiera were like the little angel and devil on her shoulders, and Danica could see both sides of what they were saying. Maggie wanted her to have fun while she could, and Kiera was afraid of her getting her heart broken again.

But if she went into it knowing it wasn't forever, that it would only last a few days, maybe she could keep her heart from getting broken. They only had one night left on the trip. Surely that wasn't enough to start actually feeling things for Pete again, right? She could just appreciate it for what it was. Maybe she could just enjoy how fantastic of a kisser Pete was, — among her many, many other talents — and then go back to Denver and her real life.

"What if it isn't over with Eddie?" Kiera said, with a strange look on her face.

Danica grimaced. "It's definitely over with Eddie."

Maggie narrowed her eyes. "*He* broke up with *her*. You think she should just be begging to get back with him?"

"I'm just saying that wedding planning is stressful, and maybe Eddie made a mistake," Kiera said. "Maybe he's waiting until you're back to try to work things out."

Danica glanced from Kiera to Maggie, a strange feeling in her gut. Why was Kiera even saying this?

"And who says she would even want to go back to that asshole?" Maggie asked, crossing her arms. "*He* doesn't deserve her, and *she* deserves to have good sex and get her groove back."

Danica held up her hands to pause them. This was turning into her worst-case scenario, where now she had to talk about Eddie, and her breakup, when she wanted to enjoy the trip and take away too much from the trip with her own problems. It was exactly what she'd wanted to avoid all along. Her cheeks were red and she couldn't remember if she'd put on blush yet. "Okay. I see what you're both saying. Thank you both for being so concerned about me, and I love you. I'll figure it out. You don't have to worry about me." She took a deep, steadying breath, staring at herself in the mirror.

Kiera sighed, like she wanted to say more, but Maggie held up her sprained wrist, the bandage wonky and uneven. "Okay, now for the real reason I was trying to find you. I can't re-wrap this. Can you be less of a hussy and more of a doctor for a moment?"

CHAPTER 18

PETE

THE PANCAKES ON PETE'S PLATE LOOKED LIKE A PERFECTLY GOOD pillow, and she considered resting her head right on their fluffy, buttery, syrupy top.

Maggie was grinning into her coffee, Kiera was seemingly entranced by the diner's tabletop, and Izzy was happily sorting through Pete's vegan bacon, trading her crispy pieces for the floppy pieces that Pete hated.

Pete yawned and Danica glanced her way, trying to hide a smile. They'd gotten very, very little sleep the night before, and she was sure that it was obvious why, given Pete's inability to keep her hands to herself this morning. Even now, her arm was slung over the back of the booth behind Danica, her fingers idly playing with a few strands of Danica's hair that peeked out from her beanie.

It was their last full day of the trip, and everyone seemed rather exhausted and resistant to heading out to ski this morning.

"Can I just say that I've really missed you guys? And that

we shouldn't wait fifteen years to all hang out again?" Maggie said, smearing apple butter on her English muffin.

"Agreed," Danica said with a smile. "Maybe we could make this a yearly thing. Kiera, do you think Aunt Jade would let us have a week at the condo next year, too?"

Kiera shrugged, glancing at her phone instead of looking at anyone. "Maybe."

Danica angled her head, watching Kiera, and Pete could see the crinkle between her eyebrows, her studying gaze. Danica had always been sensitive to others' feelings, always the first to notice if someone seemed off. It was one thing she had always loved about Danica — how concerned she was about everyone else's happiness. Pete also struggled with Danica always prioritizing others' happiness over her own.

Maggie slurped her coffee, precariously balanced in one hand while she twisted her shoulder to adjust her other arm in the sling. "Even if it's not in the mountains, we should definitely get together more often. Let's put this on the calendar every year."

Izzy shrugged. "As long as you give me enough time to save money for a ticket, I'm in," she said in between a bite of bacon. Izzy's casual tone tugged at something in Pete's chest. Izzy was the only reason Pete had come in the first place. She was concerned that a fifteen-year absence, due to her travels, had irreparably damaged her friendships. Izzy and Maggie had remained good friends, and Izzy had spent a bit of time visiting Maggie in the fall, but when it had come time to buy her tickets, she'd told Pete she might not attend because she couldn't afford it. Pete had instantly bought Izzy a plane ticket, much to Izzy's annoyance. What good was having money if you didn't spend it on the people you loved? Then, upon hearing Danica would definitely be coming, she bought her own ticket.

Although she'd tucked away most of her money in the foundation and investments, she was comfortable. Financially comfortable, at least, for maybe the first time in her life. Her childhood and early adult years had been spent in constant upheaval and change, so she was used to it. Now, she craved that comfort and stability in all aspects of her life. She loved traveling, of course, but it just didn't feel as magical when she didn't have somewhere she loved to come home to.

She glanced sideways at Danica, watching the way Danica's chestnut hair curled around her own finger, feeling the softness of Danica's sweater under her palm, the warmth of their legs touching. Her daydreams of seeing Danica again paled in comparison to the reality of reconnecting with her. Every moment spent adventuring, talking, joking, undressing... She wanted more. *Needed* more. An emotional lump lodged in her throat as she realized anywhere could be home, as long as Danica was there.

It was embarrassing to admit, even to herself, how she wanted that to be true so, so badly.

Pete tapped the toe of her Doc Martens on the floor, suddenly feeling anxious about where things stood. The sex had been phenomenal, but it always had been. And somehow, the intimacy was on a whole new level now. It was the knowing of a person, past tense, and the finding out of a person, present tense. Danica was the same, and yet a completely different person now. Loving Danica again was like rediscovering a beloved book — every chapter held a newfound significance, resonating with her heart in ways she hadn't perceived before.

She choked on her coffee as the thought flitted through her mind. Whoa, where had that intrusive love thought come from? Love? Did she *love* Danica?

"You okay?" Danica asked, gently touching Pete's knee as she coughed.

Pete nodded. "Sorry, just... wrong pipe."

As Pete regained her composure, sipping a bit of coffee, the group finished up with their meal. Kiera was being weird and mopey, but Maggie tossed down her napkin with a comfortable sigh. Maggie glanced toward Izzy. "Eager to return to the mountain?"

Izzy leaned back in the booth, fidgeting with the zipper of her fleece jacket. "I was kind of thinking we could all try something else."

Danica clutched the inflated snow tube to her chest as they stood on the top of Firecracker Hill, watching families sled down with shouts and laughter. Izzy had found a nearby shop that rented sledding tubes, and the group had enthusiastically agreed. Well, all except Danica, who looked like she might throw up in a nearby plant, should one be available.

"What could go wrong?" Maggie remarked, dragging her tube by one handle behind her. "At least falling will be easier than on a snowboard."

"It's a long hill," Danica said.

"It's barely a hill," Pete teased. "It's a stretch to call it a slight incline. After Allais Alley, this is nothing."

Danica winced, looking at Kiera, who was fixing her gloves as they watched a family of five slide down the hill in a clump of interconnected tubes.

"We should try that," Maggie said, pointing toward the family with her elbow in her sling.

"And accidentally catch one of Pete's Docs to the face? No thanks," Kiera said.

Pete shoved down her initial response that Kiera catching a foot to the face would be no accident, but she decided she'd keep the peace for Danica's sake. Kiera had been acting so strange today, either staring at her phone or watching Pete with a pointed expression. It's not like she and Danica were hiding, not holding back from a hand on an arm, a playful bump of a hip. Kiera should be used to it — it was the way they'd always acted.

"Come on, Kier, I'll put myself between you and Pete's boots," Izzy offered, and Pete watched suspiciously as they seemed to exchange a long, knowing look. She made a mental note to ask Izzy about it later.

After placing their five tubes together, Pete helped Maggie and Danica get settled in. Danica's wide eyes, sparkling with excitement despite her otherwise serious face, made her adorable. Pete waited until Kiera and Izzy were situated before taking hold of her own tube, running a few steps, and throwing herself stomach-down onto her tube, reaching to take Danica's hand as she passed.

In Kiera's defense, this *was* a terrible idea. The tubes and their riders began to fly in all different directions, creating a screaming horde of adult women flying down the hill at speeds none of them expected. Although Danica held onto Pete's hand tightly, a larger bump launched Maggie, Kiera, and Izzy in different directions. Kiera and Izzy flew from their tubes, continuing to roll downhill in the snow with shrieks. Maggie had tucked herself into a small ball, clearly afraid of further injuring her wrist after what Kiera and Izzy had just gone through.

Pete heard screaming, and it took a moment to realize that it was coming from Danica. After a brief pang of fear, she realized that Danica was yelling with... joy. She was laughing, her head thrown back, eyes squeezed shut. As they soared past their fallen friends, her hair whipped out around her coat hood, her wide mouth parted in happy squealing.

Pete wanted to memorize that sound, this feeling, the entire moment, and keep it forever. She let out an excited whoop, still laughing even as they careened from the path and tumbled from their tubes. A jolt of panic flashed through Pete's body as she saw that Danica was lying face down in the snow, limbs askew.

She scrambled on her knees over to where Danica lay, rolling her over to find that Danica was still laughing, tears streaming down her cheeks. "Are you okay?" she asked breathlessly. "Are you hurt?"

"No, I'm fine, I'm fine," Danica said, brushing at her face with her bare hands.

"You're sure?" Pete asked, her heart pounding frantically in her chest. Danica grabbed the front of Pete's jacket and pulled her down, pressing a warm kiss to Pete's frozen lips.

"I'm fine," Danica emphasized, and Pete brushed some of the hair from Danica's face. "Anyone ever tell you that you worry too much?"

"No one has ever told me that, oddly enough," Pete joked, helping Danica to stand as they wiped the snow from their clothes.

"We should rescue Maggie. She looks like a stuck turtle," Danica said, nodding her chin toward where Maggie was still tucked into a tiny ball, safely ensconced in her tube towards the bottom of the hill. Higher up the hill, Kiera and Izzy were talking with their heads close together, but Danica didn't seem to notice. They grabbed their tubes by the handles and helped Maggie, who was also fine, stand up. The three of them nearly fell over with giggles as they slipped and slid, trying to help one another regain their balance.

Pete walked back up the hill to where Izzy and Kiera were still talking, catching the tail end of a phrase from Izzy that sounded an awful lot like, "a terrible fucking idea and you know it."

"You guys alive and in one piece?" Pete announced loudly, and both women spun toward her, looking surprised. Kiera's cheeks were flushed, and Izzy was scowling.

"Should we go again?" Danica asked from behind her, dragging both her and Maggie's snow tubes.

"Definitely," Izzy said a little too quickly.

They spent the better part of the morning on the sledding hill, racing and trying to fly high on their tubes over the tiny ledge that could make them airborne. Pete's tension about Kiera and Izzy seemed to unwind with each smile on Danica's face, and when Maggie suggested lunch, Pete cleared her throat and announced that she and Danica would meet them after.

Her plan was two-fold. First, and most importantly, she wanted to steal Danica away for any alone time they could get out of their last full day. Second, if anyone could glean information about Izzy and Kiera's talk, it was Maggie, who could read people unlike any other. Or, perhaps Maggie was just the friend group's nosiest member, and therefore held more secrets than anyone else.

The second the condo door closed behind them, they were flinging boots and jackets and scarves off, already greedy with their kisses, desperate for one another.

"My bed, this time," Danica whispered against her mouth as they pressed against a wall, Pete's mouth already sliding over the soft skin of Danica's throat.

"Who said anything about a bed?" Pete teased, her knee pushing between Danica's thighs.

Danica was shameless as she moved her hips against Pete, urgent and needy. "You'd rather just fuck me against this wall?" She had a wicked smile on her face to match her sultry tone. Pete nipped at her lower lip, her hands sliding under Danica's sweater, feeling her cold sweat-slicked skin.

"If I must." Pete let out a husky laugh, her thigh rising as Danica's hips ground against her.

An hour later, Danica lay sprawled over her, Pete's breath finally slowing after drawing out Danica's first orgasm in the hallway, fully clothed like horny teenagers, then dragging her to bed as they took turns satisfying what felt like a nearly infinite need.

"I can't believe we ever left my bed after doing this last night," Pete mumbled from where her face was still pressed into Danica's hair, breathing in the rosemary and mint of her shampoo. "I don't intend to make the same mistake again."

"You think the others would ever forgive us for just

spending the next 24 hours right here?" Danica joked, her fingertips trailing over the bare skin of Pete's upper back.

"Oh? Just the next 24? I say we buy Aunt Jade's condo and never leave," Pete said, pushing up onto her elbow to get a better look at Danica.

Danica grinned. "I don't know if even your crypto-bro money could afford this place."

"The really sad part is that I bet she bought it in the 80s for a nickel and a handshake," Pete said, glancing around the room. It was far too modern to be built in the 80s, but she couldn't imagine what a giant ski in/ski out condo in Telluride would actually cost.

Danica's smile was infectious as she gazed up at Pete, a playful glint in her eyes. "That lucky bitch."

"What about you? Do you own a house?" Pete asked. "In Denver?"

"I have a condo," Danica said, shrugging. "Eddie owned a house, but I kept my place and rented to travel nurses until last month, when I moved back in." She grimaced and added, "Sorry, I bet it's weird to hear about him."

Pete shook her head. "No, he's a part of your past." She watched Danica's expression turn to one of contemplation, her mouth turning into a small frown. "What is it?"

"I'd have said the same thing about you just last week," Danica whispered.

Pete's stomach flipped in a bout of nerves. "Oh yeah?" Her voice softened. "And what do you say now?"

Danica studied her face for a moment, reaching up to trace a thumb over Pete's cheekbone. She spoke slowly, choosing her words carefully. "I'd say this trip has been a fun surprise."

Hope bloomed inside of Pete. "It has," she agreed, pressing a kiss to Danica's nose. "And... tomorrow?"

"What about tomorrow?" Danica asked, her eyes searching Pete's.

Pete's voice was strained as she uttered, "We're leaving,"

the statement a battleground of emotions: one impulse pushing her to steer clear of the scary discussion and distract Danica, the other yearning to bravely explore the possibility of a future with her.

Danica's forehead furrowed. "We are," she said slowly, drawing out the words. "And you'll go back to Seattle and I'll go back to Denver."

Pete plastered a smile on her face and nodded. She instinctively wanted to cradle her feelings like a wounded limb. "We will." She matched Danica's slow, reveal-nothing tone.

They stayed in silence for a few more moments, looking at one another, nearly daring the other to continue down that path. Danica broke the spell first, the picture of unbothered nonchalance as she turned away. "We should shower."

"Aren't we just going to work up a sweat again?" Pete asked.

Danica sat on the edge of the bed, glancing down at the place where she'd just been lying beside Pete. "Oh?" She sounded intrigued.

"You know, skiing."

Danica shook her head, her chestnut hair falling around her shoulders. "You can think about skiing today? My shins would revolt."

"Come on, Wendell. It could be one of our last runs together. We can take Galloping Goose and just enjoy it," Pete suggested, knowing that Galloping Goose was a long, long run, out on the far boundary of the resort that could easily take up the rest of the afternoon.

Danica pursed her lips, considering it. "One last run?"

Pete emphatically shook her head no, her tousled curls bouncing around her head. "You can't say that."

Danica angled her head. "Why?"

"It's a superstition. If you call it your *last* run, you will always make a dumb mistake and get injured. You have to say that you'll take two more runs but then actually skip the last one, or say that you'll see how you feel at the bottom."

Danica squinted at Pete. "You really believe that?"

"Absolutely."

A grin tugged at the edge of Danica's mouth. "That's adorable."

"Do you tell actors they're adorable for saying break a leg instead of good luck?" Pete crossed her arms with mock-affront.

Danica laughed, reaching to place a hand on her shoulder. "Okay, okay. Don't go all 'shred some gnar' on me. I believe you. No last runs."

"It's shred *the* gnar, but… sure. Wanna go on a *few* more runs with me?" Pete asked, biting her lower lip as her mouth pulled into a smile.

Danica's ocean blue eyes stayed on her. "Fine. We can do Galloping Goose and see how we feel at the bottom. But we'd better invite Kiera and Izzy or else I think they might riot."

Pete pretended to pout. "Fine."

"And I'm showering first," Danica added.

Pete grinned. "Can I join?"

Danica glanced at her watch, pretending to consider the offer. "If you must," she said with a long sigh, but Pete could tell she was teasing. Pete pushed herself up and wrapped her arms around Danica's middle, dragging her off in a fit of laughter and protest.

CHAPTER 19

DANICA

GALLOPING GOOSE WAS A LONG GREEN RUN THAT SKIRTED THE far edge of the resort, starting near the top of the top edge of the Black Iron Bowl and Bald Mountain. It had taken nearly an hour to get to, with the three chairlifts they'd had to take just to get so far near the boundaries. Mercifully, none of the lifts had broken down while they were on them, though they had shared a lift with teenage boys who had graciously offered them weed. They'd both declined with amusement.

Finally, *finally* they began Galloping Goose, and Danica was almost surprised by how flat it was, its beginning stretching wide and open with spots of trees in the middle that she and Pete wove around. She could relax on a run like this, not overthink every little bump, and enjoy herself. The view from the trail was stunning — all tall, skinny trees dusted with snow and reaching mountains with white caps and dark rock.

She felt the exhilarating lightness of flight as she skied, her breath even and steady, a comfortable rhythm established between her and Pete as they continued to pass one another.

The trail felt amazingly isolated from the resort, and this late in the afternoon, it wasn't busy. The sun was still bright in the expansive blue sky, making even the narrower stretches of the trail feel open, where they navigated between two sets of trees or a small rocky outcropping. She could almost imagine that she and Pete were anywhere, just the two of them. And most of all, she liked that feeling.

She hadn't been too sad when Kiera and Izzy had said they'd rather ski some intense black runs for the afternoon. After the moguls of Allais Alley, Danica wasn't quite in the mood to try anything more difficult than the easy, long green run Pete had suggested. More so, she was grateful to have one last run alone with Pete — or rather, one more run.

Danica stole a glance at Pete, the robin's egg blue of her jacket and bright orange pants making her easy to find, even with the glare of the sun on the snow. Danica's heart leaped when Pete glanced back at her with a warm and inviting grin, and she couldn't suppress the answering smile that stretched across her lips. Danica had promised herself that she wouldn't let the past two days let her grow too attached to Pete, but she'd been a fool. The familiar feelings started subtly, like a gentle snowfall, each flake a memory, but the accumulating weight threatened to become an over-whelming avalanche, burying her under the weight of the past.

The run veered toward the left, winding past ski chalets and mansions. Pete pointed toward a stone behemoth with a five-car garage. "Let's buy this one."

"Sure," Danica answered. "We'd never have to leave. An entire grocery store could be in there."

"Which is perfect, because then I could spend all my time at home with you, completely naked, never having to bother with clothes again," Pete whispered.

"Wow, you'd just never let me leave or get dressed?" Danica teased. "What makes you think I'll put up with that?"

"I can be very convincing," Pete called back over her shoulder.

Danica snorted in amusement, shaking her head. "I think we might need something slightly smaller."

Pete shrugged playfully, letting Danica ski past her. "Nope, it definitely has to be that big."

"And why is that?" Danica asked, slowing so that she and Pete were side by side.

"There are many, many places I've daydreamed of fucking you," Pete said with a tone that made Danica's toes curl in her boots. "And I intend to see those plans through."

Danica's face flushed behind her balaclava. Pete was just saying that, right? Her insides twisted as she tried to judge whether Pete's suggestion had a hint of seriousness behind them. Was she really suggesting a future together? Or was it just their physical connection she meant? She could see Pete's sly smile as the two of them slowed upon approaching the junction of multiple runs, working to avoid being barreled into by other skiers.

Danica quelled the thought, anxious to turn the conversation safely away from the reality of what tomorrow might bring. "Want to go back to the condo and make good on some of those plans?" Danica asked.

Pete nodded emphatically toward the Chondola lift, where both chairlift seats and gondola cars used the same line. "What do you say we get in one of the gondolas and start right away?" She bent to unstrap her bindings.

"You're shameless," Danica said, unclipping from her skis.

Pete stood and grabbed her around the waist, playfully knocking their helmets together with a gentle tap. "I just want to soak up every moment I have with you."

The muscles in Danica's cheeks were pleasantly sore — a testament to the hours spent smiling. "Me too."

She tried not to note how Pete had used the present tense.

Danica's skis and Pete's snowboard were propped

against the potted plants that Danica had desecrated just one week before. Pete's breath was warm on the back of Danica's neck, distracting her as she tried to type in the ridiculous key code for the door. Kiera was a woman of multitudes, using a code like 'boobies' for the door, but then judging her for having a casual fling with an old flame. Maybe tonight she and Kiera could have a glass of wine and clear the air. She loved Kiera, and she wanted them to get back to their normal familiarity. Though the fun with Pete was temporary — or so she kept telling herself — long-term friendships were sacred.

Pete's lips were on her neck, making goosebumps rise along her spine. How did Pete remember that would make her knees buckle? She took a moment to close her eyes, letting Pete's mouth glide over her skin, Pete's arms pulling her closer. The sweet coconut and apricot scent of Pete enveloped her.

"You'd better open that door faster or I'm going to have to fuck you up against the front porch wall for all the neighbors to watch," Pete murmured into her ear.

Danica turned her head slightly, raising a brow at Pete. "Like I said, shameless."

"Only when it comes to you," Pete said, her fingers light on Danica's chin to angle her face up for a kiss.

Danica began to turn in Pete's arms, strongly considering whether she might enjoy a touch of exhibitionism, as the front door opened. She turned, expecting to find one of her friends at the door, but she stilled, her brain taking a moment to catch up with what she was seeing.

It was Eddie.

Eddie was here, in Telluride, in Aunt Jade's condo.

Danica's skis clattered to the ground and Pete tensed behind her.

His Banana Republic quarter-zip was undone at the neck, and the stubble on his chin was a change from his usual clean-cut appearance. Judging by his chinos and loafers, he hadn't come here to ski.

"What are you doing here?" Danica asked, her voice hard.

The door opened wider, and then Kiera was standing beside Eddie, her expression completely unreadable. Her discomfort showed only in the droop of her shoulders. "I invited him."

"Why?" Danica asked.

Pete moved to stand beside Danica as she folded her arms over her chest. "What the fuck, Kiera?"

"I was hoping that we could talk," Eddie said, taking a step back to allow them in.

"Are you... okay? Do you need anything? Do you want me to come with you?" Pete asked Danica in a low voice.

Danica glanced from Eddie to Pete, where the two were sizing each other up. She rolled her eyes. "No, I'll be fine." She turned to look at Kiera, narrowing her eyes as she stepped in from out of the cold and removed her ski jacket. The urge to scream, to run, to explode with rage, or to bury herself in her room until it was all over, overwhelmed her.

She led Eddie to her room so they could speak privately, shutting the door before leaning back against it, her arms crossed over her chest. "Alright, say what you need to say. I know it was a long drive, so I'll let you get it out before you have to go back on the road."

"Actually, I flew," Eddie said, rubbing at the back of his neck awkwardly.

Danica sighed, pinching the bridge of her nose. Just the thought of the car ride back to Denver made her stomach churn, especially since she would be alone in a car with Kiera for six hours.

Eddie took a step toward her, but she put out her hands to keep him from touching her. His blinding smile flashed as he raised his own hands in surrender. "I know you didn't expect to see me this week, but Kiera reached out, and so I came."

Utter betrayal made Danica's insides clench as she considered her best friend and her ex-fiancé plotting to surprise her in this way. Kiera's claim that she was 'Team Danica' was absolute bullshit. "Why?" she asked flatly.

"I love you, Danica. I want to make things right and be with you. We can act like this never happened. It could just be a bump in the road," Eddie said. Had his eyes always been so bloodshot?

"No, why did Kiera reach out? What did she say?" Danica clarified.

Eddie sputtered. "She said that she wasn't sure exactly what happened between us, but that it might be worth coming here to try to salvage it. She said that she was worried that you were falling into old patterns, and that—"

"How did she have your number?" Danica asked.

Eddie angled his head in confusion. "What?"

"How did Kiera even have your number to contact you?"

"She reached out on Instagram," Eddie clarified.

Danica let out a forceful breath. "Show me the message she sent." Her words were steady and clipped, and she was nearly boiling with anger.

Eddie's eyes darted toward his phone. "Why?"

"Show me," Danica said, holding out her hand. She'd normally not be so demanding about seeing his phone — she'd never asked before, but she was so done. So done with this entire charade. Something felt very wrong here, and she'd spent her entire life silencing that gut feeling, but not anymore.

Eddie stared at her for a long, uncomfortable moment. Then he sighed and pulled his phone from the pocket of his khakis, typed in his passcode, and handed the phone to Danica. She opened his Instagram app and then the DMs. She noted messages from other women, but he was single after all. Seeing the women in his DMs didn't make her jealous, but her focus zeroed in on the thread with Kiera. Danica leaned back in the chair and looked through the messages. A year ago, they'd started talking to plan a surprise visit from Kiera, but then the messages had stopped until yesterday, right before the spa trip.

"I'm worried about Danica. She's making bad, reckless choices and not being herself."

Kiera made it sound like Danica had started taking hard drugs and charging strangers for sex work.

Eddie's replies grew increasingly worried as Kiera brought up specific references about Danica falling into old habits with her college girlfriend. A lump lodged in Danica's throat as she read a message from that morning: "I don't want Danica to lose you. If you want to work things out, you should come."

Rage, a violent red, filled Danica's vision; her jaw clenched tight, and her hands shook, the tremor spreading through her arms. What was Kiera thinking? The betrayal felt like a physical blow, a sharp stab of pain that left her reeling, never expecting such behavior from her best friend.

Eddie paced the room, his face contorted with worry as his lips moved, but Danica didn't hear a word as she read the messages. Her anger wasn't directed at him — not this time, at least. Eddie hadn't been a bad boyfriend; he just wasn't right for her. Her time with Pete had made her realize that no matter what the future held, she wanted a partner who challenged her, who saw her when she was guarded and worked with her to bring down those walls. Someone who she wanted to come home to, not out of obligation but out of excitement. Someone like… Pete.

As Eddie paced, she felt nothing but pity for him, as he ran his hand through his short, receding hair.

She sighed, standing. "Eddie, I'm sorry, but you need to leave."

He stopped, gaping at her like a fish out of water. "What? But what about us, Danica?"

"There's no us," Danica said, shaking her head. His shoulders slumped like he was defeated. She patted his shoulder. "I'm sorry Kiera told you to come."

"What was happening that Kiera thought was so reckless she messaged me?" Eddie asked, his tone exasperated.

She chewed her lower lip, considering exactly how much to say. "It's a long story," Danica answered.

"You can tell me," Eddie said, his eyes pleading.

Danica sighed, pinching the bridge of her nose. She was going to kill Kiera for this. "The only thing you need to know is that nothing has changed between us. It's over. You broke up with me, remember?"

Eddie looked so defeated that her pity turned to outright worry. When had he perfected that sad puppy look, complete with big, pleading eyes and a slight tremble to his lower lip? Had he ever used that before on her? "But what if that was a mistake? I can't stop thinking about you."

Danica let out a heavy sigh. "Our breakup wasn't a mistake. You being here is, though. So, I need you to leave." Eddie began to protest, but Danica gave him a sharp look.

"There's only one flight out per day, and it's already gone," he said finally.

"Okay, well, I'll book you a hotel and then you can fly back tomorrow," Danica offered.

She'd once thought Eddie was tall and self-assured, but he looked like a sad, lost boy right now.

She walked out of her room and found Pete and Izzy in the living room, standing in front of Kiera, who was sitting on the couch. Kiera looked flustered and upset. Izzy was red-faced. Danica searched Pete's face, and her heart ached at the confusion and hurt she saw there. Kiera stood and hurried from the room in a huff.

"Everything okay?" Pete asked, eyeing Danica.

"Yeah, um, Eddie's leaving." Danica said, pulling out her phone to book him an Uber and a hotel. She didn't care how much it cost, just that it was available. Was he fully capable of doing all of this himself? Of course he was, but she wanted it done immediately and correctly. She'd learned long ago that those two things only happened when she did them herself. She booked him a car and then turned toward Pete and Izzy. "I'm going to go talk to Kiera. Please, be nice."

Pete shifted from one foot to the other, clearly uncomfortable, but Izzy inclined her head politely. "I'll keep an eye out for his ride," Izzy said, and her support surprised Danica.

She turned, walking back down the hall to Kiera's room. She'd been far less nervous talking to Eddie than she was now, knowing she had to address this situation with Kiera. So many emotions were swirling inside of her. The betrayal, the rage, the frustration, and the deep hurt that crushed her most of all — they all fought for space inside her brain, and she didn't know how to quiet them in order to think properly.

Her hand closed around the doorknob to Kiera's room, and without even pausing to knock, she shoved the door open. Kiera had her suitcase on the bed and was hurrying around the room, throwing her things inside.

"What the fuck, Kiera?" Danica said, and she wasn't proud of her tone or her words.

Kiera didn't say a word, just shuffled around the room with her shoulders slumped, walking into the bathroom and throwing her makeup into a toiletry bag.

Danica followed her, leaning on the doorframe. "So, you're leaving?"

"Why would I stay?" Kiera mumbled. "Izzy and Pete hate me. You hate me. Eddie hates me."

"No one hates you." Danica's words were automatic. She was still in shock. "I just want to talk about..." She gestured back toward the door. "Why Eddie is here?"

Kiera paused, her face blotchy as she met Danica's eyes. "Well, *you* obviously hate me."

Danica stifled an exasperated sigh. "I don't, actually. I'm

pissed, but I'm trying to understand what you were thinking."

Kiera stared down into her hands, silent.

The silence was heavy and unsettling, a stark contrast to the turmoil Danica felt inside. In the four years they were roommates, and the fifteen years since, they'd been in dozens of fights. They'd had every kind of argument, from inane disagreements about air diffuser scents to all-out screaming fights. Danica paused, realizing that their worst fights had always been about Pete. Specifically, about how Kiera always claimed Danica was wasting her time with Pete.

Danica internally fumbled for some way to understand Kiera as she watched her friend shuffle through her makeup, the plastic cases clicking together in the quiet room.

"Did you do this to stop whatever is going on between Pete and I?" Danica asked as calmly as she could.

Kiera tucked a lock of hair behind her ear, catching Danica's eye in the mirror. "You lied to me," she said, her voice cracking. "You let me think that you were still with Eddie, and I saw you throwing that away for some fling with Pete."

"But you didn't stop when you learned Eddie and I were broken up. So, what do you have against Pete?"

"She's always been your greatest weakness."

Danica blinked, shocked. "That's so dramatic and unnecessary."

"You know I'm right. You see Pete and the entire world fades away, all of reality just ceasing to exist. I could see you do it again, and I thought you were doing it to Eddie, too." Kiera zipped her makeup bag shut. "Tell me you wouldn't have talked to Alex if you thought I was cheating on him."

"Fuck Alex. I don't care about Alex. I would have talked to you," Danica said, her tone defiant.

Kiera pushed past Danica in the doorway to throw her makeup bag and toiletries into her suitcase.

"Is that what this is? Is this about Alex's affair?" Danica asked, her words coming out crueler than she'd intended.

"You lied to me!" Kiera snapped, her voice getting louder.

"I did," Danica said, sighing. "I did. And that was fucked up. I'm sorry." She paused, watching Kiera move two pairs of boots around in her suitcase to try to make them fit. "I wasn't ready to tell you. I wasn't ready to tell anyone."

"Why?" Kiera asked, grimacing.

Danica sat down next to Kiera's bags and said, "I felt like I failed."

"So then why don't you give Eddie another chance?" Kiera honestly looked earnest.

Danica scoffed. "Because I don't want to, and you need to respect that."

"Is this another one of your pride things?" Kiera asked, her tone almost smug.

A surge of fury tightened Danica's muscles, her body rigid and tense. "Excuse me?"

"I thought things were good with Eddie. You two seemed happy," Kiera said. "Why would you throw that away because of Pete?"

"First of all, Eddie broke up with *me* a month ago. He said something was off, and that we weren't right together, and you know what? He was right. And second, I've been happier this week than I have in... years, and you should be happy for me," Danica explained, anger giving way to exhaustion.

Kiera rolled her eyes. "Being with Pete is like going to Neverland. No one has any responsibilities and you get to play pretend with her for a while. But she always drops you back into reality and then leaves again. Pete might be fun, but you could actually have a future with Eddie. He exists in the real world, and you're letting him just slip—"

"Stop." Danica held up her hand to keep Kiera from continuing. "Just stop. I don't want to be with Eddie. I don't even want to be friends with Eddie. And I'm not some stupid woman who has let herself be whisked off to play pretend with Pete. I'm not dumb. I know that Pete and I don't have a future."

Kiera looked at her, her jaw clenched tight. "But you and Eddie could have a future. Alex and I aren't happy right now, but we're working through it. Relationships aren't all sunshine and roses. They're hard work."

Danica stiffened, clenching and unclenching her fists. "I don't need a lecture on what relationships are supposed to feel like. You're just miserable in your marriage and you want me to be miserable, too."

A beat of silence made Danica instantly regret the cruelty of her sharp words.

Kiera looked at her with shock, like Danica had just slapped her across the face. "Well, when Pete breaks your heart again, like she always does, I'm not going to be there to pick up the phone at 3 a.m. to listen to you cry. So, I guess we really will both be miserable, won't we?" With that, Kiera zipped her luggage shut and swung open the door, finding Maggie, Pete, and Eddie just outside of it and looking guilty. Pete was focusing very intently on some vintage ski art on the wall, oddly.

Kiera huffed and stormed past them, stomping down the hall and leaving Danica sitting on the edge of the bed. For all her worries, Pete wouldn't be the one breaking her heart at the end of this week, because Kiera already had.

CHAPTER 20

PETE

EDDIE'S METAL WATCH BAND CLICKED AGAINST THE OAK TABLE, A small, precise sound in the otherwise silent room where he sat across from Pete. If she cared about this guy's feelings, she'd pity him for the obvious hurt and dejection in his expression.

So, this was Eddie. Dentist Eddie. He looked so normal in real life, though he had an air about him that screamed privilege. He'd probably grown up in an upper-middle class home, maybe he attended private school, and he dressed as though he could potentially be yacht-adjacent at any moment.

Izzy sat on the couch scrolling through her phone, pretending not to outwardly seethe after they'd ripped Kiera to shreds for inviting Eddie. Kiera had claimed that she was just trying to look out for her friend, but Pete wasn't buying it.

Maggie walked in the front door and paused in the entryway, seeing Eddie at the table. Her jaw dropped and her eyes widened. Thankfully, Eddie's back was to her as Maggie over exaggeratedly mouthed, *"Is that Eddie?"*

Pete gave her a panicked look, nodding. Kiera had offhandedly mentioned Maggie had gone shopping after lunch, but Pete knew Meddling Maggie was going to be sorely disappointed she missed so much drama.

Maggie glanced from Eddie to Izzy, then back to Pete, as if to ask where Danica was. Suddenly, Kiera's muffled voice raised enough to travel down the hallway. "You lied to me!"

Maggie gawked, mouth falling open, and she dropped her shopping bags and scurried off down the hallway. Pete was right behind her, trying to quietly hurry to listen at the door. She turned at the sound of more footsteps, expecting Izzy, but it was Eddie. She couldn't very well tell him to fuck off, not if she wanted to hear what was happening, so she instead didn't give him any room to listen at the door. The three of them lined up, crowding one another as Pete took the tallest spot, Maggie wedged between them, Eddie crouching lowest.

The two women inside of the room weren't exactly whispering, so it was easy to make out what they were saying. Eddie's entire body winced as Danica reiterated that she didn't want to be with him, and Eddie made a small *oof* sound, like he'd just stubbed his toe on the sharp corner of rejection. Pete almost felt bad for the guy.

Could she and Danica have finally gotten it right this time? She wasn't joking about the future with Danica earlier that morning on Galloping Goose — well, looking at the mansions and chalets, pretending they were shopping for real estate was certainly a joke — but she really did like the idea of a future where she and Danica could be together. She could work out of any city with an international airport, and—

"I'm not dumb. I know that Pete and I don't have a future."

Danica's words hit her like she'd just been clotheslined by a tree branch and knocked her to the ground. Embarrassment made her chest ache and tears sting at the edges of her eyes.

Maggie tensed beside her, and before Pete could say anything, Maggie stood with a hiss as they heard footsteps approach the door. Pete spun around, trying to look like she hadn't just been listening to their conversation, panic blunting her rational thinking skills. Art. There was art. She was just admiring the artwork on the wall directly outside of Kiera's room. Half a second later, the door swung open to reveal Kiera's blotchy face, and further in, Danica sitting on the edge of the bed looking very small and upset.

"Where are you going?" Maggie asked, alarmed, as they saw Kiera's packed suitcase.

"I'm leaving," Kiera said with dramatic despair, the luggage wheels abrasive and loud on the hardwood floor as she headed toward the doorway.

Maggie went to follow Kiera just as a car pulled up in front of the condo, but Pete turned back to Danica, only to find that Eddie had started into the room. "Oh no, you don't," Pete said, grabbing Eddie's arm. "Go get in your Uber, man."

To his credit, Eddie barely put up a fight before turning and walking back toward the front door. He'd probably envisioned sweeping Danica off her feet, a romantic notion that now seemed pathetic, and she felt a pang of sympathy for his loss of such an amazing woman.

Now she, too, was losing that incredible woman, the reality hitting her with the force of a physical blow. Pete wasn't some Eddie-type. Danica had said she didn't see a future with Pete, and that stung. But it didn't mean that Pete could just stop caring about her, and she didn't want to. And it didn't mean they had to give up the present, either. She exhaled, then stretched, hooking her hands on top of the door frame as she watched Danica. "You okay?"

"No," Danica said, wiping at her eyes.

"What do you need?" Pete asked, swallowing the lump lodged in her throat. "Company? Alone time? Tea? Wine? A time machine?"

Danica laughed while sniffling. "A time machine does

sound nice." She cleared her throat. "Did you... did you over-hear us?"

Pete shrugged, stretching her shoulders as she rocked back and forth on her heels, still holding the door frame. "Not much," she lied. "I was mainly body-guarding Eddie from shoving through the door and bursting into song to win you back."

There was a tiny smile on Danica's lips as she rolled her eyes and wiped at her nose again. "Listen, I—"

"Nah, don't worry about it," Pete said. "So, company or alone time?"

Danica pressed her lips together, looking around the empty room. "I think alone time. And maybe a bath before dinner, I guess."

"You got it. We can order in if you'd like." Pete used every bit of self-control to suppress the profound hurt echoing through her chest in rhythm with her heart.

Danica kept her gaze down, standing from Kiera's bed. "Thanks," she murmured, and Pete moved to let Danica past her, walking into her own room. Danica's bright blue eyes shone with tears as she glanced up at Pete before closing the door.

Pete took a deep breath, attempting to steady herself, and walked back into the main room to find Izzy still on the couch, scrolling on her phone. She'd tucked herself into a ball, her thick socks pulled up over leggings, nearly eclipsed by a massive fleece jacket that made her look like a teddy bear. Izzy glanced up as Pete walked back into the room and sat beside her on the couch.

"Did you know that crocodiles can regenerate their teeth if they lose one?" Izzy asked after a beat of silence.

Pete let her head fall to the back of the couch. "Huh. That's convenient."

"They can have up to 4,000 teeth in their lifetime," Izzy continued.

Pete's eyes closed, and she took a deep, cleansing breath. "How many do they have at one time?"

"Looks like anywhere from sixty to over a hundred," Izzy answered.

Pete let her head loll to the side to look at Izzy. "That's a lot of teeth."

"They have the strongest bite of any animal in the world," Izzy continued.

Pete frowned. "Are you doing, like, a metaphor thing?"

Izzy's eyes flicked up to Pete's, and she gave a half-smile. "You think I'm trying to make a metaphor for your feelings with crocodile teeth?"

Pete scrutinized her friend. "Are you?"

Izzy shrugged. "I just think crocodiles are cool."

"I think I wouldn't mind my head inside of a crocodile's mouth right now," Pete said, rubbing at her face.

"Their bite is ten times stronger than a great white shark," Izzy said casually.

Pete couldn't help but grin. "Did you know they eat rocks to help them sink to the bottom?"

Izzy's eyes widened with delight and her thumbs flew across her phone screen. "Apparently that's true. How'd you know that?"

Pete was grateful for the distraction. "I had an unfortunate run-in with one in the Philippines once. It didn't attack or anything, but it was a closer call than I'd have preferred. I did some research after and that one fact really stuck in my brain, because what kind of animal eats rocks for a good reason?"

Izzy furrowed her brow. "I'm so jealous that you've been to all of these incredible places. Hire me so I can travel, too." Her tone was joking, but it gave Pete an idea.

Pete brightened. "Alright."

Izzy snorted in amusement. "I was kidding."

"I'm not," Pete said, lifting her head to look at Izzy. "If

bartending long term isn't your dream, and you want a job with the foundation, you've got it."

"Don't you have, like, a board or something?" Izzy asked.

"No," Pete said. "Though lately I've been thinking I should. Want to be on the board?"

Izzy laughed. "No. That sounds awful."

"It does, doesn't it?" Pete agreed. "But I am serious. If I want to continue to grow Second Star, I need to be able to have people I can trust by my side. And I trust you more than anyone."

"I have no experience," Izzy said, looking slightly flustered.

"You're a good person. You can learn the rest," Pete said. "I'll talk to my lawyer when I get back to Seattle. I can call you and we can talk about options."

"Are you being rash because feelings are a little heightened?" Izzy asked, her tone soft.

"I mean, maybe, but I've been considering it for a while." Pete knew Izzy had been struggling with work, but she was sharp and personable. Pete had no doubt Izzy would be a great fit for Second Star.

"And you're not just saying this because Danica clearly did something to upset you?" Izzy asked, and Pete questioned for a moment if Izzy could read her mind. "You had that look when you came back from your embarrassingly conspicuous spy mission."

Pete rubbed at the back of her neck. "I overheard her say to Kiera that she didn't want a future with me," Pete said, dropping her voice to a near-whisper as hurt strangled her words.

Izzy grimaced. "And what did she say about that when you asked her?" Pete must have made another face because she watched Izzy's eyes grow larger with realization. "You didn't say anything?"

"What am I supposed to do? Pour my heart out?" Pete asked.

Izzy's brows rose, and she blinked slowly, as if she was talking to a small child. "Yes," she over-enunciated.

Pete slouched. "I tried that before. Then we didn't talk for fifteen years."

Izzy put a hand on Pete's arm. "What I'm about to say comes from a place of love…"

Pete didn't like the sound of that intro.

"Stop being a fucking idiot. Just go talk to her. You probably misheard what she said, or heard something out of context," Izzy said, slowly and clearly again.

Pete batted away Izzy's hand. "You don't know that."

Izzy leveled her with a long look.

"Okay, okay. I'll talk to her. I can't promise it will go well, though. It might just be graduation night 2.0." Pete relented, but she wasn't happy about the idea. Trying to have a serious talk with Danica about their future had gone so poorly before. The agonizing embarrassment of incorrectly assuming that Danica wanted a future after all… now that would haunt her.

Izzy squeezed Pete's arm again. "Why do you look like you're about to throw up?"

"I haven't heard enough crocodile facts." Pete let her head fall back against the couch cushions.

Just then, Maggie stomped back into the foyer and Pete glanced toward her to find that she was alone. Apparently, she hadn't been successful in her efforts to get Kiera to stay, if that was what she had been trying to do.

"Where'd Kiera go?" Izzy asked, glancing over her shoulder.

Maggie shrugged, walking into the kitchen and grabbing a bottle of red wine. All three women were silent as she uncorked the bottle and brought it into the living room.

"Don't you need a gl— oh, wow, you're really just

drinking that straight from the bottle," Izzy said, watching as Maggie slumped into the chair near the couch.

"What a fucking mess," Maggie groaned, taking another long swig from the bottle before pointing it toward Izzy and Pete in offering.

Pete took the bottle, holding the cool glass against her cheek after taking a large drink. "What a fucking mess, indeed," Pete echoed.

"Did Kiera say where she was going?" Izzy took the bottle from Pete.

Maggie shook her head. "I think she was going to stay in a hotel nearby tonight. Not the same one where Eddie is going. That man is even more helpless than I remember. No wonder Danica loved him at first."

Pete whipped her head sideways to look at Maggie. "What does that mean?"

"She loves being the competent one. She's the one with the spreadsheets and the plans and the control," Maggie said. "We love her for it, don't get me wrong."

Pete furrowed her brow. She didn't see Danica that way at all. She thought Danica liked being needed. It was as though she was continually trying to prove her place, to prove that she was a good friend who deserved to be invited. Around just her, though, Danica was far more relaxed. Playful, even. Fun.

"Glad I never suggested those matching tattoos." Izzy grimaced.

"I should go talk to her," Pete said.

"Obviously," Izzy agreed.

But at the same time, Maggie shook her head. "Not yet."

Pete glanced between the two women. "But you heard her, Mags. She said she didn't see a future with me. Don't you think I need to go talk to her before I lose her forever?"

"Kiera just blew up their friendship. Give Danica some time to process that before she has to consider your feelings, too," Maggie said, taking the wine bottle back from Izzy. "She needs friends right now, not..." Maggie gestured toward Pete, "whatever you two are."

Maggie had a point, but it made Pete feel restless. "You're the one who thought this was all a good idea in the first place." Pete crossed her arms with indignation.

"Yeah, because you're good together. To be honest, I thought if she realized how happy she was with you, she might finally leave Eddie. That guy was such a wet blanket." Maggie sighed, digging her thumb into her temple. "And then when we found out that she and Eddie had already broken up... You two were already pretty cozy, and she seemed excited about it. She seemed like the old Danica, you know? So, I encouraged her, too."

Izzy sighed. "You're all such meddling teenagers."

"Oh, I don't want to hear it, Ms. I-Kissed-Kiera-Once-And-Still-Stare-At-Her-Longingly-When-I-Think-No-One-Is-Watching."

Izzy's cheeks flushed. "I do not."

Pete's mouth dropped open in surprise as she turned to look at Izzy. "Are you in love with Kiera?"

"No," Izzy's eyes were wide as saucers. "I'm not."

Both Pete and Maggie stared at her, and Pete could see how uncomfortable she was growing under their intense scrutiny.

"She's *married*," Izzy said.

"Her husband is cheating on her," Maggie said, with a hint of boredom.

Pete nearly leapt off the couch, but Izzy froze. "He is?" Izzy asked, her voice strained.

"Yeah, and she's still staying with him for some reason," Maggie said, shrugging her shoulders. "It's so weird to me. Who would do that to themselves?"

"That's so sad," Pete commented, aware her words didn't fully capture the complexity.

Izzy tapped her fingers on the wine bottle, which they had continued to pass around. "No wonder she got so upset thinking that Danica was cheating on Eddie. She knows how it feels." Like a narrator of a Greek tragedy, her voice dripped with sorrow as she described the event, making no effort to explain their friend's despicable act.

Maggie sat up straighter, pulling a bag of candy out of her hoodie pocket. "Hey, I forgot I put these in here," she said, holding up a bag of weed gummies. "Should we get high and order Taco Bell for delivery?"

"Fuck yes," a voice chimed in from the other side of the living room, and Pete turned with surprise to find Danica standing in her pajamas, her hair tied up in a bun. A few pieces had fallen around the nape of her neck and her face, curled from the steam of the bath.

A nervous flutter filled Pete's stomach as she saw Danica. Danica's tear-stained face, though heartbreaking, only amplified her inherent loveliness. She watched as Danica sat on the floor near the coffee table and inspected the bag thoroughly, then grabbed out a handful of gummies and popped them in her mouth.

"Oh my god, Wendell! You don't even know how strong they are," Pete said with surprise, taking one.

Danica looked at her like she was being ridiculous. "Come on. They're basically just candy; how strong can they be?"

CHAPTER 21

DANICA

"This is the best thing I've ever tasted," Danica heard herself say as she crunched on the freshly fallen snow she held in the palm of her mitten.

"Better than a Baja Blast?" Maggie asked beside her as she shivered in the cold.

The four of them stood out on the deck, their breath fogging the air around them as they admired the view of Mountain Village at night. The resort was lit up only by the snowcats grooming the trails late in the evening. Snow had begun falling steadily as they'd started in on their Taco Bell feast, and now, two hours later, a fresh inch coated the world. The night smelled crisp and cold, with a hint of firewood smoke, and she wanted to bottle the moment to keep forever, delicious snow and all. Every sensation felt magnified, like the world was in syrupy slow-motion and hyper-color.

"I'd spend so much money to have a Baja Blast snow cone," Danica said, her mouth watering at the thought. "Why didn't I save any of my drink? I just chugged it and now it's gone." Her despair felt oddly heightened. She'd eaten the handful of weed gummies earlier, desperate to drown out the pain of what Kiera had said to her during their fight. Kiera's actions — the lies, the deception, her harsh, unresolved exit — left a bitter taste in her mouth, a sense of injustice and hurt.

What she'd lacked in foresight about her THC tolerance, she made up for in the very, very good mood she was in now. The few times she'd smoked weed back in college, she'd been too anxious to enjoy herself, but now she felt mellow and loose and *wow*, snow was the most delicious thing in the world. She liked the way it crunched in her mouth, melting on her tongue.

"How much snow can she eat before hyponatremia sets in?" Izzy asked beside her. "Does it help or hurt that she ate three Crunchwraps?"

Danica considered the thought, staring down at the snow in her hand. "Whoa, you guys. I just remembered that snow is frozen water."

Pete snorted in amusement, putting an arm around her waist to hold her steady. "Let's take a break on snow snacks for now, Wendell."

"Let's take a break from being outside. It's fucking freezing," Maggie said, and Izzy agreed.

Danica glanced sidelong at Pete, not feeling the cold at all. For some reason, the sight of Pete made her want to burst into tears.

"You guys go in. We'll be right behind you in a moment," Pete said, her eyes flicking to Danica's mouth. No, to Danica's quivering chin. She looked as though she may burst into tears at any moment.

Danica heard Izzy and Maggie's crisp steps through the snow on the deck to walk back inside.

"You okay?" Pete asked.

"You betcha," Danica said with forced vigor. If she looked at Pete's perfect face for much longer, she was going to really start sobbing. She tilted her head skyward, looking up at the stars. "Look, your dog is right above us." She pointed up to Canis Major, Sirius' bright sparkle ever-obvious.

Pete snorted in amusement. "You know why I always loved Canis Major?"

"It's easy to find?" Danica asked.

"Because I always wanted a dog," Pete said. "To me, kids in stable homes had dogs. Dogs were loyal in a way that I wanted. Families on TV had dogs, which meant they had chosen to care for something for a lifetime. I always thought that if I was adopted, my family would have a dog."

Danica's heart clenched, and tears stung her eyes. "Did any of your foster families have dogs?"

Pete shook her head. "Nope. The longest I ever stayed with one was three years — that was where I met Lillian. But they had a bunch of foster kids, so adding a dog into the mix probably wouldn't have been a good idea. So, Canis Major was my dog. The stars were familiar, the same wherever I went. I'd imagine flying through them late at night, all alone but not lonely."

"Why didn't you get a dog when you graduated college?" Danica asked, wiping tears at her cheeks. She stared up at Canis Major, picturing a young Pete looking up at the same constellation to bring herself some comfort. Her heart ached for Pete in those moments.

Pete shrugged, leaning on the deck railing. "I traveled too much. It wouldn't have been fair."

"And now?" Danica asked.

Pete turned, her cheeks flushed in the cold. "I don't know what the future holds. I know what I want the future to hold, but... that's something we should talk about when you haven't eaten, like, two hundred milligrams of edibles."

A long silence stretched between them, interrupted only by the muffled sounds of the other people in Mountain Village. Danica didn't know how to respond to that — didn't know if she should respond to that. Her head felt floaty, like it might untie from her neck at any moment. She reached to hold the edges of her beanie to keep her head attached. "I'm way too high for this conversation," she said finally, her cheeks burning with embarrassment.

Pete grinned. "I know. Let's go back inside."

"But I want to look at the stars," Danica whined, and Pete laughed quietly behind her, ushering her back inside as she traversed the slippery terrain of the patio.

Maggie and Izzy sat on the couch watching something on TV, but Danica took one look and decided she'd rather go lie down just in case her head decided to detach again. Pete walked her into her room, setting a fresh glass of water on her nightstand.

"Do you still have that app?" Danica asked.

"What app?" Pete asked, pulling her pajamas out of a drawer. She gestured for Danica to raise her arms, and Danica did, letting Pete undress her.

"The one you made. The night sky flying simulator?" Danica asked.

Pete looked a little bashful at the suggestion. "I do. Why?"

"I want to play it," Danica said, raising her arms again as Pete pulled her pajama shirt over her head. "I think I am exactly the right amount of high for that right now."

Pete grinned. "Okay. I'll go grab my computer in a minute. But stand up first."

With her hands on Pete's shoulders for balance, Danica let Pete remove her snow-wet sweatpants, replacing them with pajama pants. Pete had undressed her countless times, but the gentle way she dressed Danica in her pajamas now felt so tender and intimate that Danica wanted to burst into tears again.

Pete got her settled in bed, then left and returned with her laptop. "This is the only updated version I have," she explained, opening the laptop and hitting a few buttons before turning it toward Danica.

Danica's eyes widened, looking at the elaborate Start menu, tiny pinpricks of starlight swirling around the screen. Maybe it was the great design, maybe it was the great edibles, but the sheer artistry of the app was one of the most beautiful things she'd ever seen. Pete settled beside her and gave her pointers for starting, and then Danica was maneuvering her way through the stars. Though the game took liberties with time and space, it was fun as hell. She sailed around Canis Major, then down into Lepus, the constellation she'd always said was her favorite.

"I lied," Danica said calmly as she circled the Lepus Nebula, lilac and tangerine colors swirling around the screen like a giant eye.

Pete tensed beside her. "What about?"

"I said that Lepus was my favorite because it was near yours, but what I really liked about it was that the dog was chasing the hare. I used to think you'd follow me anywhere." Another blush of shame accompanied Danica's whispered words.

Pete's expression went feather-soft. "I *would* follow you anywhere, Danica." A whispered promise.

"You're just saying that. You're not serious." Danica wiped hastily at her eyes.

Pete's lips brushed over her temple. "I think we could get it right this time. I want a future with you, I want... Wait, why are you crying so hard?"

This time, the tears actually happened, coming suddenly, like she was a fizzing drink that had finally spilled over. "Don't worry, it's just the gummies. I'm totally, totally fine." A terrible lie. She was just too overwhelmed to talk about such a scary thing. She couldn't even fathom the future right now without crying harder.

"We can talk about this more tomorrow." Pete took Danica in her arms, moving the laptop off to the side of the bed.

"Let's get some sleep, huh?" she said in the gentle voice people used for upset children.

"Okay," Danica said through snot and sniffles and tears. Suddenly, she was deathly parched. She reached for her water, taking a few gulps, then settled back down against Pete. "I'm sorry I'm such a mess. I've always been such a mess."

"You're one of the least messy people I've ever met," Pete said with a chuckle, resting her cheek on Danica's head. "Take a deep breath. I'm here. I'm with you."

Danica did as she was told, clutching Pete as she drifted off to sleep.

She awoke in the early dawn hours, starving and thirsty. Her phone said it was only 5 a.m., but she was wide awake. Pete had stayed beside her all night and slept in her clothes. The thought made Danica smile with tenderness as she gazed at the woman in her bed.

In the cold reality of morning, a heavy weight settled in her stomach. The words Pete had said the night before, the future she wanted — it wasn't real. Pete had always lived in an idealistic world where love was enough, but Danica was stuck firmly in reality.

Pete deserved someone who could adventure with her. Someone who could drop everything and fly off into the night at a moment's notice. Someone who she'd be excited to follow. They were too different. Pete would grow to resent her eventually.

Pete's words last night had sent her reeling. She hadn't been in the right headspace to understand exactly what Pete had been saying the night before, but she sure was now. Pete wanted a future that Danica couldn't give her.

Danica had spent the past few days trying to imagine what a future with Pete might look like, but she couldn't picture herself fitting into Pete's life or Pete fitting into hers.

They had chemistry and a genuine connection, but was that enough?

She didn't expect that after spending time with Pete again, enjoying her company, feeling old familiar comfort and sparks would lead to this. She had thought that she could have a fun fling that might help her feel confident and happy and distracted. Instead, a tender, vulnerable emotion had crept up over the past few days, settling in with confidence the night before. An emotion that terrified her more than anything. A feeling she was too scared to let take root.

Kiera had already left her so raw and hurting. She couldn't risk that kind of loss again. Not from Pete. It would hurt far worse.

Pete slept deeply as Danica silently gathered her belongings and slipped from the room. She carried her suitcase to avoid the sound of the wheels on the hardwood and noted the rich, nutty scent of brewed coffee. The sight of Izzy at the island, enjoying coffee and a magazine, sent her pulse soaring with anxiety. She'd been hoping to make a clean getaway.

Izzy glanced up to where Danica awkwardly clutched her suitcase in her arms. "Are you leaving?" she asked quietly, her tone falling somewhere between curiosity and understanding. Far nicer than Danica felt she deserved.

"Yeah, it's a long drive," Danica said awkwardly.

"Pete still asleep?" Maggie asked from behind her, and this time Danica nearly dropped her suitcase.

She nodded, feeling the familiar warmth of shame in her cheeks. "Yeah. Sorry, I just..." She didn't know what to say. That she was a coward? That she was panicking about what Pete had said the night before?

"What a week, huh?" Maggie said with a gentle smile, making Danica put her suitcase down for a hug.

Danica let out an exhausted laugh. "What a fucking week."

"Here, I'll help you carry that out to your car," Izzy said, appearing beside her and lifting her suitcase.

"Oh, you don't have to — thank you," Danica stammered in surprise.

"Let me know when you make it home," Maggie said, watching Danica pull on her ski jacket.

Danica nodded, giving Maggie another hug. "You, too. Give Gwen and the kids a hug for me." She opened the front door and led Izzy to where her SUV was parked in the small parking lot. At least driving herself wouldn't make her as car sick as when she was a passenger. She planned to stop halfway in Grand Junction to grab a late breakfast or early lunch, and try to make it home by early afternoon.

How Kiera was getting home, she didn't know and didn't care at this moment. Not that she was any better than Kiera now, leaving Pete without saying goodbye. It was a different kind of leaving, but it was still the same. Easier than staying and seeing where it would lead. Easier than confronting the inevitable questions she had no answers for. No big fight in the quad to remember and analyze for years after. No regrets about missed moments. Just... leaving. She rubbed her temples as the ache in her chest deepened. Maybe this was the problem with always taking the "easy way out." They couldn't hold on to just the good memories forever. They couldn't freeze time. They couldn't keep pretending like everything would be fine when they knew it wouldn't.

But this way, she thought, this way, at least they could focus on the good things, right? They could remember the sweet moments, the easy laughter, the way everything had felt lighter, simpler. The way it had been before she'd let herself get too close. Before she'd allowed herself to care. Because once she cared, once she felt it all, the exit was never easy. It never would be.

She hit the remote start to get her defroster going, then unlocked her trunk for Izzy to place the suitcase inside. She chucked the suitcase carelessly into the car, then turned to give Danica a serious look.

"She cares about you," Izzy said, her voice firm.

Danica blinked in surprise. "What?"

"Pete. Obviously, Pete. I won't pretend to understand what you're doing just leaving like this, or what you two discussed last night, but I do know that she cares about you, and now you're sneaking out like a thief in the morning. She doesn't deserve that."

Danica stepped back to shut the trunk of her car. The familiar sting of unshed tears pressed against her throat, thickening the air. "I know."

"So, why do this to her, then?" Izzy said, crossing her arms.

"Because we don't have a future together," Danica said impatiently.

"Says who? Because I know she's not saying that. In fact, I bet she's already planning how to move to Denver to be with you," Izzy said, her brows furrowed as her eyes stayed steady on Danica.

Danica blinked away the tears that had begun forming in her eyes. "I can't ask her to do that. It'd be like putting a bird in a cage."

Izzy huffed with exasperation. "Pete isn't a bird. She's a human being who loves you."

Danica's eyes stung from the cold and the tears welling within them. She used her ice scraper to aggressively clear the ice from her windshield.

"You're lying to yourself," Izzy said, her voice raised and her cheeks flushed.

Danica stopped to glare across the car's hood. "You don't even know me."

"I've known you since we were eighteen. I know you pretend to be some person who has it all together and that you can't handle when your life isn't perfect."

"Spare me the soapbox life lessons," Danica said, fuming. Izzy's words were dangerously close to mirroring the little voice in the back of her head that always told her she wasn't trying hard enough. "I wasn't ready to talk about Eddie—"

"I'm not talking about Eddie! I don't even care about him. Just because you don't show it doesn't mean you aren't struggling."

Danica paused, staring at Izzy. Her body shook with cold. She was not wearing the right shoes to be getting lectured in a parking lot in below freezing temperatures. "Why do you care?"

"I care about Pete, and she cares about you. And I know that she's spent the last fifteen years trying to get over you by running all over the globe, working hard to build and help others. Then it dawned on me last night when she told me wants to travel less, be more stable and build a life. There's only one person who she'd do that for." Izzy pulled her fleece jacket tighter around her against the chill of daybreak.

Danica moved to the other side of the car to continue clearing her windshield. "I don't want her to compromise anything for me."

"Believe me, I don't either. But you have to let her make her own decisions," Izzy said. "Instead, you're being a stubborn, proud idiot. Just like you usually are."

"Wow, Izzy. Thank you for the pep talk." Danica clenched her jaw.

"Just…" Izzy sighed with frustration. "Just think about it." Izzy's expression had softened, which made Danica second-guess her reluctance to listen.

"There's nothing more to think about." Danica opened the driver's side door, tossing the ice scraper onto the passenger side floor.

"You know what I mean. Don't shut Pete out again."

Danica shook her head, anxious to get away from this conversation. "Have a good one, Izzy."

Izzy grumbled something about how *at least she'd tried* and turned to walk inside.

Danica turned up her seat heater, rubbing her hands together to feel warmth again. She wiped at her eyes, confused by what Izzy had said to her. Izzy had voiced Danica's worst fears — that everyone saw through her facade. Had she been the one to shut Pete out before? Pete had been far more casual about a future with Danica when they'd had their big fight in the quad on graduation night, but she'd at least wanted to see what would happen. It had been Danica who had told her she was being an idealistic, immature idiot.

Was she doing the same thing all over again?

She paused, glancing back at the condo, half-expecting to see Pete standing there, but the door was closed. The snow crunched under the tires as she turned out of the lot and onto the road toward home.

It didn't matter. She wouldn't ask Pete to change for her, and Pete couldn't ask her to sacrifice her stability. They were just too different. They wanted different things.

Didn't they?

CHAPTER 22

PETE

PETE AWOKE TO SHAKING. IN HER SLEEP-ADDLED STATE, HER FIRST thought was of the Cascadia Earthquake, here to take her at last. She jolted upright, confused to find that instead of a catastrophic tectonic event, it was just Izzy and Maggie jumping on her bed. Well, Danica's bed.

Danica. The one she'd been chasing without realizing it all this time.

"Come on, get up so we can get a few runs in this morning before our flight," Izzy said.

Pete looked around, still confused. "Where's Danica?"

Maggie and Izzy both paused their quaking, looking at her like they felt sorry for her.

"Where is she?" Pete repeated, throwing her blankets off. She'd slept in her clothes last night, too afraid of leaving Danica's side, too afraid of the feelings that she'd let herself voice. She'd held Danica all night, not allowing herself to think of what daylight might bring.

Pete knew — deep down she knew exactly where Danica was, but she had to hear them say it.

"She left early," Maggie said in an exceedingly gentle voice.

Pete blinked, a resonating ache in her chest nearly stealing her breath. Why would Danica leave without talking to her? She grabbed her phone to call Danica, a shock of pain as the call went straight to voicemail.

Maggie and Izzy were watching her warily, like they were ready to comfort her, should she ask. She cleared her throat and pushed her hair out of her face. "Did she say why she left?"

Izzy shook her head. "No." Her tone was flat, and Pete could tell she was angry.

Maggie shot Izzy a look. "It's a long drive home," she said, ever the peacekeeper.

"I think you both just need some time. Come on, let's go forget about the real world for another couple of hours," Izzy said.

Pete noticed Maggie wasn't wearing her sling and was flexing her wrist. Maggie shrugged her shoulders. "I feel fine. I'll take it easy."

Pete looked back down at her phone, at the contact she had saved for Danica. It had a picture she'd taken of her lying on the ground whining about snowboarding, and made Pete smile as she looked at it. Now, she didn't know if she would even need Danica's number. By leaving without a word, Danica had sent a very clear message about her priorities, and Pete obviously wasn't one of them.

Pete swallowed. "Sure, just… Give me a moment."

A hollow space seemed to open up inside her chest, a cold draft sweeping through her body as if Danica had taken more than just her presence with her. It wasn't the silence that stung — it was the absence of the goodbye.

She had imagined a thousand different endings, each one filled with something, *anything*, to acknowledge what they had shared over the last few days. But this? This was an abrupt, jagged emptiness.

She grabbed her phone as if she could call Danica, ask her what happened, demand some kind of explanation. But the words wouldn't come. They just felt stupid, unnecessary, as if to ask would only remind her that there had never been a promise, never a guarantee.

Danica hadn't even said goodbye. The thought dug into Pete's skin like a splinter, sharp and painful. She had expected something more — maybe not a dramatic farewell, but a moment. A kiss. A word. A fucking explanation. Instead, the only thing she had was the heavy, oppressive quiet, the echo of her own thoughts filling the room like a distant hum.

She should be used to this. She had been waiting for this, hadn't she? She knew better. But it felt different with Danica. There was something in the way they had talked, the way they had laughed, the way everything felt so effortlessly right between them this time.

So, why had she just… walked away?

Pete could feel the sting of something sharp gathering in her throat, a mix of confusion and hurt, but she swallowed it back. Crying wouldn't bring Danica back.

But the ache lingered.

Her heart kept pacing in her chest, a steady drumbeat of *What now? What now? What now?* and the answer was nothing. Nothing at all.

Her eyes drifted to the spot on the bed where they had fallen asleep together, tangled in the covers like two things that had fit perfectly into each other. The memory should've felt sweet, but it only hurt now, like a bruise she couldn't stop rubbing.

The promises of the night before looped endlessly in her mind, too heavy to let go of, too sharp to ignore.

She composed herself and stood, the moment feeling so

final. Maybe the wind in her face, the rush of adrenaline, and the quiet of the mountain would do her some good.

Maggie insisted they stick to blues, taking it easy on her healing arm and Pete's emotional state. "We don't need two injuries today," she'd said. She was right, but Izzy and Pete both grumbled on the lift. They planned to hit a few trails, grab lunch at Bon Vivant, then head out.

Izzy handed Pete a small shooter of whiskey, but Pete declined, opting for honey water in her flask instead. A sudden stop of the lift brought back the memory of Danica's earlier panic attack on the chairlift, a near-hysterical episode averted only by Pete's distraction of picking a fight. Had that only been this week? It felt like so long ago.

"Do you think a very mild concussion could cause enough short-term memory loss to forget most of this week ever happened?" Pete asked, pointing to a patch of trees nearby. "Nothing life-threatening. Just enough for a bit of amnesia."

"Yikes, buddy," Izzy said.

Maggie patted Pete's shoulder. "It wasn't all bad. Remember when I got to ride on that rescue toboggan?"

Izzy glanced sideways at her. "Or karaoke night? I'll never forget nearly blowing a vocal cord screaming to Alanis."

"It would have been a little *ironic*, but that vocal cord would have gone out as a hero," Maggie said with a self-satisfied giggle.

"Remember when I had to play a full round of truth or dare with socks on my hands?" Izzy asked.

"Oh, or when I hit you right between the eyes with a snowball?" Maggie added excitedly.

Pete cracked a smile at that one. "Okay, maybe just short-term memory loss centered around one... maybe two people, then."

"I mean, I'm pretty sure the message of Eternal Sunshine would say that you can't have the good memories without the bad ones," Maggie said, swinging her skis.

Izzy sighed, her breath swirling in the cold air in front of her face. "We could save a tree and I could just club you over the head with my board."

"A very kind offer," Pete said with a huff of amusement. "Very environmentally-friendly."

"Sustainable concussions. You could market that," Maggie added. "Like dolphin-friendly tuna. Tree-friendly ski injuries."

The lift shuddered into action again, pulling them forward, and they fell into a companionable silence. Pete tried to rein in all of the runaway ideas she had about chasing after Danica. How long did you chase someone who never stopped running?

"Maybe our next trip should just be the three of us," Maggie said finally, and Pete nodded in agreement. "Has anyone heard from Kiera?" Maggie glanced toward Izzy.

Izzy shook her head. "Nope. I have no idea. Maybe she and Eddie caught a ride back to Denver together or something."

"Maybe," Pete said, chewing her lip thoughtfully. She idly wondered if Danica would ever forgive Kiera for what she'd done.

A new thought popped into her head, causing tears to sting at the corners of her eyes. She didn't know if she'd ever see Danica again. Maybe she'd just been something Danica had to get out of her system. A fun plaything to leave on vacation. She'd really been a fool for thinking they were beginning something new. They were just temporarily picking up where they'd left off, that was all.

Lift 4 lowered into the station and the three of them made their way to the run. Thankfully, the ease of Boomerang, a wide blue run, loosened the tension in her shoulders as she took a wide, carving path down the run, enjoying the fresh inch or so of snow that had fallen the night before. Izzy and

Maggie were right. This was the best way to clear her mind and spend her last day.

After completing their run, they hopped on Lift 5, and Pete felt invigorated. Sitting between Izzy and Maggie, she wrapped an arm around both of their shoulders. "Thank you for putting up with my bullshit this week. I love you both."

"I love you, too, bud," Maggie said, patting Pete's thigh.

"Don't get all sappy now," Izzy said, but she laid her head on Pete's shoulder for a quick moment.

"You know, this week may not have gone the way we all thought it would, but I wouldn't trade it for anything."

Izzy and Maggie murmured their agreement as the lift lowered and the three clambered their way out of the lift station.

"Last one down buys crepes," Maggie called playfully, pushing toward Polar Queen with a laugh. Izzy and Pete scrambled to clip their bindings, and Izzy hopped into place, following behind Maggie.

Pete paused, watching her two friends interlace paths down the mountain, and she could hear their laughter. In that moment, surrounded by snowcapped evergreens, white-tipped mountains, and the crispness of the cold air, her heavy heart felt a bit lighter.

Pete loved flying. She'd never been afraid of flying, but she'd been on so many planes she'd begun to take it for granted. Still, it was just a little more exciting to be on a small plane taking off from one of the most gorgeous places she'd ever been. The plane from Telluride to Denver was tiny, with only about 30 seats on board, and she felt extra bougie as she settled back into the leather seat, pretending she was on a private plane with her two best friends. What would teenage Pete think of the life she lived now, spending a week in a luxury condo in Telluride to ski, then flying on a tiny plane back to Denver?

She and Izzy shared the two-seat side of the plane while

Maggie took the single seat across the aisle. The engine was eye-level out the window and loud, but didn't block the stunning mountain surround as the plane lined up on the runway. The landing strip was short, and Maggie had panicked about it when they'd flown in, so Pete reached across the aisle to offer her hand to Maggie now, knowing the takeoff would be fast and likely just as steep.

"So long, Telluride," Izzy said toward the window as the plane lifted at the end of the runway. Maggie's grip tightened on her hand and Pete smiled reassuringly.

Immediately at the end of the runway was a ravine with a creek, and then it was granite and snowy mountains as far as she could see. Unfortunately, they were pointed in the wrong direction to see the resort, even as they craned their necks to look back for one last goodbye.

Here, so high above it all, everything from the week seemed to fade. The laughter, the excitement, the worry, the pain... Thousands of feet in the air now, everything mattered just a little less.

Pete closed her eyes, letting the sound of the engine drown out her thoughts. She'd go back to Seattle. She'd continue building Second Star, hire Izzy, find a happy medium between travel and home. Maybe she'd get out to see Lillian soon. Maybe she'd get a dog, finally.

She'd be okay.

She always was, eventually.

CHAPTER 23

DANICA

"You look terrible."

Danica turned to find her favorite nurse practitioner, Annie, standing in the doorway of their shared office with two cups of coffee. She rubbed at her eyes, her vision still blurry as she reached for the cup. Annie paused, then handed her both.

"Did I miss something? Is something wrong?" Annie asked, brushing her bright white hair out of her face as she tossed her scrub cap into her desk.

"I'm fine," Danica lied.

Annie surveyed her. "Isn't this your third overnight in the last week? Is that even legal?"

Danica shrugged. "I took a week off last month for that ski trip, so I have to make it up to everyone who covered my shifts."

Annie hooked a thumb toward the hallway with the on-call rooms. "You know we can sleep at night, right? You look like you haven't closed your eyes for—"

"You don't actually have to finish that extremely flattering compliment you were about to give me," Danica said, scoffing in amusement. "Hey, did you see the new blood test numbers for baby Kirby?"

Annie glanced at her watch. "Don't you try to distract me."

Danica couldn't help but grin. She knew damn well that Annie had already been on the watch for hypocalcemia with one of their favorite patients and she'd figured that it would be an easy distraction. She sipped the bitter, burnt coffee that most likely came from the team room, where the well-meaning new resident had taken to making the worst coffee in the world.

It was nice to be back here after her week away. It felt... not exactly normal, but familiar. Life inside the NICU could feel like a vacuum. Nothing outside of the unit existed for the time she spent there. She could entirely devote herself to her patients, to figuring out the puzzles of strange dips in calcium levels, to sit and talk to her patient's parents to come to an agreement for the best treatment plan. It was exactly the situation she needed right now — too intense and challenging to spend any extra time thinking about Pete.

She'd taken on so many additional shifts because her time outside of the NICU felt like it passed in slow motion. Just two days ago, she'd cried in the produce section of the grocery store while Roxette's "It Must Have Been Love" blared from tinny speakers overhead. Flustered, she'd abandoned her empty cart and driven home in silence. She'd racked up so many shifts taking over for colleagues that they'd all be indebted to her for months.

Though her sleep in the on-call room was shallow and broken, it was far better than the sleep she'd been getting at home. Valentine's Day had come and gone, reminding her just how alone she was.

Six weeks had passed, and Danica still woke up some mornings with the faint, lingering scent of Pete's coconut and apricot shampoo, as if a part of her was now permanently imprinted on Danica's belongings.

But that moment, the one where she left without a word, haunted her like a ghost. It had been so easy to leave. Maybe too easy. She'd told herself it was because she was the one who couldn't do this — couldn't have this. Not with Pete, not with anyone. There were reasons, all these carefully constructed reasons: she wasn't ready, she wasn't good enough, she didn't know how to stay without losing herself in the process of trying to live up to Pete's ideals.

But every night, when she let herself think about it — really think about it — her heart ached. And sometimes she couldn't tell if it was regret, or something else, something deeper.

The quiet replayed in her mind. How she had silently packed her things, then slipped out without a goodbye. How she'd told herself it was the only way — get out before it hurt too much, before she got too attached. But she had gotten attached, and it had hurt anyway. More than she'd expected. More than she'd wanted to admit.

She could still hear Pete's laugh, warm and soft, echoing in her chest, like a part of her heart had stayed behind in that room.

Danica had tried not to think about Pete for weeks, tried to bury the memory in the mundane rhythm of her life, the intensity of her work. But there was always a gap, an open space where something important should have been. Her mind wandered back to their last conversation, how Pete had said she'd follow her anywhere — until she'd left so Pete couldn't make good on that promise.

Every time she thought about Pete, a tightness in her chest made her want to reach out, to say the things she hadn't said before, but she was too scared to ruin it even further. What if Pete had moved on? What if Pete hated her for what she'd done? What if Pete had just been wrapped up in the moment and never really intended for them to have a future?

Her fingers hovered over her phone, thinking about texting — just a simple, stupid "Hey" or maybe an apology, something to bridge the gap between them — but she always stopped herself. Every message she drafted felt inadequate, like no combination of words would ever explain why she had run, why she had cut things off the way she had.

Maybe Pete wouldn't even want to hear from her. Maybe it was better this way, to let the past stay where it belonged.

Then there were moments when Danica couldn't shake the memory of Pete's touch, her smile, the way everything had felt so damn real. The ache in her chest grew sharper, more insistent. It didn't make sense, but it was there, and it was unavoidable.

She wanted to believe it wasn't too late. That maybe, just maybe, Pete was still thinking about her the way she was thinking about her. The longer she waited, the more she wondered if she had already lost that chance.

There was something about Pete. Something that made Danica feel safe, seen. And that scared the hell out of her.

The hardest part wasn't just that she had left — it was that she didn't know how to come back.

"So, Friday works, then?" Annie was saying.

Danica blinked, coming back to the present. "Sorry, what's Friday?"

"The dinner party at my house. Michaela will be there," Annie explained. Michaela, her niece, had recently moved to Denver and Annie had been trying to set them up ever since she found out Danica and Eddie were officially over. Danica had told her for weeks that she wasn't interested in dating anyone, but Annie had promised that they should at least try to be friends. Danica interpreted the insistence as Annie's belief that all queer women in her life would get along, and if Michaela was anything like Annie, she was sure that was true. The fact was that she just wasn't ready. She couldn't open that part of herself again.

"Oh, right," Danica said, nodding. "Yeah, I couldn't get out of the plans with my parents." Her parents wouldn't have cared if she'd postponed their biweekly dinner to go meet new friends — in fact, they'd been encouraging her to venture into exploring what a healthier work-life balance could look like. She just wasn't ready to be set up with someone. It wasn't fair to the other person, and it also made her feel ashamed to admit to herself that it wasn't that she was getting over a broken engagement *and* a recently reopened heartbreak wound.

Friday was the start of six days off in a row, and she was dreading having so much time alone with her thoughts. Maybe she'd beg one of her other colleagues to switch a shift with her halfway through to break up the monotony.

"Next time, then?" Annie asked.

Danica nodded. "Next time."

Distracted, she tugged at the drawstring to her scrub pants, retying them in a tighter bow. She glanced at the clock. She had to attend a scheduled C-section in about twenty minutes, and wanted to complete the statistics for a bedside meeting before the end of her shift for an expectant mother in the antepartum unit.

Marina, the nutritionist, popped her head into the office. "Oh, hi Danica. Annie, I wanted to talk to you about Kirby's calcium levels."

Danica stretched, yawned, and tipped the coffee cup up to finish the last drops of the blessed caffeine. "I'm going to go check on a chest tube seal before this birth. See you in the OR, Annie?"

Annie gave her a thumbs up, and Danica stood from her desk, her clogs clicking against the floor as she tucked a few loose strands of hair back into her scrub cap.

She'd chosen this. The sharp scent of disinfectant, the soft hush of sliding glass doors, the rhythmic beeping of monitors, the occasional alarm — everything in its place, predictable, structured. It calmed her soul. Before the trip last month, it had been enough. The hospital was her world, a place where she could bury everything — the noise in her head, the weight of her loneliness, the ache of unspoken words.

But now, as she rubbed hand sanitizer onto her palms and pulled a pair of gloves from the dispenser, something unsettled her. The hollow feeling had started small, like a pinprick, but it was growing. She couldn't ignore it, even as she checked the chest tube with practiced hands. Her patient was stable. Everything was fine. Yet her mind drifted back to the last days of her time off — the long conversations, the laughter, the deep connection she'd felt with her friends, with Pete. It had felt real, something she hadn't experienced in a long time, and it had left a void now that she was back to this — her routine, her walls.

She hadn't reached out to Kiera, not after the way they'd left things. The betrayal hanging between them was too much to face. More than that, she missed Pete. Not just the romantic moments, but the way Pete had made her feel seen. It had been so easy, so comfortable. It was something Danica didn't even realize she needed until it was gone.

Her heart tightened. She hadn't expected it to hurt this much. The hospital, the patients, the daily grind — it was all still there, still familiar. Now, it felt emptier somehow. She didn't want to admit it, but the life she had built felt like it was missing something, someone. And that terrified her.

She glanced down at the monitor again—stable vitals, nothing to worry about. But her chest felt heavy in a way the machines couldn't measure.

Her pager buzzed with the code for an accidental extubation in room 27, for a baby just down the hallway. Her mind focused and she forgot entirely about her self-pity as she spun, nearly crashing into the respiratory therapist in the hall.

She had work to do. Important work. She couldn't just wallow in self-pity all day. She'd chosen this, and she had to stop dwelling on past regrets and mistakes and What Ifs to be here in the present. She'd owed her patients — she owed herself — that much.

Danica got a notification that her groceries were being delivered. She was still avoiding the produce section like a coward after she'd cried into that heap of cabbages. She had about two hours to get herself ready and also make the salad she'd offered to bring to her parents' house for dinner — her step-dad had called earlier to remind her and bribe her with one of her favorite meals. Maybe she'd get drunk and sleep in her old bedroom so that she wouldn't have to face six entire days alone.

She opened the door expecting to find grocery bags but stilled as she saw Kiera standing on her doorstep, her hand raised as if she was about to knock. She wore a long wool coat over a matching lounge set and sneakers. To top off the look, she wore a navy-blue baseball hat that just said "Sports!" Danica had never seen her in a hat, and the sight was uncanny, like Kiera was wearing the costume of a casual person.

Kiera's shoulders lifted in surprise. "Um. Hey," she said, tucking a strand of her short hair behind her ear like she didn't know what to do with her raised hand. She fidgeted and adjusted her glasses.

"What are you doing here?" Danica asked, more shocked than angry, even though her tone tip-toed the line between the two emotions.

"Can we talk?" Kiera asked, looking past her into the condo. "Inside, preferably? I'm about to lose a toe to frostbite out here."

Danica's grip tightened on the salad bowl and she didn't move from the doorway. Two warring thoughts battled inside of her — how relieved she was to see Kiera again and how angry and hurt she still felt about what Kiera had done.

Kiera stood, wringing her hands, as Danica stared at her in silence. Danica's eyes locked on the gesture, noticing that Kiera's hands were bare. No wedding ring. She glanced back up to meet Kiera's gaze.

Her best friend had dark circles under her eyes, which were red-rimmed and puffy.

Footsteps interrupted them as a confused man delivering her groceries approached, his arms full of two paper bags holding her salad ingredients. She waved, taking the groceries while thanking him, then turned back to Kiera with her arms full now.

"I have to make a salad," Danica said, feeling like it was a stupid excuse even as the words left her mouth.

Kiera silently shifted her weight from foot to foot.

"How are your radish slicing skills?" Danica asked. She was not ready to be the first to say she was sorry. Not this time.

"I'd say above average," Kiera said, her eyes darting past her and into her condo.

"Want to help me get this salad ready?" Danica asked, and as Kiera nodded, Danica waved her in.

Five minutes later, the only sounds in the kitchen were the rhythmic chopping of the knife against the cutting board as Kiera cut vegetables, and the faucet as Danica rinsed the lettuce in the salad spinner. Danica was waiting for Kiera to apologize, or to explain, to say *anything*, but Kiera just stared down at the small red root vegetables on the cutting board.

Danica pumped the salad spinner, the bowl humming as it spun the water from the lettuce, then slowed to a stop. She glanced back toward Kiera, but Kiera was still dutifully slicing radishes.

Finally, Kiera finished, opening cupboards to find a bowl to put the sliced radishes in. She opened four cupboards before finding where Danica kept her bowls, and Danica just leaned against the counter watching, without chiming in to help.

Kiera turned, finally, and furrowed her brow slightly. "What else do you need to prepare?"

"You don't even like radishes," Danica said, setting the salad spinner down a little too loudly on her granite countertop.

"I eat salads," Kiera said defensively.

Danica couldn't stand it anymore. She was going to have to be the first to bring it up. "Why?"

Kiera angled her head. "Why do I... eat salads?"

"Why did you tell Eddie to come to Telluride like I needed saving? Like I didn't deserve a say in my own relationship?" Danica asked, not falling for Kiera's attempt to disarm her.

"Something important happened in your life, and I didn't know. And because you didn't tell me, I thought you were cheating on your fiancé." Kiera shook her head, crossing her arms over her chest. "I was pissed off, and freaked out, and confused, and betrayed."

Danica blinked back tears. "I didn't lie to you to hurt you. You invited Eddie to hurt me."

"I'm so sorry for that. I wasn't trying to hurt you." Kiera turned, leaning back against the counter. "I was genuinely worried about you. I thought you were doing to Eddie what Alex had done to me, and I knew what it felt like to be on the other side of it, and it wasn't fair to Eddie. And then you told me you'd broken up after I messaged him, but I still thought that maybe if you and Eddie could work out... Maybe so could Alex and I... I don't know." She reached under her glasses to wipe her eyes.

Danica sagged against the counter. "Well, I'm genuinely worried about you, too. Alex is having an affair and you're—"

"We're getting a divorce. Alex and I." The confession came

fast, like a dam had broken inside of Kiera. Her voice shook as she continued, "I'm divorcing Alex. I served him papers about a week after getting home from Telluride."

Danica gaped at Kiera, and upon noticing that her chin was wobbling in an effort not to cry, she stepped forward and wrapped Kiera in a hug. What was she supposed to say to that? That she was proud of her friend? That she was sorry? Neither felt exactly right.

"I fucked up," Kiera said, sniffling into Danica's shoulder. "I'm so sorry. I'm so embarrassed that I thought I knew better than you did about your own relationship."

Danica just held Kiera tighter. "I fucked up, too. I made a mistake by not telling you, causing you to think I was cheating on Eddie. I don't know why I did that to you."

"I was so mad at you." Kiera's voice cracked into a whisper.

"Same." Danica confessed, her voice muffled in Kiera's sweatshirt.

Kiera let out a shaky laugh. "I was mad that you didn't just tell me. You can tell me anything, and you kept it from me. That makes no sense, you dummy. And I was jealous that you were happy when I wasn't, if we're being honest, and feeling a little betrayed that you were having fun with Pete again after how many years it took for you to get over her."

Danica pulled back, wiping at the tears welling in her own eyes. "I know. I thought Pete and I were just having fun, and that I had it all under control, and I just... I got scared. Being there didn't feel real, you know? I could just have fun and focus on the present. I could pretend like my real life didn't exist, and that Pete and I could exist in some vacuum where I could come home after and not feel..." She paused, struggling to find the right words. "Heartbroken all over again. But you were right. Pete and I don't work in real life, and I should have guarded my feelings better."

Kiera pulled off her glasses, cleaning the fogged-up lenses

on her sweatshirt. Her face was still blotchy, but now she had a slight grin on her face. "Yeah, about that."

"About what?" Danica asked suspiciously. She pointed toward the wine rack with her eyebrows raised in question. Kiera nodded, and Danica pulled out two glasses and a bottle of a red blend.

Kiera moved around the kitchen island to sit on one of the stools. "I've been talking to Izzy about you and—"

Danica paused mid-step, staring at Kiera in disbelief. "You've been talking to Izzy?"

Kiera rolled her eyes. "That's what you're focusing on?"

"You've been talking to Izzy about... me?" Danica asked as she uncorked the bottle. Her hands were shaking with a sudden jolt of nerves.

"About you and Pete. You're our best friends," Kiera said like it was an obvious statement.

"This feels more like a Meddling Maggie thing," Danica said, pouring the wine.

"Oh, believe me. She's been in on it, too."

"And what if I don't want to be in on whatever it is? Or if Pete doesn't?" Danica asked gently, picking at a speck of invisible dust on the countertop. How could Pete ever forgive her for slipping away without a word, especially after Pete had opened up about wanting a future together? Danica felt like a coward, and she'd be shocked if Pete ever found it in her heart to forgive her. She lifted her wine glass to her lips, but paused. "Wait, what has Izzy said about Pete? Hypothetically."

"You know, that's the interesting part. I thought Pete would run off and spend a year in Zambia or something," Kiera said, drumming her fingers along the stem of her wine glass. "But she seems to be settling down in Seattle. Traveling less. She bought a houseplant."

The pain that she was still making assumptions about Pete felt like a punch to Danica's solar plexus. She rubbed at her sternum. But what had Danica expected? That Pete would show up with a boombox outside her window? That Pete would show up and beg her to reconsider their future together? That Pete would move to Denver without her knowing and they'd run into each other at Jazz in the Park? All of these daydreams, playing out since her return home, left her with a childish, immature feeling, a sense of longing for something she couldn't quite grasp. Who needed to grow up now?

Kiera sipped the wine, watching Danica's expressions closely. "She and Izzy are leaving for a three-week-long trip to Costa Rica tonight. The first few days are basically just a fun, relaxing part of the trip, I think."

Danica nodded again. "She and Izzy?"

"She's training Izzy to take over some of the international travel duties," Kiera said, giving her a pointed look.

"Okay?" Danica said, not quite understanding.

"Pete told Izzy that she wants to travel less. You know, really have a life in one place," Kiera said.

Danica snorted in disbelief.

Kiera gave her a challenging look. "She seems serious about it. Anyway, she and Izzy have a layover in Denver."

"Oh?" The sound came out as a tiny squeak.

"Yeah, they'll be here for about three hours starting at..." Kiera glanced at the clock on the stove. "Well, in thirty-four minutes."

"What are you saying?" Danica asked, standing up straight, her brain feeling fuzzy.

"I'm saying, Costa Rica is really nice this time of year. It's the dry season, so there's lots of time to lay on the beach."

"Yeah, must be nice for those of us who don't have work," Danica said, lying.

"Do you remember that year I went with you as your date to your work Christmas party? Before you started dating Eddie?" Kiera asked nonchalantly.

Danica raised a brow, confused.

"Somewhere around the third espresso martini, Annie and I became friends on Insta. We still message occasionally. Her grandkids are really cute. Anyway, I asked her to secretly figure out when you'd have a few days off, you know, just in case. She double-checked for me a few days ago, so I know you have the next six days off."

Why did Danica suddenly feel like Kiera was moving a chess piece across a board? She gave her friend a questioning look.

Kiera glanced at her phone. "Oh good. Izzy was able to reschedule her flight for later in the week," Kiera added. "She had a bit of a stomach bug this morning so she is going to meet Pete later. Poor Pete is going to spend a few days in Costa Rica all alone."

Danica frowned with a dubious expression. "Why are you telling me this?"

Kiera looked tentatively hopeful. "Look, I fucked things up in Telluride. And so did you, leaving without a word. Let's make it right."

"So, let me get this straight. Pete is sitting at DIA waiting to get on a plane to Costa Rica where she has a few days of relaxation, and Izzy is pretending to be sick so that she'd be there all alone? And now you're suggesting I... what... buy a last-minute ticket to Costa Rica and join her?"

"Maggie bought you a cheap ticket so you can get through security. It's in your email."

Danica let out a surprised laugh, shaking her head. "You're all crazy."

Kiera beamed.

"What makes you think Pete even wants to see me?" Danica asked, running a hand through her hair, exasperated.

"Listen, Dani. I know you're not... spontaneous," Kiera said carefully. "But I — *we* — think you will regret it if you don't at least try."

"And so even if she does want to see me, we spend a few days in Costa Rica together, which is *still* not real life, and then what?" Danica asked, her throat tightening with emotion at the thought of trying to make it work with Pete. At the thought of failing. Again.

"That part is up to you," Kiera said.

Danica shook her hands, feeling the familiar tingles of the beginning of a panic attack. "I don't... I don't know. I don't do well without plans."

"What would you tell me in this situation? Or Maggie? Or even Izzy?" Kiera asked calmly.

"I'd tell you to suck it up," Danica said automatically, then guffawed at her own words. "Oh my god. This is crazy to even consider. I don't have anything packed." Was she seriously thinking about doing this?

In all of her daydreams, Pete was the one who showed up to beg to try again. But maybe in real life, she had to be the one with the proverbial boom box. She'd never think of a plan like this on her own, but thanks to the imperfect, meddling, busybodies she called friends, she might have a chance at fixing things with Pete.

"Your mom packed your suitcase for you." Kiera's eyes were sparkling with amusement, her mouth twisted in a wry smile.

Danica picked her jaw up from off the floor. "But what about you? You showed up here to get moral support for your divorce, and I'd just be leaving."

Kiera looked slightly sheepish. "I'm not going anywhere. Alex isn't fighting me on custody, and sometime when the divorce is final, the girls and I are moving to Denver to be closer to my folks and Aunt Jade. Actually, Aunt Jade is bankrolling the lawyer *and* the move. I'm going to spend this weekend house-hunting."

Danica was completely shocked. "Really?" She hopped up and down excitedly. "You're moving to Denver? Man, I love your Aunt Jade. Wait, do you have a teaching position here yet?"

"I have a few interviews. I'll figure it out. I know I want to be closer to my parents, but also you. If you want… that," Kiera added.

Danica moved around the kitchen island and wrapped her best friend in a hug. "Are you kidding me? I'd love that."

"Which means we have plenty of time to talk more about me and us later. If you want to make it to the airport on time, you'd better go," Kiera said.

Danica felt a rush of emotion and tears fall down her cheeks as she hastily brushed her hair out of her face.

"Are we doing this?" Kiera asked, standing and staring at Danica intently.

It was a terrible idea. It would never work. She'd make a fool of herself. She'd put herself out there only to face the worst rejection of her life. In public. Again. It was a gut-wrenching thought, the idea of standing there, exposed, heart on her sleeve, only to be met with pity or indifference. The humiliation would burn, sharper than anything she'd ever experienced. But it was more than that, wasn't it? It wasn't just about rejection. It was about the ache of unspoken words, the weight of everything left unsaid between them. The weight of everything she'd left unsaid by leaving without a goodbye.

And yet, Pete was worth it.

The chance to try again with Pete — the chance to really try — was worth it. Because Pete wasn't just someone she had a crush on or some passing infatuation. Pete was… everything she hadn't known she needed. The way Pete saw her, understood her in a way no one else had, the way they just fit. It had been too real to ignore, too important to just walk away from. And in the loss of connection that had stretched between them after she'd left, Danica had come to understand that more clearly than anything.

To try again meant facing all of her fears, all of the walls she'd built to keep herself safe from the mess of relationships and emotions. It meant putting herself in a position where she could either heal or break all over again. But what did that even look like? Did she want Pete to know everything? To know that she wasn't just sorry for walking away but that she was terrified of feeling so much, of letting herself need someone in a way that made her feel vulnerable, out of control? She wanted Pete to understand that she wasn't just asking for another shot at love — she was asking for the chance to be seen, to fully let in the one person who had always seen her.

Because that was what it all came down to: the chance to be seen. To be understood and accepted for all the parts of her she'd hidden away, for the fears and mistakes and all the jagged edges of perfectionism she kept locked up. And Pete, somehow, had already seen all that. Had seen her for who she really was, and still wanted to see more.

Danica swallowed hard. If she didn't take this chance, if she didn't step into that vulnerability, she'd spend the rest of her life wondering, *What if?* And that thought — that was unbearable.

Yes, she'd risk the humiliation, the rejection, and everything in between. She'd face it all if it meant one more chance to show Pete who she really was, what she really wanted. A fierce determination burned within her, a silent promise to herself. To try. To try again, and maybe — just maybe — make it right this time.

Danica composed herself, taking a deep breath. Her throat was tight with anxiety and her heart raced with excitement, but she was ready. "Okay, but I'm driving."

CHAPTER 24

PETE

The hard, unforgiving chair dug into Pete's thighs as she sat alone at the bar of a restaurant near her gate, her posture mirroring the heavy weight of her melancholy mood. Families laughing, couples talking, children running — the terminal buzzed around her, yet she felt utterly alone. The noise only highlighted the emptiness she felt, amplifying the silence in her head.

She was a seasoned solo traveler, with countless hours in airports under her belt. Today felt different, though. Maybe it was because she was in Denver — so close to Danica she could hardly stand to stay in the airport instead of showing up at her window with a boombox. Not a great idea, given Danica's sudden exit, leaving only the lingering scent of her rosemary shampoo and a void inside Pete.

She sipped her beer, its hoppy bitterness a momentary distraction from her thoughts. Maybe she was just feeling out of sorts because Izzy had been sick that morning and had to delay joining her on the trip. They'd successfully taken two trips in the last six weeks to introduce her to the foundation's partner organizations in Greece and Croatia. Izzy had been a natural. She had a way of understanding people that Pete respected, and others seemed to respect her, too. They'd been closely working together to delegate tasks and get Izzy completely onboard, and Izzy was rising to the occasion just as Pete knew she would.

Pete's fingers occasionally tapped her phone, but there was nothing new to distract her. Izzy had her notifications on silent, probably sleeping on her bathroom floor if she was as sick as she'd claimed. She glanced at the screen again, flicking open her news app as she watched the minutes go by with agonizing slowness. Her eyes scanned the same stale headlines as repetitive flight announcements droned in the background.

She observed couples close by, their hushed words and soft laughter emphasizing her solitude. The idea of a honeymoon, of traveling with a partner just for fun, remained a distant, elusive dream for her.

She'd been lonely and mopey ever since her Telluride trip. She'd bought a houseplant just to feel something, and now she worried it wouldn't survive the three weeks she'd be in Costa Rica. She used to travel without a second thought, but something had shifted inside of her when she'd realized that she wanted to spend the future with Danica. With Danica's silent departure, her hopes, plans, and dreams of a future together had evaporated. Her feelings for Danica seemed to unlock desires she'd long suppressed — a stable, quiet life with someone she loved. Now she was a moody mess, sitting in an airport bar.

Letting out a soft sigh, she dug into her bag in search of a distraction, her fingers coming across an unread book, a partially filled water bottle, and a crumpled receipt. Leaning back in the hard chair, she briefly closed her eyes, the dull ache of loneliness settling in her chest.

She thought she heard a familiar voice say her name, then

mentally chastised herself for daydreaming. Wait. There it was again, she realized. She opened her eyes and turned in her seat, scanning the bar.

"Pete *fucking* Pancott," the voice hollered, and this time, Pete was sure that it was Danica. Confused, she finally spotted her standing at the entrance to the bar area. Danica's messy bun, oversized sweatshirt inexplicably advertising Costco hot dogs, and straight-leg jeans with a grass stain on one knee signaled that she'd been in a bit of a hurry.

Pete's heart stuttered in her chest. "I... you... What? What is happening?" she said with an incredible amount of eloquence. "Wendell?"

Pete stood from her chair, frozen, her heart pounding as she watched Danica step into the bar, looking as unsure and vulnerable as Pete had ever seen her. The air around them seemed to still, and for a moment, everything else faded—the blur of travelers rushing past, the hum of overhead announcements, the sharp scent of coffee and jet fuel. It felt like time itself was holding its breath. Danica wasn't just standing there, though — she was *waiting*.

Pete stared at her in shock and delight and absolute confusion. "Are you flying somewhere?"

"I'm sorry for just showing up like some kind of stalker. Izzy sent me a screenshot of your exact location on Life360, so I knew you'd be at this bar, and..." Danica trailed off, awkwardly fidgeting with a pulled string in her oversized sweater.

"Okay?" Pete said. "That really only opens up more questions." Pete's pulse quickened, the weight of everything they'd left unsaid suddenly crashing down on her. She wanted to pull Danica into a hug, demand answers to the questions that had been eating away at her, but she was paralyzed. *Why now?* Pete's mind raced. Things had felt so right between them in Telluride, but so much had changed since Danica had left without a word. So much had been left in the air, unspoken. And yet, here Danica was, standing in front of her, all the walls Danica had built suddenly crumbling under the weight of something else: hope.

"I wanted to apologize for leaving like I did. That was wrong of me. I shouldn't have left without saying more. I woke up, and I panicked, and I thought it'd be easier for both of us if I spared us the awkwardness. I should have just been honest with you and let you see me struggle, but I was... I was scared. I mean, after that graduation night quad break up, I spent fifteen years regretting every word I said. I didn't want to chance it. I guess what I'm trying to say is I'm an idiot," Danica said, pausing to pick up Pete's beer and take a large gulp.

Pete was pretty sure she had a dazed expression on her face. Danica's words seemed to hang in the air between them, soft but heavy, as if they carried all the weight of the last six weeks. Pete felt a rush of emotions, a mix of relief and disbelief, but most of all, a deep, painful ache that settled in her throat. She'd spent so much time wrestling with the silence, the unanswered questions, the feeling that maybe Danica hadn't cared as much as Pete had. And now, hearing that sincere, raw apology felt like the floodgates opening, letting out all the hurt and hope she'd kept buried. She wanted to speak, to say something, but the lump in her throat made it impossible. Instead, she just stood there, staring at Danica, her heart pounding, her mind racing. *Was this real? Was she really here, really apologizing?* Part of Pete was terrified that this was just a brief moment of vulnerability, that Danica would pull away again and slip back into the distance. But another part of her — a part she hadn't allowed herself to acknowledge until now — was ready to believe, ready to let go of the hurt and take a chance on something that still felt so *right* between them.

"I'm not adventurous. I'm boring. I like vanilla ice cream and I get excited over new pajamas and I work too much.

You're not boring. You're brave and caring and so, so fun to be around. When I'm around you, I want to be fun. I want to be a better, more fun me. You see me, and you see that I'm boring, and you've never tried to change me. You've just always steadily encouraged me to try new things, to trust in myself. I love that about you," Danica said, shifting her weight from foot to foot, restless and uncomfortable.

By then, other patrons, without embarrassment, faced Danica as her voice grew louder and surer. Pete glanced toward the bartender, who had been drying the same cup for the last three or four minutes.

"And I know I was a coward to leave. And I honestly can't imagine how to make our lives work together, and that terrifies me. I love plans, and you go with the flow, and I didn't know how to find a way where we're both happy. I know in Telluride, you said you saw a future with me, and I wasn't there yet, but the past six weeks without you have made me realize I was wrong. I do see a future with you. I was letting this idea of perfection get in the way of the raw, messy happiness we could have." Danica paused, looking pained by the idea of letting Pete see her, but bravely pushing through the discomfort. "I want to figure out our future *together*."

Pete's cheeks were flushed, her heart racing in her chest. She never imagined Danica saying those words. She felt both thrilled and terrified by the possibility before them.

Pete's breath caught in her throat. Did she really want this? Did she want to try again? The answer hit her with a sudden, undeniable force. *Yes.* She wanted it more than anything. But now she had to figure out if she could forgive the silence, the distance, the fear that had kept them apart. "You do?" she asked, needing to hear it again.

"You make me want adventure and spontaneity. I mean, I checked in on my phone while stopped at a red light on the way here, and I don't even know what's in my suitcase, and I... I'm like, really far out of my comfort zone right now, but you make it all seem possible. You make everything *seem* possible, because you *believe* everything is possible, and I love that about you. I don't want to pressure you into something you're not ready for, but if you're game for one last run, so am I."

Pete softened, smiling at Danica as the words spilled from her mouth. She was incredible and brave to come all this way just to do this. Pete knew Danica hated every aspect of this situation — the vulnerable public declaration, the awkward surprise arrival — and Pete found it all incredibly endearing and lovable. Still, she couldn't resist a tiny bit of teasing. "You know the one last run superstition."

"We might get hurt, we might make a dumb mistake, but I want to fucking try." Danica was smiling, her eyes flashing with tears, her cheeks flushed.

Pete felt the last worry leave her mind, reaching to push a strand of Danica's hair behind her ear. Danica stared at her, her ocean blue eyes brimming with unshed tears, waiting expectantly. She was so beautiful, so open and vulnerable. They'd figure it out. They would struggle and fight and celebrate and learn from each other. She had no doubt.

"I love you, too," Pete said finally, pulling Danica against her.

"That's not what I said," Danica argued weakly, her arms wrapping around Pete's waist.

"Didn't you?" Pete teased, leaning to kiss Danica, urgent and messy and real. They fit like two halves finding themselves whole once more. Several people around them began clapping, and she let herself give into the joy of the awkwardness, kissing Danica without worry.

"I do love you. I've loved you for so long," Danica said against Pete's lips as they paused for a breath.

"How did this all happen? How did you know Izzy canceled, and I'd be alone?" Pete asked. She'd almost rescheduled her own flight, but Izzy had insisted she go ahead and have a few days to herself to relax.

"Those meddling friends of ours," Danica said, her grin both wry and mischievous.

Pete's eyebrows drew together. "What do you mean?"

Danica shared all the details of Kiera unexpectedly showing up at her door while they shared the rest of Pete's beer, but then Pete realized something. "Wait, you booked a flight to Costa Rica? With me?"

"Yeah, what other flight would it be?" Danica asked with a laugh.

Honestly, Pete thought that Danica might have bought a cheap flight just to get past security and talk to her, but the idea of Danica coming to Costa Rica made Pete swing her around in excitement. Danica laughed, the sound causing Pete's heart to explode with happiness. "What seat did you get?"

Danica shrugged. "Uh, I'm not sure. It didn't let me pick."

Pete nodded seriously. "Okay, we've got to go fix that while we can. I'm not spending another moment without you by my side."

Danica beamed up at her, raising onto her tip-toes to kiss Pete once more.

Holding hands, they hurried, breathless with happiness, toward the ticket counter. Danica initially protested the first-class upgrade, but Pete shut that down quickly, stating that it was the only way they'd be able to sit together. Danica was going to have to get used to getting a little spoiled.

As they boarded the plane, Danica whispered, "Do you think it's okay that I'm wearing a sweatshirt that says 'I got that dog in me' in first class? Don't they have rules?"

Pete couldn't help but laugh. "Somehow, I don't think they'll kick us off the plane for that, Wendell."

"I've never been up here with all the fancy people," Danica admitted as Pete ushered her into their row, giving her the window seat. The flight attendant appeared with champagne, and they each took a glass. "There's champagne? Wow, don't let me get used to this or I'm going to become so insufferable."

Pete snorted with laughter as she watched Danica's exuberant bouncing — a joyful, carefree energy radiating from her. "It suits you."

Danica stopped, a thoughtful frown creasing her brow as her eyes darted around, as though in search of something specific. "I usually hate flying, but look at all this leg room, and they give you bubbles right away. Maybe there's a hot tub behind one of these curtains."

Pete laughed, taking Danica's hand in her own and kissing her fingertips. "The hotel has one, you know, in case you need a happier thought during this flight."

"I can't wait," Danica said, glowing with excitement. She rested her head back against the seat, her expression soft. "I can't wait for every little thing with you."

EPILOGUE

DANICA

One Year Later

THE ROCK FELT COOL AND COARSE UNDER DANICA'S FEET AS SHE crouched, peering into the tide pool. She gasped, leaning closer to peer at the cobalt blue sea star stuck to the bottom of the pool, its five long legs shimmering in the sunlight streaming through the shallow water. Pulling out her camera, she hunched, trying to shield the starfish from the sun to get a good photo.

"Find anything good?" Pete called out from nearby.

"I _finally_ found a giant sea star!" Danica exclaimed, giddy with her success. She peered through the camera's viewfinder, watching in awe as the bright blue creature shifted against the rock, crawling deeper into the pool, away from the excited paparazzi action.

Pete cheered, and Danica turned, looking to spot Pete standing in the shallow water, a surfboard hooked under her arm. Her dark wet curls stuck to her forehead and cheeks, and her wide grin made Danica's chest ache.

"One last wave before we grab dinner?" Pete asked, shielding her eyes as she looked back at the water of Dreamland Beach. The low tide today was around 4 p.m., and Danica had been climbing around the tide pools for nearly a half hour, exclaiming about snails and crabs. All afternoon she'd felt light and relaxed and so, so happy.

"Let's stay for the sunset." Danica turned back to the tide pool, on a hunt for her dream tide pool creature, a brightly colored sea slug.

"If you insist," Pete teased, wading carefully through the shallows.

This last-minute trip to Bali was a whirlwind of spontaneous decisions and quickly booked flights. Over the last year, Izzy had shouldered most of the travel for Pete's nonprofit, but Pete, with a particular fondness for Bali, insisted on taking that trip herself. When she'd suggested they take an extra few days for a vacation, Danica had swapped shifts with another doctor for six days off in a row. She'd even allowed Pete to use miles to upgrade her seat to first class — after all, they were celebrating.

So much had changed in the past year. Pete had moved to Denver, and they'd lasted nearly six months in separate condos before deciding to move in together. Today marked one year exactly from the day that Danica had taken a chance on their future. She'd hopped a flight to Costa Rica with Pete, where they'd split their time between the hotel bed, exploring the rainforest, and lounging on the beach. Pete had even tried to teach Danica how to surf during that trip, but it would take a lot more practice before she felt confident enough to try out the waves at a place like Dreamland Beach.

Danica was grateful every day that they'd decided that trying again was worth the risk. Worth the mistakes and hurt and struggle. And in the end, they had found a lot to compromise on — Pete had suggested they take it one day at a time, figure everything out as they went.

Reality had far surpassed anything Danica had ever dared to imagine — having Pete by her side felt like a dream she wasn't sure she deserved, but couldn't ever imagine living without. Pete was everything she hadn't known she needed: fiercely supportive, effortlessly spontaneous, and somehow always in tune with her, reading her moods like they shared the same heart. Some days, Danica caught herself simply staring, overwhelmed by how effortlessly they fit, as though every piece of her had been made to align perfectly with Pete's, and she marveled at how they *worked*—how it felt like coming home every time they were together.

The turquoise blue waters of the Indian Ocean were particularly stunning today, and Pete had been ecstatic about the conditions all afternoon. Pete's joy was contagious, and Danica's cheeks hurt from smiling.

Danica made her way from the rocky ledge of the tide pools back toward the cave where they'd set up in the shade. Dreamland Beach was tucked into a sequestered alcove of steep rocky cliffs, brown and sun-bleached giants that made the coastline feel like its own little world. Small caves hollowed out the cliff faces, and though there were umbrellas for rent, Danica much preferred the cool seclusion. She sat down on her towel, squinting into the sun to watch as Pete dropped into a wave. Though Danica was far enough away that she couldn't make out details, she could picture the strong muscles of Pete's legs as she carved her way across the wave, the concentrated furrow in her brow as she flew across the water.

Danica wondered briefly if the next college friends' trip should be to Bali, or at least somewhere tropical. Skiing was fun, but did anything compare to a lounge-on-the-beach vacation? She could almost picture Izzy and Pete surfing, Kiera and Maggie getting a massage as they lounged by the water, the entire group drinking cocktails in the pool of the overlooking resort.

Pete bailed from the wave, leaping into the water, and Danica waited for her to surface before she relaxed again, leaning back onto her elbows. She watched as Pete carried her board back over to where Danica lay. Pete sat beside her a few minutes later, shaking water from her hair like a shaggy wet dog.

Danica laughed, attempting to protect herself from the water, but Pete playfully held her down on the towel by grabbing her wrists.

"Did you see my wave?" Pete asked, her eyes wide with excitement.

"You were flying." Danica beamed with pride and elation, the same happiness that was mirrored on Pete's face.

Pete leaned down to take Danica's mouth in a gentle kiss. "I love you. I love being here with you, sharing this."

"I love you, too," Danica said, lifting her head slightly to kiss Pete once more.

Pete sat down beside her and grabbed her phone. "I miss Gladys. Do you think she's doing okay?" She watched as Pete swiped open her phone and began to scroll through photos of their newly adopted pittie mix, an older, fawn-colored, adorably dumb sweetheart of a dog. Pete paused on a photo of Gladys smiling up at the camera, her eyes squeezed shut, a Lamb Chop toy held tightly in her mouth. The photo was blurry, like most photos of Gladys tended to be, since she never stopped wiggling with happiness.

"I'm sure Gladys is being spoiled rotten by Aunt Lillian," Danica said, leaning her cheek on Pete's shoulder.

"It's our first time away from her, though. She knows we'll come back, right?" Pete asked, and Danica lifted her face to look up at Pete, her entire body flooding with adoration.

"I bet she has eaten so many treats that she's hardly even noticed we're gone," Danica assured her, kissing the bare skin of Pete's shoulder.

Pete sighed, closing her phone and tossing it back towards their backpack and scooter helmets.

The world seemed to slow as the sun lowered toward the horizon. The sky shifted into a canvas of warm, golden hues, bathing their skin in an amber glow. The colors intensified as the sun sank lower, painting the sky in purple and orange spreading along the horizon, bright clouds soaking up the color. The soft breeze smelled like saltwater and wet earth, the shouts of the surfers quieting as the beach slowly emptied. The reflection of the sunset in the water looked like molten gold, darkening into inky blue as the sun sank below the horizon.

In the twilight before the stars began to reveal themselves, Danica closed her eyes, wanting to memorize this moment to keep it forever. "I feel so happy I could just float away," she whispered.

"Don't worry, I've got you." Pete rested a hand on Danica's knee. Pete's skin, warm from the sun, contrasted with her own, which was growing cool in the evening air. Pete's touch was a tether, her presence a reminder of all the bliss they'd shared together so far.

Danica felt the promise of a future unfolding — endless, uncharted, and waiting for them to claim it, together.

THANK YOU!

Thank you for reading One Last Run. I hope you loved Danica and Pete's love story as much as I do!

Read on for a special sneak peek of the next book in the series...

SHIFT THE TIDE - SNEAK PEEK

Izzy Tierney is doing everything right. She's got a job she's proud of and a passport full of stamps from her frequent work trips. Everyone keeps telling her she's living the dream — but it's starting to feel more like drifting. Constant motion is just another way to avoid standing still long enough to feel lonely. She tells herself she's content, but something's missing — something she's never quite let herself want.

Kiera Phillips is caught in a swirl of uncertainty. Newly divorced and living with her two daughters in her parents' house, she's trying to rebuild a life she no longer recognizes. A new city, no job, no real plan — and now even her closest friendships feel distant. She's doing her best to hold it all together, but the truth is, she feels completely lost.

Then, an invitation from the group chat: a weekend getaway to a beach house in San Diego. Izzy and Kiera agree, thinking it's just a short escape — how bad can it be? But what starts as a casual weekend quickly pulls them into deeper waters. Reconnected bonds stir up old emotions, buried truths, and unanswered questions. By the end, neither woman knows where she stands.

When real life rushes back like an unstoppable tide,

they're left wondering if they can truly leave the past behind — or if their lives are about to change for good. What happens when the weekend ends, and you're left standing at the shore, knowing the tide has shifted?

SHIFT the Tide is a spin-off story of *One Last Run*, featuring two characters who kept stealing the show. It can be read as a standalone or the second in the series.

SHIFT THE TIDE - SNEAK PEEK

CHAPTER 1

KIERA

EVEN ASLEEP, KIERA COULDN'T STOP RUNNING TOWARD something she might never have. Kiera was barefoot on cheap carpet, swaying to music she couldn't quite place. Izzy was in front of her, close enough to touch, with a red Solo cup in one hand, her hand resting lightly on Kiera's hip. The room was crowded, overheated. The music pulsed through the floorboards, but they were still, eyes locked.

When Izzy leaned in, Kiera didn't flinch. She kissed her back like she'd been waiting for it, like nothing else mattered. It was slow and certain and just a little messy. They smiled into it.

Then the sweetness in the air shifted. The music faded. Something too bright crept in around the edges...

Kiera opened her eyes to the scent of incense curling against her nose, sweet and leathery.

She stared at the ceiling for a long moment, still half-dreaming. Then came the singing. Off-key, far too enthusiastic. Her dad, down in the kitchen, launching into "Here

Comes the Sun" with the kind of energy usually reserved for toddlers and Broadway auditions.

The pillow muffled her groan as she pulled it over her face.

She stayed like that for a few seconds longer before forcing herself upright. The mirror caught her as she passed: loose t-shirt, yesterday's mascara, a smudge of dried toothpaste from someone's small hand on her shoulder. She rubbed at it without much conviction.

Downstairs, the day was already in full swing. Her mom stirred oatmeal on the stove with quiet focus, the incense stick anchored in a mug that said *World's Okayest Mom*. Her dad was crouched beside the fridge, balancing on the balls of his feet like he was about to leap into a yoga pose.

"Morning, Sunshine," he said cheerfully.

"Barely," Kiera muttered, heading straight for the coffee maker.

Kiera's mom, ever the devoted herbal tea drinker, gave her a look as she poured herself a generous cup of coffee. "You know, caffeine just adds to your stress levels."

"So does existing," Kiera said, taking a deep sip.

Eliza burst in a moment later, crayon drawing in hand, her cheeks pink with excitement. "Mama! I made you something."

Kiera set down her mug. The paper was an explosion of marker colors, purples and golds, with two figures in the center with dark hair and a glittery crown.

"We're fairy queens," Eliza explained proudly.

"Of course we are," Kiera said, pulling Eliza in for a quick forehead kiss. "And it's *beautiful*."

Quinn arrived just behind her, dragging a blanket and clutching a scribbled mass of green and black lines.

"I'm a monster truck," she announced.

Kiera nodded in quiet agreement, giving Quinn's hair a ruffle. "Well, naturally. I wouldn't expect anything less."

They settled at the table. Her dad produced strawberries from the fridge like a magician pulling scarves from a sleeve. Her mom set bowls down with soft clinks and gave Kiera a familiar glance — the kind that meant, *What's your plan today?*

Before the question came, Kiera preempted it. "Same as yesterday. Apply for jobs. Wait for the universe to respond."

"You could call the co-op," her mom said, not unkindly.

"I could."

The silence that followed wasn't hostile. Just familiar.

After breakfast, the girls migrated to the living room and began rearranging couch cushions with single-minded purpose. Their voices rose and overlapped — Eliza demanding structural integrity, Quinn arguing for more aesthetic sparkle. Kiera sipped her coffee and let them build.

She opened her laptop at the dining table, the screen lighting up to the same set of open tabs she'd left the night before: district job boards, a half-filled spreadsheet of application deadlines and dead ends.

Her inbox had two new emails. One was a coupon for a local pizza place. The other was from a charter school she didn't remember applying to.

She opened it anyway.

Thank you for your interest... At this time, we have decided to move forward with other candidates.

Kiera cleared the table while her parents shifted into small talk. Her dad launched into a summary of a documentary on sustainable farming he'd watched the night before—something about vertical gardens and aquaponics. Her mom nodded along, skeptical but patient.

It was all normal. All familiar.

Still, Kiera felt miles away from herself.

In the living room, Eliza and Quinn were mid-construction, balancing throw pillows between dining chairs, the couch, and an ottoman that had already been commandeered as a throne. Kiera leaned in to help, draping a blanket higher than Eliza could reach.

They beamed at her like she'd built it single-handedly.

There were moments, like this one, where the noise in her head softened. Where their laughter filled up the room enough to drown out the rest. They were okay. That was something.

Resilient in a way only children could be, Kiera thought. They took each change in stride — new house, new school, new rules — and somehow still found ways to delight in it. She envied that ease. That capacity for bounce-back. Hers had long since eroded.

Eliza knelt beside her, folding another blanket with serious concentration. The same curve to her brow, the same clipped way she pressed her mouth when she focused — it was like looking at a younger version of herself. Quinn, on the other hand, was all chaos and stubborn joy, more like her father than Kiera liked to admit.

Kiera sat back on her heels, watching them.

The divorce hadn't been contentious. That, in its own way, had been worse. Alex had stayed in Omaha, entirely fine with Kiera taking the girls to Denver. He hadn't fought her on custody, hadn't fought her on much of anything. He'd agreed to split the house sale evenly and start over with his new life, his new girlfriend, his version of a clean slate.

Kiera had walked away with the girls and not an ounce of regret.

Sometimes she thought that should've felt like a win. Other times it just felt like abandonment.

She'd refused alimony. Aunt Jade had offered to help, of course — had paid for the legal side of it all without blinking — but Kiera hadn't let her pay for anything beyond that. She couldn't. Not even when Aunt Jade had dangled the promise of a down payment.

Without a steady job, signing a lease or taking on a mortgage felt reckless. So she'd stayed. Her childhood home turned into something temporary but indefinite, her parents reminding her daily, in small ways, that she was welcome, that she had time.

In return, she cooked. Cleaned. Folded everyone's laundry while the girls were at school or when she wasn't picking up a sub shift. She made it work. Or tried to.

Her phone buzzed from the coffee table.

A message from Maggie.

Maggie: *Hey! What time do you get in on Friday? Can't wait to see you!*

Kiera picked it up slowly, thumb hovering. The trip had sounded like a good idea when it was just an idea. A beach house in San Diego. Ocean air. Her old college friends, Maggie, Danica, Pete, and Izzy. Her parents had practically forced her to go, promising they'd manage everything here. That it would be good for her.

Now it felt less like a vacation and more like a performance.

Kiera: *Hey. I get in around 2 p.m. Can't wait to see you, too.*

It wasn't a lie. But it also wasn't the full truth.

Another buzz.

Danica: *Hey, I wanted to check in before the trip. You're coming right?*

Kiera's stomach tightened. She hadn't expected to feel nervous about hearing from Danica, but there it was, the familiar worry and shame.

They used to talk every day. Now, messages like this carried the careful tone of people still holding one another at arm's length.

Danica had been her anchor for years, the person she called when things cracked or collapsed. But lately, their conversations felt careful, like their connection was fragile and precarious all at once.

She thought about Telluride. About how fast everything

had unraveled. Back then, she hadn't known Danica had broken off her engagement. She'd only seen the way Danica and Pete moved around each other — too close, too easy — and something in her had buckled. It had reminded her of the lie she'd lived in for so long with her husband's affair, of holiday parties and polite smiles, of everyone knowing before she did.

So she'd done something she couldn't take back. She'd reached out to Danica's ex, told him maybe he should come. At the time, it had felt like the right thing — like fairness. Like truth.

She hadn't meant to hurt anyone, but intentions didn't matter much after impact.

She hadn't known it was betrayal until it was too late. And even now, the weight of it lingered. Quiet. Unresolved.

She typed out a reply, slow and measured.

Kiera: *Yeah, I'm excited to be there. It'll be a nice break from real life.*

Danica responded almost immediately.

Danica: *Seriously. Work's been crazy. Looking forward to this weekend, though. It'll be good to see everyone.*

Kiera hesitated, fingers hovering over the keyboard. She started to type *Looking forward to reconnecting*, then deleted it.

Kiera: *Yeah, it will.*

She placed the phone face-down and leaned back into the couch. The room felt quieter now, despite the continued rustling and chatter from the fort-in-progress.

She couldn't shake the sense that this trip was less about fun and more about proving something—to them, maybe even to herself. That she could still be part of the group. That she could belong, despite what happened.

Despite Izzy.

• • •

LATER THAT AFTERNOON, Kiera sat on the floor of her childhood bedroom, legs crossed beside the open suitcase on the bed. Clothes were half-folded, half-forgotten in small piles —tank tops, a swimsuit she hadn't worn in years, a dress she wasn't sure still fit.

She wasn't thinking about packing. Not really.

Her thoughts circled Izzy, uninvited and persistent. She hadn't meant to dwell. But the quiet of the room made it harder to ignore the knot in her stomach, the flickers of memory that caught her off guard.

Izzy hadn't reached out. Not since Kiera had called her in a panic, asking how she could make things right between Danica and Pete, and they'd conspired to get the two back together. Now, a year later, Kiera had been too ashamed to make the first move. That silence had settled between them like dust, coating everything with a thin layer of discomfort.

The idea of seeing Izzy again — of sharing a house, a table, a conversation — made Kiera's palms sweat. Would Izzy still look at her like she was someone to be tolerated more than trusted? Would she look at her at all?

Kiera tried to picture the version of Izzy she remembered best — head tilted, lips curled into a half-smile, that rare, genuine laugh that softened everything sharp about her. It came back a little too easily.

She folded a shirt more forcefully than necessary and muttered under her breath, "It's not about Izzy." But it was, a little. It always had been.

Her gaze drifted toward the dresser. A photo sat in a slim white frame — her and Danica on the Oval at CSU, arms slung around each other, mid-laugh, wind-tossed and sun-drenched. They looked like people who still believed everything would work out.

She didn't feel like that person anymore.

A quiet knock broke the stillness. Her mom stepped into the room holding a mug.

"I thought you could use this," she said, setting the tea down on the nightstand.

"Thanks," Kiera murmured.

Her mom sat beside her, folding her legs like she might stay a while. "The universe will provide a path forward. Have you been practicing that manifestation ritual I taught you?"

Kiera arched a brow. "The one where I write, 'I will get the teaching position of my dreams' a hundred times a day?"

Her mom gave her a look, both amused and unimpressed. "I wonder what I did in a past life to raise such a skeptical daughter."

"You probably manifested me wrong," Kiera said dryly, and her mom laughed.

"Now, why are you moping in here instead of playing Scrabble with us?"

"I'm not moping."

"You love beating us at Scrabble, honey."

"I'm just packing," Kiera said, though she hadn't made much progress.

Her mom followed her gaze to the photo on the dresser, her expression shifting into something gentler. "Are you excited to see everyone this weekend?"

"Of course," Kiera said automatically.

Her mom didn't push, just nodded. "Tonya always says to look ahead."

Kiera blinked. "Who's Tonya?"

Her mom looked exasperated. "My new spiritual guide. I've told you about her. We meet over Zoom."

Kiera gave her a long, blank look.

Her mom sighed. "Anyway, Tonya says the future responds best to clarity. You just need to decide what you want."

"I'm trying," Kiera said. "But it's hard to look ahead when I feel like I'm failing the girls. And when it seems like I've disappointed everyone I care about."

Her mom didn't hesitate. "You're not failing them. You're doing your best. They're happy, Kiera. That's what matters. And as for disappointment? Never. Surprised, sometimes," she added with a smirk. "But never disappointed."

Kiera blinked back sudden tears.

"If those women are truly your friends," her mom continued, "you'll find your way back to each other. This weekend could be the start of that."

"I hope so," Kiera said, her voice thinner than she meant it to be. She turned back to her suitcase. The packing still wasn't done. But the tea was warm, and the silence felt a little less heavy than before.

Her mom gave her hand a gentle squeeze and stood. "And if you need your dad and me to come pick you up from the slumber party early, just say the word."

"Mom, that was *one* time."

SHIFT THE TIDE - SNEAK PEEK

CHAPTER 2

Izzy

Izzy Tierney felt weightless, her surfboard slicing through the water as though it were an extension of her body. The wave — perfect, glassy, and cresting just right — held her in a fleeting, magical balance. The salty air kissed her skin as she leaned into the turn, her toes gripping the waxed surface of her surfboard. This was what happiness felt like. Pure, uncomplicated, blissful.

She rode the wave all the way to shore, leaping off her board at the last second and landing knee-deep in the foamy surf. With a grin, she turned to watch the ocean reclaim her wave, the sea as endless and inviting as the sky above. Life wasn't perfect — she was still figuring out her place at Second Star — but here, she was content. Or at least, she was supposed to be.

The beach stretched out before her, quiet except for the rhythmic sound of the waves and the distant chatter of tourists from the small surf school set up a few hundred feet away in the direction of Carmen Beach.

Izzy dropped her board next to her beach towel and sat down, the sand warm beneath her. Santa Teresa wasn't a typical lounging beach — there was more of a rocky stretch than the perfect beaches that existed all throughout Costa Rica — but she liked that. It was a surfing haven, and she barely had to compete for a towel spot.

She'd been in Costa Rica for two weeks now, working with Pete's nonprofit, Second Star. She'd only been with the organization for a little under a year, and she still felt like an imposter most days. The organization provided funding for children's homes to offer extracurricular activities, and Izzy's job was to ensure the partnership was working well for the organization and adjust at will. The two children's homes in Costa Rica were in San Jose, but she always preferred to spend at least one or two days of her trip surfing on the Nicoya Peninsula, particularly at her favorite beach this time of year, Santa Teresa. The work was fulfilling, the weather flawless, and every day ended with sunsets that seemed to be painted just for her. It was the kind of life she'd dreamed about during her restless nights as a bartender back in San Francisco.

The buzz of her phone from her beach bag pulled her back to reality. Izzy leaned over to grab it, the screen lighting up with a message from Maggie.

Maggie: What time do you get in on Friday?

Izzy stared at the message for a long moment, the afterglow of her perfect wave fading into something more complicated. Another trip with the group meant seeing Maggie, Pete, Danica... and Kiera.

Kiera Phillips. Just the thought of her name sent a ripple of restlessness and something warmer, more bittersweet, through Izzy. They hadn't spoken since the Telluride trip, where Kiera had managed to alienate most of the group by playing referee between Pete and Danica, who hadn't yet figured out that they were meant for each other. Kiera's attempts to keep them apart had felt to everyone else as misguided and unnecessary, but Izzy had seen the strain in Kiera's eyes, the way she was trying — maybe too hard — to keep the group dynamic from changing.

Izzy sighed, tossing her phone down on the towel. She stretched out on her back, letting the sun dry the last traces of seawater on her skin. Of course, she wanted to see her friends. Maggie's chaotic humor, Pete's unshakable confidence, Danica's steady presence. But Kiera? That was... complicated. They had kissed once in college — a fleeting, impulsive moment during a party. Izzy still remembered how soft Kiera's lips were, how her laughter had turned into something quieter, more tentative, before their mouths met. It hadn't gone any further, and neither of them had brought it up again, but Izzy often wondered what might have happened if they had.

Her phone buzzed again. Another text, this time from Pete.

Pete: Mags told me she texted you. Don't make me come drag you to the beach house myself. I'll do it.

Izzy couldn't help but laugh. Pete's blend of tough love and relentless support was one of the reasons they'd been best friends for so long. If Pete was going, there was no way Izzy could say no. She tapped out a quick reply to Maggie.

Izzy: Early. I'll rent a car and meet you at the beach house.

As she slipped her phone back into her bag, a flicker of nerves stirred in her chest. Seeing Kiera again would be... something. Maybe a chance to clear the air, maybe just a new way to get knocked sideways. Izzy wasn't sure. Lately, she wasn't sure about a lot of things. But she'd already spent too much time keeping people at arm's length. And whatever this turned into, she'd face it. Let it come. Let it pull her under, if it had to.

. . .

THAT EVENING, the world around Izzy softened into a slow, golden hush. The air, thick with salt and the scent of blooming jasmine, clung to her skin as she wandered back to her rented bungalow — a small, sun-bleached space with uneven wooden steps and a crooked porch light that flickered at dusk. It wasn't fancy, but it was hers for a few days, and it was quiet. Peaceful.

Izzy grabbed a cold Imperial beer from the tiny fridge, the bottle sweating instantly in the humid air. She stepped outside to the creaky hammock strung between two posts and sank into it with a sigh. The hammock rocked lazily with every movement, the worn fabric familiar against her bare legs. Before her, the sky stretched endlessly, painted with ribbons of lavender, peach, and molten orange as the sun melted into the Pacific.

She'd spent a lot of time alone lately — not because she wanted to, exactly, but because it felt simpler. Less complicated. Being around people, even people she loved, sometimes made everything feel louder inside her head. Out here, with no one expecting anything from her, she didn't have to explain the ache she couldn't quite name. She could just sit in it. Let it hum quietly under the moon and pretend it wasn't still waiting to be answered.

It should have been enough — this life she'd carved out, simple and beautiful. The kind of existence that was supposed to quiet the constant itch of restlessness inside her. But the moment she let herself relax, her thoughts found their way back to the one thing she didn't want to think about.

To Kiera.

Izzy tried to push the thought away — tried to focus on the soft crash of the waves or the slow hum of crickets starting their nightly chorus — but her mind kept pulling her back. The memory of Kiera's hopeful, awkward smile in Telluride haunted her like a half-finished song. She hadn't expected to miss her. Hell, she hadn't expected to *think* about her.

And yet... there she was, lodged in her brain like a splinter she couldn't remove.

Her phone buzzed on the armrest. She almost ignored it. But when she glanced down and saw Pete's name flashing on the screen, she sighed and answered.

"Hey, troublemaker," Izzy said, trying to sound light, like she wasn't coming apart under the weight of her own thoughts. She ran a hand through her short hair, tugging at the blonde strands.

"You better not be ditching on me," Pete shot back, her voice carrying a familiar warmth wrapped in playful gruffness. "I will personally fly down there and drag you to San Diego if I have to."

Izzy forced a laugh, pushing her hair out of her face and adjusting herself in the hammock until the fabric cradled her more securely. "Relax. I'm coming. You know I wouldn't miss a chance to witness all of you make fools of yourselves."

The pause on the other end was slight but noticeable. "You've been quiet," Pete said, her usual teasing tone dialed down. "Not just missing calls. Like... *gone* quiet. Is this one of your disappearing acts?"

Izzy tipped her head back, resting the cold beer bottle against her forehead. "I'm here," she said, which wasn't the same as *I'm fine*, but still not the truth. "Just laying low."

Pete made a small, unimpressed sound. "Laying low or pushing everyone out before they get too close?"

Izzy's jaw tensed. "I'm not pushing anyone out. I've just been surfing for a few days, and you know what I do for work. I'm just enjoying being on my own."

"You're always on your own," Pete said gently. "And for someone who claims to love it, you don't sound all that happy about it."

Izzy didn't respond right away. The sun had dipped below the horizon, and the sky was sliding into blue-gray. She watched the tide move in slow, steady pulses — indifferent, unbothered, sure of itself in a way she wasn't.

"How's married life?" Izzy asked, clearing her throat.

"Okay, deflection queen. I get it. And Danica and I aren't married yet. You'd know. You'll be my best person up there," Pete said.

"That's cute. I will gladly hold your bouquet for you," Izzy teased.

"I'm very excited to get you a bit drunk and play therapist about your weird deep-seeded issues this weekend." Pete said.

"Did you just say deep-seeded?" Izzy said, her smile clearly evident in her near-laugh.

"Yeah."

"Deep-seated. Like the seat is deep."

"That doesn't make sense. It's seeded, like you plant the seed really deep," Pete said, stubbornly.

"No, bud. That's…"

"Stop trying to distract me from your deeply sown issues," Pete said with a laugh.

The tightness in Izzy's chest loosened. She was excited to see Pete again, and Maggie, and Danica. Kiera would just be a part of the weekend she could avoid if necessary, she supposed. The sun had disappeared completely now, leaving the sky streaked with the soft gray of early twilight. The waves crashed on, steady and constant, unbothered by human fears and mistakes.

"I'm here for you anytime, okay?" Pete's voice was gentle now. "You're doing a damn good job in Costa Rica, and I know you're like a bazillion miles away but you're not in this alone. In anything alone, if you don't want to be."

"Fine. Now, let me off this invisible therapist couch," Izzy groaned, but Pete's words did warm her.

They hung up a minute later, but Izzy didn't move from the hammock. She sat there for what felt like hours, watching as the sky shifted from gold to blue to deep, endless black.

And when she finally went inside and climbed into bed, Kiera's name was still tangled up in her thoughts, stubborn and quiet like the tide pulling back to shore.

SHIFT THE TIDE - SNEAK PEEK

DANICA NAMED THE CONVERSATION, "THE GAY AGENDA (AND SNACKS)".

DANICA

Okay, listen up, everyone. We need to lock down the plan for SD tomorrow.

PETE

MAGGIE

Is the plan not just… go to the beach and vibe?

DANICA

No. We need logistics. Who's getting groceries? Who's picking up the rental car? What time does everyone land?

MAGGIE

I'm bringing sunscreen and vibes. That's all I'm committing to. I will not be opening a spreadsheet.

DANICA

We cannot survive on vibes alone.

PETE

Challenge accepted.

KIERA

I can coordinate the snacks.

PETE

As long as they aren't too healthy.

MAGGIE

Yeah, let's get a rundown of your ideas before we commit.

KIERA

Fruit, or my parents have me addicted to these gut biome bars that are actually pretty good.

PETE

Boooooring. It's Donettes or bust.

MAGGIE

Let's just Instacart things over a beer when we get there. Ta-da. Check that one off, D-sizzle.

DANICA

GUYS. Focus. We also need to coordinate who's driving from the airport.

PETE

Uber. Next problem.

DANICA

Will we all fit in an Uber? Does anyone have Uber vs Lyft feelings? Which is better for the workers?

PETE

Shh. The vibes have spoken.

KIERA

I can can fit everyone in my rental car.

DANICA

THANK YOU, Kiera. It's so nice having a responsible adult here.

MAGGIE

Wow. Passive-aggressive much?

DANICA

It's not passive-aggressive, it's just *aggressive aggressive* because you're all impossible.

MAGGIE

So, what's the alcohol situation? Are we planning tequila or rum vibes?

DANICA

THIS IS NOT THE PRIORITY.

PETE

Tequila. Obvi.

IZZY

Why isn't "who's picking up the booze" at the top of the list?

MAGGIE

Izzy! You DO look at your texts!

DANICA

I'm actually going to lose my mind.

MAGGIE

We love you, Dani. You're doing amazing, sweetie.

DANICA

I feel like I'm organizing a circus.

PETE

You knew who we were when you chose to love us.

KIERA

You got this, Danica. I'll help with food and logistics.

DANICA

THANK YOU, Kiera.

PRE-ORDER SHIFT THE TIDE

Want more? Shift the Tide releases April, 18, 2025. You can pre-order it here:

Pre-order Shift the Tide

ACKNOWLEDGMENTS

Shoutout to my wife for being my real-life romance novel heroine. You inspire every perfect moment for my stories, and every silly moment, too.

I could not have written this book without the help of my incredible editor, Lemon. Lemon, your eagle-eye and cheerleading made this book my best yet. I am so grateful for your help and extremely glad we met on LiveJournal nearly twenty years ago. What the fuck? Twenty? We are old.

Also I'd be remiss not to thank my college situationship for still being such a positive light in my life and a role-model for living an authentic life. Merry Christmas, btw.

As always, my sister is amazing and I love you. Thanks for all the driving chats and for also understanding that "Hi,nothing'swrong!" is a perfectly normal greeting.

Yin, you were such a lifesaver for answering all of my neonatology questions and also literally keeping my child alive in the NICU and making up new lyrics to "We Don't Talk About Bruno" with us.

And most importantly, thank you, dear reader, for sticking with me after all these years. Your emails, comments, and DMs are so appreciated and motivational. The wait between this and the next book won't be three years, I promise promise promise.

ABOUT THE AUTHOR

Bryce Oakley is a Goldie-award winning author of sapphic romantic comedies and self-proclaimed pepperoni pizza connoisseur. She lives in Colorado with her partner, daughter, and a small herd of rescue animals.